The Last Duke

(THE 1797 CLUB BOOK 10)

By

*USA Today Bestseller
Jess Michaels*

THE BROKEN DUKE
The 1797 Club Book 3
www.1797Club.com

For more information, contact Jess Michaels
www.AuthorJessMichaels.com

To contact the author:
Email: Jess@AuthorJessMichaels.com
Twitter www.twitter.com/JessMichaelsbks
Facebook: www.facebook.com/JessMichaelsBks

Jess Michaels raffles a gift certificate EVERY month to members of her newsletter, so sign up on her website: http://www.authorjessmichaels.com/

DEDICATION

I do not know how it is possible that we have reached the end of The 1797 Club series. It seems like just yesterday that we met these men and their wonderful ladies. But here we are and there are so many people to thank.

To Michael, for just being who you are. Thanks for keeping me...sane? Do we call it that?

To Mackenzie Walton, editor extraordinaire, catcher of all plot holes and just a great friend. To Millie Bullock, copyeditor and my Mama. To Kelsey Strothmann, also copyeditor and keeper of scary red balloons.

To Jenn LeBlanc, for shooting the cover and meme images for all these books. We have so much more sushi to eat and bestying to do. Also thanks for making me bite the hardest bullet in this particular book. It made it a lot stronger. Love you!!

And finally to all of you who have come along for the ride with me on this life-changing series. You've laughed and cried with me, shared your favorite moments and kept me on the path to see this series through. I hope you have enjoyed my "dukes" as much as I have. And that you'll come along for the next ride and the one after that and the one after that for as long as I have finger strength to keep typing.

PROLOGUE

Summer 1810

Sarah Carlton stood at the edge of the ballroom, watching her dreams drift away as couples spun around the dancefloor. Her heart ached, and even the two glasses of punch she'd drunk in the last half an hour could not take the edge off her disappointment, fear and regret. They only made her mind cloudy.

She'd had one task when she came out to this party at Abernathe with her mother, and that was to make herself attractive to the gentlemen in attendance. That had been her only obligation since her coming out two years before. She and her mother needed the security a good match could offer, and time was running out. After all, every Season she got older, and every year new Diamonds appeared in the crowd that made Sarah look uninteresting and even less attractive, with her unimportant name and miniscule dowry. At the rate she was going, even that small settlement would be nonexistent.

She glanced across the room to find her mother in the crowd. Alice Carlton looked so tired. Even when her mother smiled, Sarah saw the dullness in the expression. The listless surrender to a dark future. Sarah could do nothing about it unless she wed.

Her desperation had been at its peak, and then she'd come here and found a spark of new hope, new life. The Duke of Crestwood had actually shown her some interest. The *Duke of Crestwood*, with all his money and status! He had danced with her, chatted with her. It was all friendly, nothing particularly serious, but she'd allowed herself to feel optimism for the first time in months.

And now that was gone. Stolen by a woman who had no need for such hope.

Sarah glanced across the room. Lady Margaret, the sister of the Duke of Abernathe, stood with her brother and his wife. Looking stunning, of course. For a moment, a dark streak of jealousy and anger flared up in Sarah's chest, and she shook her head.

Margaret…Meg to her many friends…had always had the opposite life to Sarah's, it seemed. She'd had money and privilege from the start. Her bright personality gave her popularity to boot. And she had support from her beloved brother. Abernathe had even arranged a marriage for her with the Duke of Northfield. What more could a person want than that handsome, rich, settled kind of man?

Apparently, *Meg* could. Just days ago, scandal had erupted at the party. Margaret had been caught after spending a night unchaperoned with…Crestwood. And in a flash, the lady had not only blown up her own engagement, but any hopes Sarah had allowed herself to have of a future.

Meg would marry Crestwood. Immediately, to reduce the scandal. And Sarah was back to desperation and despair as her time ticked away.

Sarah huffed out a breath. Her life had never been an easy one, and when she was just a tiny bit in her cups, it felt so much more unfair.

Abernathe and his wife Emma stepped away from Margaret, and Sarah jolted forward. She had no idea what she would say to Margaret, but she felt compelled to move at any rate. Pushed by drink and disappointment.

She reached her side and folded her arms as she glared at her. "Good evening, Lady Margaret."

Oh dear. She could hear the slur in her words. Apparently Abernathe wasn't watering down his drinks, and Sarah hadn't had much to eat that day.

But it was too late to go back now as her target stiffened and turned toward her. Meg had been frowning and now that expression grew deeper as she looked Sarah up and down. Dismissively, Sarah thought. Just like most everyone in the Upper Ten Thousand did.

"Miss Carlton, isn't it?" Meg asked, her tone strained.

Sarah nodded once and then stepped up to stand beside her. For a moment, they observed the dancefloor together in silence. Sarah tried to figure out what it was she wanted to say to this woman who had crushed her dreams so effortlessly.

"Are you enjoying yourself?" Meg asked.

Sarah glanced at her. Was she serious? As if she hadn't been fully aware of the connection Sarah had been working to build with Crestwood? As if she hadn't seen them talking and laughing and forming what Sarah had prayed could be a bond? All that just before Meg had swept in and…well, one couldn't exactly steal a *person*…

She shrugged. "I *was*."

There was no mistaking the peppery accusation in her tone. Sarah hadn't quite meant to put it there, but between her desperation and the alcohol, it was undeniable.

"Oh," Meg said, and Sarah felt her watching from the corner of her eye. "Is there something *I* can do for you, since our hosts are currently dancing?"

Sarah turned to her, and her gaze narrowed. Something she could do? *Something she could do*? As if she hadn't done enough. As if she hadn't ruined enough, for her own family and for anyone else in her periphery.

"You had a fiancé," Sarah hissed, trying to meter her tone

and finding it difficult in her slightly inebriated state. "A perfectly good fiancé who was a duke. I think an even richer duke than Crestwood, if my mother is to be believed."

Meg clenched her fists at her sides and her frown turned deeper. She looked at Sarah with what felt like pure disdain. "You and I do not know one another well enough to be having this incredibly impertinent conversation."

Sarah's eyes went wide. Of course, the conversation *was* impertinent. She was far beneath Meg in station, and it wasn't as if she had a real claim on Crestwood. Only the hopes she'd had for a future. Her last hopes.

That spurred her on where she normally wouldn't go. "I don't care if it's impertinent. Great God, is any man safe? Will you bore of the Duke of Crestwood soon enough and move on to another? Will you suck up all the eligible men in the countryside and leave none for anyone else?"

The moment she said the words, Sarah wished she could take them back. *This* was why she rarely drank. It loosened lips. And yet she didn't do the prudent thing and walk away.

"You have *no* idea what you are talking about," Meg snapped, and she had the audacity to look annoyed. "Crestwood and I have been friends a very long time and—"

"*Friends*, my lady? Only *friends*?" Sarah whispered, her voice cracking as frustrated and desperate tears filled her eyes. In the end, she knew there was no point to this display. She had no power, no money, no prospect.

No future. She had no future. And that had probably been true long before Crestwood and Meg had gone and gotten trapped in a cottage overnight together. The weight of that truth sank in and nearly buckled her.

"You are overwrought," Meg said firmly. "And perhaps you've had too much punch."

"I am *not* overwrought," Sarah muttered. "I just don't like to see someone grab for everything in the world because she thinks she can just take, take, take. My only consolation is that this scandal is so desperate that you may never recover. And when they whisper about you, I shall be the first one to tell them what *I* observed with my own two eyes."

"That is enough."

Both women turned, and Sarah's breath departed her lungs entirely. The Earl of Idlewood was now standing just at Meg's side, and he was glaring down at Sarah.

She'd been a keen observer of Society for a long time. In her position, she had to be. Almost everyone made her nervous, for most were far higher than she in station, but no one gave her stomach as many flutters as this very man. Unlike his friends, the men of their duke club, he was very serious. Almost wiser than his years. He was always watching, always present in whatever situation he encountered. He rarely talked to her, but when he did it was…*mesmerizing*.

And God's teeth, but he was handsome. Even when he was staring at her like she was a bug to be crushed, his lean face and intelligent brown eyes were impossible not to note.

"L-Lord Idlewood," Sarah said, forcing her gaze away from both his judgment and his distraction. "I did not see you there."

"I would wager not, or you would not have said such wretched things," Idlewood said softly. "Walk away now and go back to your mother. I'd also suggest you start planning on how you're to tell her."

Sarah shivered at the quiet command of his tone. At the horrors his words implied. "Tell her?"

Idlewood arched a brow. "When the Duke of Abernathe finds out you were attacking his sister, your invitations to many events are going to disappear. I assume you'll need to tell your mother why."

Sarah's heart felt like it stopped in her chest as she stared at him. He almost looked bored, despite the fact that he was saying words that were world destroyers. Would he truly speak of her indiscreet behavior to Abernathe?

Everyone knew the duke was protective of his sister. He

was a golden child, untouchable in even the deepest scandal. If he wished, he could bring down all the final, delicate threads of hope that remained for Sarah.

Idlewood held her stare as he said, "Now run along."

Sarah couldn't breathe. Couldn't think. Couldn't do anything except purse her lips together as she turned on her heel and slowly walked away. As she did so, the tears she had been fighting filled her eyes and she blinked to keep them at bay.

She'd spent her adult life trying to do the right thing. The proper thing. The ladylike thing. She did all that because she knew it was her only chance at any kind of future.

And now with one tipsy moment of foolishness, it seemed she had collapsed all her prospects and fantasies. She would have to face those consequences, because she had no doubt that the Earl of Idlewood would make good on his threats.

And her world would come crumbling down at last.

CHAPTER ONE

June 1813

Christopher Collins, Earl of Idlewood, sat at his father's bedside, watching the old man's breaths become more and more labored. The Duke of Kingsacre had been failing for such a long time, his illness taking pieces of him year by year, month by month, day by day. But it had progressed so slowly Kit had somehow allowed himself to feel that this day would never come.

And yet here it was. It felt like someone was tearing out his heart. Kit bent his neck, pressing his forehead against his father's arm.

The old duke coughed and his fingers flexed against Kit's hand gently. "You…have been…a good son," he whispered, his voice raspy and heavy with strain.

Tears stung Kit's eyes and he lifted his gaze to his father's face. "I can only hope I will be half as good a duke as you are," he said. "I am certain I will fail at it."

His father's expression softened and he smiled gently. "Never. You could…never…fail. Where…is…Phoebe?"

Kit straightened and looked toward his father's chamber door. As if on cue, it opened and his younger sister, just five years old, stepped inside. She clung to the hand of her governess.

Kit frowned. His father had hired Sarah Carlton to fill that position after her final fall from grace. She'd joined the household just two months before. The duke had not asked Kit's opinion on the subject.

He did have one, of course. He *always* had opinions when it came to Sarah. But right now he shoved them away, just as he had been since her recent arrival to the estate. He did not have the energy or time to deal with her.

Not when his father deserved all his attention.

"Papa?" Phoebe whispered, her voice breaking as she turned into Sarah's skirt.

Sarah reached down to stroke her hand along Phoebe's red hair. "It's all right, poppin," she said softly. "Go see your papa."

"Phoebe…love," his father called out gently.

The little girl did not turn away from her hiding place against Sarah's legs. If anything, she clung harder to the fabric.

Kit shoved to his feet. He understood his sister's fear, and yet he wanted to force her to go to her father. To say her goodbyes for both their sakes.

Sarah shook her head slightly and lifted a hand to stay him. He pursed his lips at her nerve, but remained where he was as she dropped down to her knees so she was the same height as his sister.

He moved forward, but could not understand what Sarah murmured to her charge. Phoebe drew back, looking her governess in the eyes before she slowly nodded. Sarah turned her toward the duke and gently tapped her forward.

Phoebe moved to the bed and Kit stepped away to allow his sister a moment of privacy with her beloved Papa. He looked at her as she spoke to him softly, tears beginning to form in her brown eyes. The eyes so like his own and their father's.

She was not his full-blood sister. She was not legitimate, but the result of an ill-chosen affair. And yet Kit adored her. His father adored her. Kit knew what it was like to lose a parent so young, and he wished he could keep her from that pain.

"Is there *anything* I can do, my lord?"

He jolted and turned his face to find that Sarah had moved to stand beside him. He caught a whiff of the warm lilac scent of her bright honey-blonde hair. She always smelled good. She always had.

Not that it mattered. He paid attention to her because she'd been in Society, linked to his friends by a moment of bad behavior. Once she'd fallen from grace, he'd watched her because she worked for his father.

There was no other reason to be interested in her.

"No," he said softly.

Phoebe had her arms around their father's neck now. She had buried her face into his slender shoulder, and Kit could see that sobs wracked her little body. His own eyes burned with tears and he caught his breath.

"I'm so very sorry," Sarah whispered.

He nodded, using all his focus not to show his reaction to her pity. "Thank you, Miss Carlton. Will you take Phoebe now? She shouldn't be here when he…when he goes."

Sarah stepped forward. She moved to his sister's side and touched her shoulder gently. "Come along, dearest. Let us leave your papa and your brother now."

Phoebe looked up at Sarah, her face streaked with tears. Then she nodded and took Sarah's hand. As they turned, the duke reached up and touched Sarah's arm. Kit stiffened as she turned back.

"Yes, Your Grace?" she whispered, her voice shaking.

"Thank you for your kindness, my dear," he said. "I know you will take good care of my daughter…after. And my son."

Sarah jerked and Kit took a step forward at the surprising statement. He waited for her to respond, and finally she covered his father's hand with her own. "Of course, Your Grace. I will do everything in my power to see that they are well. Good…goodbye."

"Goodbye," he responded, and closed his eyes.

She cast Kit a quick look, then slipped away, his sister in tow. Which left Kit alone with his father again. He sat down by his side, smoothing a few thin locks of hair from his forehead.

"I swear, Father, I have no idea why you hired Sarah Carlton of all the governesses in the world," he muttered, uncertain if his father was sleeping and could even hear him.

The older man's eyes came open at the statement and a ghost of a smile fluttered over his lips. "Don't you? I…hired that girl…because…you'll need her."

Kit pressed his lips together. "If you say so."

"Let her…*help* you," he said. "Don't let the past…destroy…the future."

Kit shook his head. He'd spoken to his father about Sarah before, of course. Mentioned her bad behavior with Meg years before. Talked to him when he saw her at balls. He'd probably pointed out her position when her mother died and left her destitute. But certainly his father couldn't think there was some kind of bond between them.

Not that it mattered now. If it comforted the old man to believe Kit would have some kind of help, then he was not going to disabuse the man of the notion. Even if he was wrong on every level.

"I'm not ready for you to go," Kit admitted, feeling the tears stream down his face at last and not caring.

His father looked up at him, searching his face, like he was memorizing it. Then he smiled. "But it's time. I love you…my…dearest…boy."

His breathing went shallow as he said it. His eyes slid closed. Kit jolted, clinging tighter to his hand. "No," he whispered. "Oh no, no, no. Please…please don't."

His father didn't respond now. He didn't open his eyes. Kit counted his breaths, counted the endless spaces between them. And then, there was nothing left to count. In quiet, in peace, in a moment that would change Kit forever, his father slipped away.

Kit rested his head on his father's chest, a lifetime of love between them playing out in his mind. And now it was gone, only a memory, with no new moments to ever be shared again.

He lay like that for a what felt like an eternity, then he stood up. He stared down at his father. He looked so peaceful there. The pain that had accompanied his long illness was gone from his face. He looked younger.

With a shuddering sigh, Kit stepped from the chamber into the hall. Only the servants were lined up there, gathered in groups, weeping. He drew a breath of relief. At present they had a full house. When it became clear his father's life was close to an end, his friends had come in from all over England. His brothers, the 1797 Club dukes.

They'd filled his home and his father's last days with gentle kindness and soft laughter. Kit appreciated it, but he wasn't yet ready to see them. To tell them what he was about to say to his father's loyal servants.

He drew a deep breath and felt their sadness increase. It was clear they knew what he was about to say before he did.

"My father has passed," he said, his stomach turning as he said those words for the first time.

His butler, Barrymore, stepped forward, his face solemn. The man had been with the household since before Kit was born, and he could see the servant's true heartbreak in every line of his face. "The household staff will see to your father's last wishes," he said. "Our deepest condolences to you and to Miss Phoebe."

Kit nodded. "Thank you, Barrymore."

"Of course, my lor—*Your Grace.*"

Kit froze. *Your Grace.* That was his title now. He was the duke. A role he had been prepared for by the very man who now lay dead in the room behind him. A role he felt woefully ill prepared for in this moment of pain and loss.

The household staff moved away, scuttling off to make arrangements. He was left alone in the hall. Except he realized he was not alone. Sarah was standing at his sister's door, her hands folded before her as she just…watched him.

"We'll need to tell her," he said, looking away from her.

"Yes," she said softly. "Would you like me to be present when you do so?"

He froze and glanced at her. His father's words about her rang in his ears. That he would need her. It seemed like nonsense at the time, but right now less so.

At last he nodded. "Yes. I think that would be a good thing. She will need…she'll *need* both of us."

Sarah inclined her head. "If I might make a suggestion?"

"Please," he whispered.

"Take a moment, Your Grace," she said, taking half a step toward him before she stopped herself. "You have suffered a great loss."

"I knew it was coming," he said.

She tilted her head and a flash of anguish crossed her face. "Somehow I doubt that is a comfort. Phoebe will know soon enough. Take a moment, won't you, and I will be waiting in the nursery to help in any way I can."

She turned and left him there, alone at last in his grief. And as he let the moment she had granted wash over him, he dropped to his knees and he wept.

Sarah's hands shook as she sat on the floor with Phoebe, helping her stack a tower of blocks and then watching the little girl knock them down. Phoebe was a unique little girl, for she had always liked toys that might be labeled for boys as much as those for girls. She ran and played and laughed without thought for propriety or the state of her gown.

But right now that big spirit was muted. Phoebe's mouth was turned down deeply and she shifted in her seat like she was waiting. Like she already knew what her brother would come in to say to her.

Sarah shut her eyes. Christopher Collins…Kit…was now the Duke of Kingsacre. Her employer. After all they'd been through all those years ago, after so many times he had looked at her with disdain plain on his countenance…now her fate was up to him.

It was an untenable situation, indeed. And yet all she could feel when she thought of him was empathy. He'd been so close to his father, everyone knew that. The look on his face when he said the old duke was gone was…heartbreaking.

So despite her conflicted feelings about him, she was bound by honor and duty to do all she could to ease this troubling time for him and for his sister. What happened after? Well, that would be what it would be.

The door to Phoebe's chamber opened and Kit stood in the entryway. From Sarah's position on the floor, he looked like a god. So tall, his shoulders so broad, his entire being formed by lean, wiry muscle and hard angles.

And then she looked into his face and saw all-too-human heartbreak. She pushed to her feet and said, "Phoebe, your brother is here."

Phoebe looked up at him and her little frown drew down further. "Go away, Kit."

Sarah caught her breath and jerked her gaze toward the new duke. He flinched ever so slightly but did not respond in a harsh way. He very patiently stepped into the room instead and shut the door behind him.

"I cannot go away, dearest," he said softly, and he glanced at Sarah. She nodded in encouragement. "I have some news for you."

Phoebe froze, her hand hovering over the tower of blocks she had built. "No."

Sarah pressed her lips together. It was obvious how difficult this was for Kit. And how horrible it was going to be for Phoebe. The little girl knew it, too, on some base, powerful level, which explained her petulant response. Normally she was exuberant and friendly.

"Phoebe," she said gently. "Stand up. Your brother has something important to say."

Phoebe slashed her hand out and the tower she'd built fell, blocks scattering halfway across the room with the force of her angry response. "No! Go away!"

Kit met Sarah's eyes and she saw the devastation within. That and the helplessness that his sister's response engendered. She moved toward him even though being close to him had always been a situation fraught with dark emotions.

"She knows," he said softly, shaking his head. "She knows."

Sarah glanced over her shoulder. Phoebe was now sitting on the floor, back to them, arms folded across her little chest. "I tend to agree with you," she whispered back. "I don't know what your father said to her earlier, but she is a child, not a fool. She knows that the time is near. Seeing you here must make her think her world has changed."

He jerked his gaze to her and his brown eyes locked with hers, holding there, pleading and pained. "Her world *has* changed, Sarah."

Sarah jolted at the use of her given name—he always referred to her formally. That slip was evidence of his state of mind. For a moment all her hesitations about the man, all her memories of an ugly encounter long ago, faded. All that was left was a connection to him, a desire to soothe the anguish that lined his handsome face.

After all, she knew it well.

"Not all her world," she whispered. "Your job, my job, from this day forward, is to reassure her that her life will be different, but not destroyed. That her home is still here, that she is loved and cared for. That she will not find darkness in all the corners where there was once light."

He hesitated, then nodded. "Yes," he murmured. "Let me try again." He stepped forward and sat down next to his sister.

He picked up one of the blocks and smiled. "These used to be mine," he said, nudging her with his arm gently.

Phoebe glanced up at him at last, her upset tempered somewhat by his statement. "They were?"

He nodded and stacked one on top of the other. "Papa gave them to me, I think. I used to build big towers. Just like the one you just knocked down. I doubt any of mine were as good as that one, though."

Phoebe smiled just a little, as if that idea that she could beat her big brother at anything was triumphant. He let out a long breath.

"Phoebe… Poppin… Papa is dead." He said the words softly but firmly. "Do you know what that means?"

She bent her head and her little shoulders began to shake. But she murmured, "Papa said I wouldn't see him again until I go to heaven. But that he'll be watching over me."

Kit let out another shuddering sigh. "Yes, that's right."

Her cry echoed in the quiet room, a sound of pure heartache. "But I want to see him now. I don't want to wait."

Kit grabbed her, dragging her into his lap, and the siblings wrapped their arms around each other. He rocked her as she cried, and Sarah held a hand to her mouth as her own tears flowed. She was not so far removed from her own loss. This reminded her keenly of a night when she'd watched her own mother's light go out.

"I know, love," he said, voice strained with emotion. "I don't want to wait either. I want him here too. But…but I promise you that I will take care of you, just as he would have done. I will love you just as much. And you can depend on me."

She pulled back a little. "So I don't have to…go away?"

He jolted as if he'd been struck by lightning. "Go away? Why would you go away?"

"Because I don't have a papa anymore," she explained. "And—and girls without papas have to go away."

Kit's face twisted with pure horror and Sarah gasped.

Phoebe had never said such a thing to her about these unfounded fears regarding her place in the world. Good God, no wonder she had been so afraid of losing her father.

Kit cupped her cheeks. "Look at me, Phoebe. You never have to go away. You will always be with me and I with you. I *need* you here."

She nodded and hugged him tightly. Sarah let out a long breath. The worst was over. Phoebe's grief would follow, of course, as the reality of what it was like to not have a father anymore struck her. The girl had never known her mother— Sarah had heard that the woman had given her up to the duke at birth.

But time would heal. And probably heal the little girl faster than it did her grown brother. Children were more resilient that way.

Kit sighed and glanced over his shoulder at her. She caught his gaze and nodded, hoping that little movement would reassure him that he had done well. For a moment, he allowed the kindness she hoped to offer. But then his expression hardened. He returned to the man who had been judging her for years.

She turned away and slipped from the room. It seemed her future was not as set as Phoebe's. And with the old Duke of Kingsacre gone, everything she had begun to rebuild could be dashed as swiftly as Phoebe's tower.

CHAPTER TWO

Kit stood at his father's grave, staring down at the coffin which had just been lowered in. It was littered with flowers, tossed in by the attendees of the funeral. His was the last to go in and then his father would be covered in dirt and he would be gone.

Kit's stomach turned with the realization, just as it had been turning nonstop since he said his goodbyes and watched his father's life disappear. Since that afternoon, he had been busying himself with duties. Making decisions for the funeral. Allowing his friends to try to comfort him.

Try. Fail.

Everything in Kit hurt. His body, his heart, his mind…his soul. What would he do without this man, this wonderful, decent, loving man who had served as Kit's rock for three decades?

He almost buckled, almost threw himself into the grave so that he could be covered in the dirt with his father. Before he could succumb to those desperate impulses, though, one of the men stepped from the small crowd of funeral-goers behind him, and he felt the comforting hand of a friend on his forearm.

He glanced over to see the owner and nodded to the Duke of Abernathe. James was one of his dearest friends, a brother, just like all those in their club of dukes. As leader of their group, of course it fell to James to be his support in this time of need.

"What can I do?" James asked softly.

"Nothing," Kit whispered, and his voice sounded so far away. He fought to control his emotions, knew he failed at least a little. "He's just…gone."

"I'm so sorry, Kit," James said, his voice low and kind.

Kit nodded, distracted as he looked from the coffin to the rose in his hand and back again. He didn't want to let it go. He didn't want to let his father go. And yet he had to. That was his duty. With a shuddering sigh, he held out the flower and at last dropped it with the rest.

"Godspeed, my dear friend," James said to the coffin, squeezing Kit's arm harder.

Kit gathered his composure and turned to look back at the crowd. They were mostly his friends. He could have invited the entire shire, of course. Men and women were clamoring to show their respect to his father, to pay tribute to him as they tried to figure out what kind of duke Kit would be. He'd allow it at some point. Perhaps in a week or two he'd want to have a more public memorial. His father would probably tell him he owed their tenants and acquaintances that courtesy.

But for now all Kit wanted was his friends. His closest friends. His brothers. The men James had gathered together what felt like a lifetime ago in a club of future dukes. He was the last to take that title, and now they were all here to support him, to surround Kit with family.

And yet he felt empty. Adrift. Even more so when his gaze fell to Phoebe. Normally children weren't allowed at a burial, but he refused to keep her from her chance to say a final goodbye. But God, there was nothing so heartbreaking as a five-year-old in black. Despite their conversation in her nursery three days before, she had been very quiet since. She clung to Sarah's hand now, her expression blank and forlorn.

"She will be all right," James reassured him. "And she has you and Sarah, all of us, and your staff to support her when she isn't."

"Sarah," Kit repeated with a shake of his head. In truth, he had been thinking a great deal about Sarah since his father's death. Tangled, jumbled thoughts. "My father said the oddest thing about her on his deathbed."

James wrinkled his brow. "You discussed Sarah with your father on his deathbed?"

"I asked him why he'd hired her as governess—" he began, and watched as James jerked his gaze back to the crowd. To Isabel, their friend Matthew's wife. The Duchess of Tyndale had been close friends with Sarah before their circumstances had shifted so vastly.

"And what did he say?" James asked.

"He said I needed her," Kit said with a small snort. "*I* needed her. Not just Phoebe."

James was quiet a long time. "Hmmm."

Kit arched a brow in his friend's direction. "Hmmm? What does that mean?"

"Well, you have always had an uncommon interest in the woman," James said softly. "I have never understood why you despise her so much."

Kit bit his tongue. He'd never told James what Sarah had said to his sister. Meg had asked him not to, so he'd kept his mouth shut for her sake. Only hers.

"I don't despise her," he explained carefully, trying to put out of his mind how gentle Sarah had been with his sister. With him. "I just do not think she belongs here."

"I would not say that in front of Isabel," James said. "She and Sarah are old friends from her wallflower days—she might have words with you if she thinks you might do Sarah a wrong."

Kit harrumphed as an answer. It was true that Isabel would likely defend Sarah if he moved to end her position here. That was not something he wanted to manage at present. He needed peace. Quiet. Support, not a fight. Right now he was too overwhelmed for a fight of any kind.

"I've got so much to do," he muttered, happy to change the subject. "My father was so hands-on in every aspect of his duties. He talked about the dukedom to me for years, and yet I know I will still miss something."

"You won't. My father didn't give me any direction and I haven't harmed my position one bit. The idea of it is more overwhelming than the reality. Besides, you have nine dukes here at your side, any one of them ready to help at the slightest flick of your hand."

Kit smiled at the idea, but he couldn't help but still be troubled. "And yet you won't be here forever. At some point, I'll have to face it all alone. Kingsacre is the largest holding of any of our friends. It has the most tenants, the most tangled duties."

James turned toward him with a frown. "Kit, for God's sake, take a break. Your father arranged everything. I know Baldwin and Ewan were looking over his accounts no more than a few days ago. Everything is in perfect order. You need time to grieve before you jump headlong into your duties."

Kit shook his head, watching as the other mourners began to trail off toward the house. He stepped forward to follow them, forcing James to fall into step beside him if he wanted to continue the conversation. Which, of course, he did. James was King of the Dukes. Right now Kit was the subject he thought needed him most.

And yet there was nothing his friend could do.

"I don't want to take time," Kit said, hardening himself to the pain in his chest. "I just want to do him proud. That's all I can do now. Starting today."

Sarah stood at the sideboard in the East Parlor. It was one of the biggest gathering places on the estate, save for the ballroom, and it was filled to capacity by dukes and duchesses.

But it was still as the grave they'd all left not an hour before.

The only child in attendance was Phoebe, as the others had been put to their naps before the funeral. Now Sarah's little charge sat on the Duchess of Abernathe's lap, speaking solemnly to her as the pretty, sweet woman nodded with great interest. Sarah sighed with relief, for she knew having so many kind and attentive adults was good for the fragile little girl.

"I so love seeing you."

Sarah jolted back to her companion. Her old friend Isabel, now the Duchess of Tyndale, smiled at her. Sarah forced the same. "I do too," she said.

She meant it. She desperately missed her best friend—she had for a year. But Isabel was not her equal anymore. She was elevated far past Sarah, so no matter how much she wanted to link arms with her and whisper all her fears and troubles, she resisted the urge.

"I do wish it were under better circumstances." Isabel pursed her lips and glanced across the room at the new Duke of Kingsacre.

Kit was standing with the dukes of Donburrow and Northfield presently. Donburrow had a muscular arm slung across his shoulders and the men were not talking, but just…standing together.

Sarah couldn't help but be happy he had such support in this moment. She knew it all too well and had wished for the same when she'd felt it.

"Sarah?"

She shook her head and drew her attention back for a second time. "Yes, it is a terrible shame about the previous duke," she said. "He was the best of men. Never anything but kind to me in the short time I was in his employ. Thank you for helping me obtain this position."

Isabel wrinkled her brow. "You have thanked me a dozen times already. I think that quite covers your obligation. I am your friend, Sarah. I only wish you would have let me help you more."

Sarah flinched. When her mother had died nine months before, Isabel had suggested Sarah simply come and live with her and her husband, Matthew. It had been an enticing suggestion, of course. But unfair. Sarah knew her future. She'd known it for a very long time.

It was service for her. And so she had come out of her mourning swiftly, pushing aside her grief for her dead mother, and searched for months for a position. Ultimately, Isabel had introduced her to the previous Kingsacre, and here she was.

For as long as it would last. The new duke suddenly glanced up and his dark gaze slipped to her. His face grew more serious, more closed off, just as it had in Phoebe's nursery a few days before, and her heart skipped a beat.

"You may have a chance to help me again," she said as she darted her eyes away. "I'm not sure I will be governess here for much longer."

Isabel cocked her head. "You don't think Kit will keep you on, despite the bond you've formed with Phoebe?"

Sarah tried not to feel the sting that gripped her every time she pictured walking away from the sweet little girl in her care. "He doesn't like me. You know that."

She looked across the room to where the Duke and Duchess of Crestwood stood together. Meg reached up and smoothed an errant curl from her husband's forehead, and he smiled at her. Of course, Sarah felt no jealousy when she saw the exchange. In the three years since that ill-fated ball when she'd confronted the duchess, the deep love the couple felt for each other had become not a scandal but a story of triumph in Society.

They clearly adored each other. Sarah knew enough now that time had passed to see what a great loss it would have been if circumstance had turned her way. She begrudged them nothing. How the duchess felt about her, of course, was a subject up for debate.

"You think he still holds that silly moment from ages ago against you?" Isabel asked.

Sarah shrugged. "Who knows? In the time I've been here, the man has avoided me to the point it could be considered funny. I once watched him walk all the way around the outside of the garden to avoid encountering me. He doesn't even look at me most of the time." She sighed. "There was only one time when his façade cracked and that was the night the duke died. And it was only because he needed my help when he told Phoebe what had happened. I suppose he mostly treats me like a servant, which of course I am."

Isabel shook her head. "It's such an odd thing to hear, for Kit is normally so good-natured and kind. That he has focused so much on one moment from years ago seems so out of character."

Sarah wasn't certain about that assessment. "I suppose I might offend him in some other way."

"He is difficult to read," Isabel said. "You might only be seeing the effect of the strains of the last few years. He's had so much on his mind since his father began to slip away day by day."

Sarah bent her head. Yes, that she could grant him. And she respected the way he had been with the old duke. Kit had hardly left his side, trying to tend to his comfort. He had been a marvelous son. She thought of her own mother. Of stroking her hair as she struggled. Of the day the struggle ended.

"Losing a parent is…" She trailed off, for she could not finish the sentence.

Isabel caught her hand. "Oh, Sarah."

Sarah straightened her shoulders and gently drew her hand away. Once again, she forced herself to remember her position in the world. The one that could not allow her to collapse in front of the Duchess of Tyndale. Or anyone else, for that matter.

"It's fine," she lied. "I am fine. Even if I weren't, you have other things to attend to." She looked across the crowd to where Isabel's husband was standing. He was watching the pair. "Including your family. The Duke of Tyndale seems to need you. I shall leave you to him."

She bobbed out a tiny curtsey and turned. She felt Isabel watching her as she slipped away. Felt the pain of rejection radiating from her friend. Felt the same pain squeezing her heart. But what could she do? They could not truly pretend that nothing had changed. Everything had.

And if she didn't find some comfort in her place, she could lose it. The new Duke of Kingsacre would surely be looking for any excuse to sack her.

She moved to the back of the room, where she could stand ready to be of service to Phoebe if she were needed but would no longer draw the attention of the invited guests. But before she could vanish into the wall, Kit said something to his friends and moved toward her.

She caught her breath as he crossed the room in a few long strides. He was coming for her. Oh God, would he dismiss her right here in front of all his friends? In front of Isabel? Was this the end at last?

She smoothed the front of her gown as he reached her, looking down at her for a long moment that felt charged with electric energy. At last the silence stretched too long and she hustled to fill it.

"Hello, Your Grace," she said.

He flinched at the address, and for a moment the mask slipped. She saw intense pain on his handsome features. Loss and grief and torment that she knew all too well.

In that second, she wanted to comfort him. Take his hands and whisper to him that she knew. That when everyone said it would be all right, it was a lie. She wanted to run away with him, run until neither could feel the pain anymore.

And then the mask returned and she blushed at her inappropriate response to it.

"Miss Carlton," he said, brusque and formal as he glanced back over his shoulder toward the group. "I realize I have been remiss in speaking to you since my father's...my father's passing. I think we should talk."

She blinked up at him, her heart racing so fast and so hard that she feared he could hear every beat of it. "Oh," she squeaked. "Right now?"

"Yes," he said. "There is no time like the present, especially since my sister seems to be busy with Emma and Adelaide at present."

Sarah swallowed hard and nodded, for there wasn't a way to refuse him. He was her employer, after all. He had all the power.

"Of course, Your Grace."

"Very good," he said. "Then please come with me."

Kit motioned Sarah into a smaller parlor just down the hall from where his friends were gathered, and watched her walk inside. She turned in the middle of the room to face him, her hands clenched in front of her.

She was trying to be strong. He could see that in the twitch of her cheek, the way her fingers fluttered against each other in their gripped position and how her gaze darted to him and away. Like a little bird flitting back and forth.

She was nervous. She was also very pretty. Her blonde hair was bound simply at the base of her neck, but there were a few honey strands that framed her face, highlighting the angles of her cheekbones. She had full lips that were a warm pink color.

He blinked as those facts rolled through his mind. None were surprising. He wasn't certain of the first time he'd noticed the young woman standing before him. Certainly they had shared many a ballroom or parlor in the years since she first came into Society. His attention had focused fully on her that night of the ball when she'd spoken harshly to Meg, though.

After that, he'd watched her. Noticed when she entered

rooms, felt when she left them. When her hairstyle changed. When she had a new gown.

"How is Phoebe?" he choked out, trying to clear his mind of the riot of thoughts clattering around in his head. Jumbled by grief, certainly.

Her eyes widened a fraction, like she was surprised by the question. She cleared her throat. "As well as can be expected, Your Grace." She hesitated a moment and then her expression shifted. Softened. "Despite her tender years, she is a very bright little girl. She seems to be a bit easier since you told her she would not be sent away."

He paled. "God's teeth, the very idea that she would be. Where would she get such a notion?"

Sarah shook her head. "I cannot imagine. A child's mind twists in its own way. Some offhand comment or something she saw in a story…who knows."

"Well, I'm glad that my words comforted her in some way." He dropped his gaze away. "I try to reach out to her, but…"

"It's difficult," she finished softly. "You've had a great deal to do since…well, since that day."

He drew a long breath. This was *not* why he'd asked her here to talk to her. This momentary connection where she comforted him with her gentle words, her soft tone. He took a long step away, putting his back toward her.

"Well," he said, sharpening voice. "We will need to be very careful with her for a while."

"Of course," she said slowly. He turned to face her and found she had edged toward the door. "Will that be all?"

He arched a brow at the hopeful expression on her lovely face. The fact that she wanted to escape him was evident. It sparked a reaction in his belly that made him set his jaw.

"No," he said firmly. "My friends will be staying here a while. Is that going to be a problem?"

The color drained from her face slowly and she swallowed, the action making her throat flutter. Her slender, lovely throat.

"What do you mean, Your Grace?" she asked, her voice catching ever so slightly.

He stepped forward. "I saw you and Isabel talking, and you were looking at Simon and Meg. I couldn't help but think of what I stumbled upon one night not so long ago and if that will impact your ability to perform your duties."

For a moment she merely stared at him, hands trembling. Then she widened her stance a fraction, as if bracing herself for whatever would come next.

"I assume you are referring to the incident that occurred between myself and the now-Duchess of Crestwood years ago?" she asked, her voice surprisingly strong.

He arched a brow. "I am, indeed."

"I assure you, Your Grace, that we aren't going to have a problem," she said. "I know my place very well and what I am expected to do to keep it. Is that all?"

"For now."

She blinked at his answer and a momentary terror entered her gaze. Then it was gone and she nodded. "Very good. If you need nothing else from me, I shall go collect your sister and see if she can be coaxed to try to sleep for an hour or so. She is overwrought, and I think it would do her good."

"Very good."

She turned and moved to exit the room, but at the doorway, she stopped and faced him once more. "Y-Your Grace, I realize you have been overwhelmed by your duties these past few days. I wanted to tell you again how very sorry I am for your loss. I-I know what it is like to lose a much beloved parent. Good afternoon."

She walked away, leaving him to gape after her in surprise. Oh, of course he had been given condolences many times in the days since his father's death. Virtually everyone on his grieving staff had spoken to him and all his friends had done the same. He was certain he would hear many more words like hers in the days, weeks and even months to come, for his father had been much beloved in Society.

But no one had yet framed his loss in the light of their own. No one had expressed empathy of that kind until she had. He looked to the spot at the door where she had spoken to him, and sighed.

He didn't want the woman here. She made him…uncomfortable in ways he could not articulate in words. But now that she had left him alone in the room, he also felt a little…empty. Like he had missed an opportunity he hadn't known existed.

He shook his head as he cleared away those odd thoughts. They meant nothing.

CHAPTER THREE

If Sarah had believed there might be trouble to come out of the Duke of Kingsacre's gathering of friends, the two days following his father's funeral disabused her of that notion. Kit had not spoken to her since their encounter in the parlor. They had returned, somehow, to the same level of relationship they'd had before.

He watched her. She felt it, though she had no idea what it meant. The rest of the party tiptoed around, quiet and solemn. They kept to themselves and asked for no special quarter from their host or his staff.

"I suppose I should feel good about that," she muttered to herself as she moved down the hall toward Phoebe's nursery.

Yet she didn't. She still felt the guillotine hanging over her neck. Kit could drop it on her at any moment and end her employment. Without a reference, that could mean an end to her life as she knew it.

Her stomach turned.

She ignored the nausea, the anxiety, and opened the door to Phoebe's chamber. She'd put the little girl down for bed half an hour before, but she wanted to check on her, make sure she'd been able to sleep. That had become a struggle since her father's death.

Sarah stepped into the chamber and stood a moment, letting

her eyes become accustomed to the darkness in the room. When she could make out shapes of furniture, she tiptoed forward until she stood beside Phoebe's bed in the firelight.

To Sarah's great relief, the girl was fast asleep, her little thumb tucked between her lips. Someday Sarah would have to discourage that behavior, but for now she had no intention of taking away any habit that offered comfort to her charge.

She leaned in and smoothed a lock of hair from the little girl's face. She did care for Phoebe. In the time she'd been here, they'd grown very close, closer since the death of her father, when Phoebe had begun to turn into herself more and more. Sarah could only hope she wouldn't be dismissed and not just for her own sake.

She sighed and slipped back out of the room. As she gently shut the door and turned, she started. Coming from the room across the hall was the Duchess of Crestwood.

Meg smiled as she stepped closer. "Miss Carlton," she said in a low tone. "I was just checking on my son. Were you looking in on Phoebe?"

Sarah swallowed hard. She had not had a conversation with this woman for three years. She'd avoided an encounter strenuously. And yet here she was in the hall with her and the duchess was smiling like nothing terrible had ever transpired between them.

"Er, yes," Sarah managed when she gathered her composure. "She's been having trouble falling asleep lately."

The duchess's smile fell. "Poor little lamb. She must miss her father fiercely."

Sarah nodded. "Indeed, that is true. Though I think having a full house of friends is helping her a great deal. She so enjoys having the younger children here."

"She's wonderful with them," Margaret said immediately. "I overheard her telling Emma yesterday that she can help because she's a big girl, not a baby anymore."

Sarah smiled. "That sounds like Phoebe."

She shifted as she realized how familiarly they were speaking. Too much so, considering their past and the lady's position. Sarah took a step back and was about to make her excuse to leave the hall when the duchess tilted her head.

"You seem to be very close to Phoebe, despite being employed here such a short time. I'm sure that offers her great comfort."

"I hope so," Sarah said, glancing back at the door, her personal worries gone for a moment.

When she looked at the duchess again, she saw a small smile on her face. "If your duties for the night are finished, I think everyone would love it if you joined us. The group is having after-supper drinks in the parlor."

Sarah couldn't help it when her jaw dropped open at the unexpected invitation. "Oh no, I couldn't," she said.

The duchess lifted her brows. "No?"

Sarah shook her head. "I cannot imagine it would be appropriate, nor that the Duke of Kingsacre would appreciate his sister's governess inserting herself into such a gathering."

Margaret's face wrinkled. "Gracious, Miss Carlton, that is ridiculous. I am inviting you—it isn't as if you would be striding in of your own volition. And you were raised as a member of Society, known to everyone in that room. You are one of our dear Isabel's friends and I know she loves to see you. I *insist* that you join us."

"My dress," Sarah said as she looked down at her plain, serviceable black gown. Although it wasn't as fine as the lady before her, she was grasping for any last straw that might save her from the perseverance of this woman.

Margaret looked her up and down. "Looks no different than mine. Everyone is wearing mourning attire. It isn't an exhibition. Please?"

Sarah's shoulders rolled forward on the please. She had avoided Margaret so strenuously in the years after their ugly encounter, she'd almost forgotten how friendly and persuasive she could be. Now she found herself nodding.

"Of course, Your Grace," she said on a sigh, and stepped in next to the duchess as they began to move up the hall together, back toward the stairs.

Margaret turned to face her. "Oh no, you mustn't Your Grace me. You are off duty now that Phoebe is asleep and we are amongst friends. Meg, I insist."

Sarah gaped. *Meg*? Great God, she could only imagine the ramifications that doing as she was asked would create. Especially if Kit heard her speaking so impertinently. Still, she couldn't refuse, so she simply nodded. "If you would prefer it."

"I would," Meg said, smiling as they made their way down the stairs and through the hall to the parlor.

As they neared it, Sarah could hear voices from within. To her surprise, their tone was lighter than it had been in the past few days. Gentle laughter filtered into the hallway. Life was coming back into the house, as it always did in the end.

She knew better than most that life went on, even when it hurt.

Meg led her in, and as she slipped in behind her, she was shocked when the duchess announced, "I have found Miss Carlton and convinced her to join our party now that her charge is asleep."

Sarah blushed as the group as a whole called out their greetings. Only one person did not acknowledge her entry with a friendly hello or wave. That was Kit. The duke was standing in the corner of the room with a few of the other men, and he speared her with a gaze she couldn't read.

He was going to let her go. She knew it. He was only barely tolerating her before and now she had broken protocol entirely. She rolled her shoulders forward as she slipped to one side of the room away from the other guests. How she wished she could just curl into a tiny ball and roll away.

Especially when the man stepped away from his friends and began to cross toward her.

"Miss Carlton," he said as he reached her.

She shook her head, clenching her hands at her sides. "The Duchess of Crestwood insisted I come down. She asked me, I did not encourage her."

He brought his lips together with a shake of his head and actually looked confused by her statement. Then his eyebrows lifted and he glanced up and down her body. Appraising. Cool.

How many times had he looked at her just like that? Judging her.

"Yes," he said slowly. "Meg said that, of course. I wasn't coming over here to interrogate you on your sudden appearance in the room."

"Oh," she whispered, ducking her head as heat suffused her cheeks.

He was silent for a beat, and then he said, "How is my sister?"

She lifted her gaze and found him watching her intently. That was one thing she could grant him. He took the subject of his sister very seriously and clearly loved the little girl deeply. It was a very attractive facet to his complicated personality.

"A little rambunctious," she admitted.

He gave a small smile and her heart fluttered. This man had very seldom allowed that expression around her. It made him even more handsome, which hardly seemed fair.

"Well, my sister has always been a bit wild," he said with a shake of his head. "Not that I'm complaining. Her spirit kept this house filled with light, even as my father grew sicker."

Sarah swallowed hard. Once again, she was moved by this man's acceptance of his half-sister. Many men, especially ones as concerned with propriety, would be speaking to a governess about how to tame Phoebe's wild heart. And one day, of course, the girl would need to temper herself. But he seemed in no hurry to rush that transformation.

"Her spirit is wonderful," Sarah agreed, "for it is filled with sweetness, and that is lovely. However, right now I see something else beyond your sister's normal playful impishness."

He frowned. "You think it part of her grief."

Sarah nodded. "Yes. She misses her father desperately."

"I know how she feels," Kit said with a sigh that revealed far more to Sarah than she thought he meant to. Then he tilted his head and examined her face. "I suppose you do, too. Your mother passed not that long ago."

She caught her breath. "Nine months," she admitted softly, and the pain shot through her like it was yesterday.

He shook his head. "I admit I hadn't thought much about that until you reminded me of that fact after my father's funeral. Under normal circumstances, you would still be in mourning."

Sarah felt her cheeks brighten further. "Well, we do not get to choose our circumstances sometimes," she whispered.

"I suppose not," he said. "But you seem to make the best of it. You take very good care of Phoebe. I hope you know I recognize that fact."

Sarah's lips parted in surprise as she stared up into his face. For the first time in years he was not holding himself away from her, letting her know he hadn't forgotten her bad behavior. In that moment he felt all the more…human. Their loss had connected them in ways she never would have expected, nor hoped for.

"I'm very glad to be here for her," she said. "She has become so dear to me."

His expression softened further. "I see that when you're with her. And how dear you are to her. Even in the past few days, only you can coax a smile from her. Make her seem like a little girl again, not just a lamb lost in sorrow."

"Time will…well, I won't say heal. I hate that saying," Sarah admitted. "But it will soften her heartbreak."

He ducked his head. "I hope that is true. For her and for me. Do you—"

He broke off his question and she tilted her head. "Do I?"

He cleared his throat. "I'm sorry, I was going to ask you a

forward question. One that has an answer I'm certain I am not owed."

She could have left it at that. Could have nodded and found an excuse to walk away from what felt like a potentially dangerous situation. Only she didn't. She examined his face a bit more closely. His jaw was clenched, but it wasn't in anger or disgust with her. It was with pain. His dark eyes had flitted away from her. But he broke the connection because it was too much for him, not because of a judgment he was making against her.

She saw his anguish, the one that mirrored her own, and found herself saying, "Ask the question, Your Grace."

He flinched. "I hate being called that. My father was His Grace. And yet this is what it is."

She nodded. "I'm certain someday it will not seem so foreign or distressing."

"I hope so," he whispered. Then he met her stare again. "Do you have any suggestions on how to…how to manage the grief?"

She caught her breath. *That* was not the question she'd ever thought he would ask of her. And not with such clarity and gentleness. There seemed to be no ulterior motive, just a real desire to discuss the subject with her because he had realized she was the closest one to it in his circle.

She understood that need to call out and find comrades in loss. She'd so wished for her own not that long ago. Now one was standing before her. Dashing and confusing and…just…*there*.

"Well," she said, shifting beneath his intense regard. "In my case, I had little choice but to swiftly move on. I think my…my situation was known to most. I had to procure a position as soon as possible, for money was nonexistent after her death."

"That must have been difficult," he said, his brow wrinkling like he hadn't truly considered that before.

She shrugged. "It was. But in some ways it was also…helpful. Searching and eventually finding my place here was a distraction that I desperately needed. Still need, truth be told."

"Well, I certainly have a great deal of distraction in front of me," he said. Then he shook his head like he'd heard his words and how they sounded like he meant she was the distraction. "I, er, mean with all the duties I must take on."

"Of course," she whispered, breaking her gaze from his for it now felt too intense. "But..."

"But?"

She worried her lip. "You cannot try to forget all your pain. It will not be possible."

"You've tried?" he asked.

She felt that very pain rise up in her chest. "Oh yes. But any time I walk too far from the grief, try to ignore it is behind me, when it snaps me back it is all the worse. Almost unbearable. So I recommend that you do not try to pretend it away, no matter how busy your duties make you."

"You mourn in the midst of your life," he said.

The turn of phrase brought her up short. "Yes," she said. "That is exactly right. I mourn my mother, in my own way."

"How?" he asked. She blinked, for the sting of tears had begun in her eyes. For a moment she struggled with it, and he turned his face. "My apologies. It was another impertinent question."

She shook her head. "No. It helps me to speak of it, and perhaps it will help you to hear it. My mother's favorite flower was yellow primrose. When I came here I saw that your garden was filled with them."

He bent his head. "I admit I am no expert in flora."

She smiled a little. "No, I would think such mundane things would not interest you."

The moment she said the words, she wished she could take them back. They revealed too much of her. Revealed that she'd watched the man over the years, been aware of his keen mind.

He held her stare for a beat. Two. "It is a failing, I think. My father loved flowers."

"He did," she said, ducking her head a little. "One afternoon he was walking with his nurse in the garden and saw me there amongst the primroses. He asked me about my interest and when he heard why I was drawn to that particular flower, he kindly told me I could make myself a bouquet for my room any time I liked. So one way I remember my mother is to pick a few of the flowers for my chamber each week."

His lips parted, and for a moment she thought he looked…upset. She shifted a little. "If you do not wish to allow that now that you are duke, of course I will not continue. I can enjoy the flowers while out on walks with Phoebe. I do not need a bouquet by my bed."

"You think I would deny you that small pleasure?" he asked.

She shrugged. "I am in your employ, am I not? You do not owe me *any* pleasures."

His mouth set in a thin line and there was no mistaking his irritation this time. He held her gaze a moment, then shook his head. "You may continue, Miss Carlton. I would not stop you from picking a few flowers now and then. The garden was meant to be enjoyed."

"Thank you," she said softly. She stared at him a moment. He was so very difficult to understand, to read. After all, he'd spent years watching her with such judgment and now he was here, pressing her on personal matters. It was a strange thing. One that didn't give her any sense of increased stability when it came to her future.

"I also re-read her last letter to me," she said, bringing the subject back to her mother.

He frowned. "I'm sure I have letters from my father around," he said. "But I have been here for months—I do not have a letter that says a goodbye."

She shook her head. "Perhaps it doesn't need to be goodbye. I think a letter that is just something normal would be more comforting in some way."

"Hmmm," he murmured.

"And then I have a mourning ring." She shifted, raising her hand slowly so he could see the little ring on her right hand. The crystal decoration was cheap, but beneath it was a lock of her mother's hair.

"The color is like yours," he said softly as he reached out and took her hand to look closer.

Sarah jolted. Kit had never touched her before. And now he held her hand in his, no gloves to separate them, and an odd shiver worked through her entire body.

"Does this comfort you?" he asked, releasing her and taking a step back.

For a moment, she thought he meant his touch. Oddly, the answer leapt to her mind and screamed *yes*. But then the moment passed and she somehow she found her breath. "Yes. All these things make me feel…closer to her. I'm sure you will find details that will do the same for you."

He inclined his head. "Well, thank you for the advice. I'm certain it will be of assistance during these trying days."

"Of course, Your Grace."

He nodded once, a swift and cold dismissal, then turned and walked away, leaving Sarah to blink after him in confusion. She was no more certain of what would happen next than she had been when he'd approached her. But dizzied by the strange encounter and the odd sensations the handsome new duke created in her.

CHAPTER FOUR

Kit stood along the terrace wall, staring down at the dim shadows in the garden below. After his conversation with Sarah, he had come straight here. He needed escape. From his well-meaning friends, but also from the odd feelings his talk with her had created.

He didn't *like* Sarah. He had reasons for that. And yet when he spoke to her he'd felt…comforted somehow. He'd let go of the past and just…been.

Her words about the nature of grief, of forgetting and not forgetting, had sunk deep into his soul. She'd spoken to him of distraction and all he could do was look at her, so pretty in her mourning attire, her blonde hair bright against the dark, her blue eyes filled with empathy and understanding.

"Do you want to be alone?"

Kit stiffened and turned to find that Baldwin, Duke of Sheffield, had stepped out of the parlor and was standing by the door, watching him. Kit shrugged. "If I said yes, would it matter?"

Baldwin lifted his brows. "Of course it would. I would not force my presence on you. At least not right now."

"Later then," Kit said with a dry laugh.

"If any of us thought you had spiraled into your grief for too long, probably *any* of us would seek you out to bring you home to us." Baldwin sighed. "But you have only recently lost your father. You are allowed to want to be alone. So I'll leave you."

"Wait," Kit said, gripping his hands against the rough stone wall and returning his gaze to the garden. "I'm sorry I am…difficult."

"You aren't," Baldwin said as he moved to stand beside Kit. "The *situation* is difficult. I know what it is like to lose a beloved father. It may have been many years ago, but the pain is still there."

"So I can look forward to feeling this way a very long time," Kit murmured. "That is not comforting."

Baldwin was quiet a moment. "Our situations are not the same," he said softly. "I loved my father, and he was connected to us in a loving way. But from almost the moment he died, I discovered all his lies, his debts, things that would destroy our family. My mourning for him was truncated, intruded upon by the betrayal I felt in his bad actions and the responsibility that fell on my shoulders to correct all of them."

Kit shook his head. "I cannot imagine how devastating it must have been to discover your father's weaknesses so soon after his death. You suffered alone for a long time."

Baldwin sighed. "I created a prison for myself far more than he ever did. And then Helena set me free. As did the kindness of my dearest friends."

Baldwin squeezed his arm gently and Kit nodded. The group as a whole had taken part in helping their friend invest a loan. In just two years, Baldwin had already paid them back in full, so Kit knew some part of the answer to his next question.

"Your new investments are paying off, aren't they?"

Baldwin nodded. "Yes. Thanks to all of you and the suggestion that I invest in Mr. Danford's ventures, my coffers are refilling every month. And that helps, of course. The pressure is coming off. But it is really my life with Helena that has helped me most in my grief."

Kit flinched. He was happy for his friend, of course, but this statement didn't help him. He had no woman in his life to offer comfort. His mind flitted to Sarah, but he pushed that away.

"I'm glad she offers you succor," he said softly. "She is a wonderful woman and you deserve your happiness."

"She is the best of women," Baldwin mused, staring up at the stars for a moment with a faraway smile. Then his attention snapped back to Kit. "I saw you speaking intently to Miss Carlton."

Kit shot him a side glare, for the statement felt rather accusatory. "She is a member of my household staff."

"And that's why you were holding her hand," Baldwin said.

Kit walked away a few steps, trying not to remember how soft Sarah's skin had been. How that lilac scent of her hair had filled his nostrils and softened the harsh edges of his emotions.

"I was looking at her mourning ring," he muttered. "I don't even like her."

Baldwin tilted his head and his gaze narrowed. "Yes, so you've been saying for years. You've made quite a study of watching the young woman as she navigated her final years in Society."

Kit shrugged. "I don't think so."

Baldwin lifted both eyebrows. "Every time you saw her, you pointed out her presence. I saw you watching her. If you didn't keep telling everyone you didn't like her, I might have even thought you had a *tendre* for her."

Kit faced him with an outraged snort. "For Sarah Carlton?"

"Yes. Honestly, Kit, I've never heard a good explanation for why you feel as you do toward her."

Kit shook his head. Despite his words to Sarah that night long ago, he'd never made any attempt to destroy her. Partly because Meg had asked him not to intervene. Partly because he didn't want to be the one to…to hurt Sarah.

He blinked at that realization and hardened himself to it and to her. "I keep my reasons to myself, but trust they are there. They no longer matter, though. Miss Carlton is in my employ, and that is how she will be managed. I don't need you lot getting bored and trying to create a situation that simply isn't there."

"Whatever you say, Kit." Baldwin looked out over the garden again. "Whatever you say."

Kit ignored the dry delivery and focused instead on the stars overhead. It was only the high emotion of losing his father that was making everything feel so odd. That was making him draw closer to Sarah. There was nothing more to it, no matter what silly stories his friends wanted to say.

No matter what his own tangled dreams tried to tell him.

Sarah glanced at the parlor door with a frown. Kit had been outside for a very long time. He wasn't alone, of course. The Duke of Sheffield had followed him out.

Not that it mattered to Sarah, of course. Her relationship to Kit was no different than it had been before. One conversation about the nature of grief, one brief flash of connection, couldn't change years of uneasy interaction. Kit was still her employer. He still didn't like her.

Nothing had changed at all.

"Sarah?"

She turned, happy enough to be distracted from her odd thoughts, and smiled as the Duchess of Willowby approached. Aside from Isabel, this lady was the one Sarah was most comfortable with. The woman was a healer and she and her husband had joined the family a few weeks before the old duke's death to see if the duchess could ease his pain. The woman had been nothing but kind and generous to the family, and to Sarah.

"Your Grace," Sarah said. When Diana lifted her brows, she laughed. "Diana."

"Better," Diana chuckled. "How are you holding up?"

Sarah shrugged. "Well enough, I suppose. The household

staff is all in mourning, though not as deeply as the family."

She glanced again at the door to the terrace, thinking of Kit's drawn face as they discussed the loss of his father. Despite their past, she felt for him.

Diana touched her hand. "I'm certain that this brings up painful memories of your own."

Sarah bent her head. She had already had this painful conversation once tonight. She didn't feel like repeating it. "I think of my mother, of course. Perhaps that will help me in my duties with Phoebe."

Diana wrinkled her brow. "I suppose that is true. No one would understand the death of a parent more." There was a brief, faraway look in her eyes for a moment, then her gaze cleared. "I saw you talking to Kit earlier, as well. I'm sure you will be a great comfort to them both."

Sarah caught her breath. She'd been so wrapped up in her conversation with the duke, she hadn't stopped to think that it had been held in a public room with everyone watching. Judging, perhaps. Making their own assumptions.

She shook her head. "I doubt the duke would seek my comfort. He is not fond of me."

Diana wrinkled her brow. "Is he not? Well, I was not part of your circles until my marriage, so I do not know the circumstances. But he didn't seem to be averse to your company a few moments ago."

There was something in Diana's tone that made Sarah's heart jump a little. She stared at the observant, clever lady and tried to find words to combat her implication. Because that implication was very clear. Diana was saying she'd seen a connection between Sarah and Kit.

Which was preposterous beyond words. That was why she struggled with the very concept.

"He is…in an untenable position, I suppose. His father hired me and we all know how Kit—" She broke off immediately. Had she truly just called the man Kit to his friend's wife? Oh, that was always how she referred to him in her mind. An old, unacceptable familiarity she had adopted for years.

But to do it out loud? When her position had so greatly changed? Heat suffused her cheeks and she wished to sink into the floor.

"I think between friends it is easier to refer to the dukes by their first names," Diana said softly, her green stare holding firm on Sarah's. "There are so many Your Graces in this room, your head would likely burst if you tried to refer to them all individually without confusing yourself."

Sarah swallowed. Well, her friend had certainly given her one excuse for her bad behavior. She would cling to it, even though in her heart she knew that clarity wasn't why she always thought of the man by not just his given name, but his nickname.

She pushed those thoughts aside. "The new duke," she began slowly, "was close to his father, and if he wishes to sack me, then I suppose that would be difficult for him to do so. That was all I was trying to say."

"Sack you?" Diana repeated. "Gracious, is that how deep whatever this animosity you think exists goes?"

Before Sarah could answer, the Duchess of Crestwood slipped up beside Diana and slid an arm around her. They two gave each other a warm squeeze and then Meg smiled at Sarah. "I was eavesdropping shamelessly, as I am wont to do. I heard the word *animosity* and got very curious."

Sarah caught her breath. Oh God, this was the moment she had been dreading for years. Now Meg would have Sarah's bad behavior thrown firmly in her face. It would be horrible and awkward and probably end in Sarah's dismissal. How could it not?

"Sarah was just telling me that Kit has some secret reason for not liking her," Diana explained. "Enough that she fears the security of her position here."

Meg's eyes went wide. "*No*. That cannot be. Whatever could you and Kit hold against each other?"

Sarah's mouth dropped open and she stared at the duchess with wide eyes. Meg didn't remember that awful night? How could she not? Sarah recalled each and every detail in fine relief. Every awful, tipsy word she'd said so long ago haunted her dreams, especially when she knew she'd have to talk to Meg or one of her friends.

Now, it was possible the duchess was just a fine actress, but she gave no indication that she was pretending not to recall the night that had changed Sarah's life forever. The one that had put her in the path of a wrathful Kit. Meg just stared at Sarah with empathy and kindness and true confusion.

Sarah hesitated, for she had no idea what to do. Did she remind Meg of what she had done? Wouldn't that only make everything worse? If she didn't remind her, did that mean she was lying? Wouldn't that only give Kit more ammunition against her if he found out?

Her head spun and she swallowed hard. "Once upon a time, His Grace and I had a rather unpleasant encounter," she said slowly, trying to walk a fine line between the truth and the *whole* truth. "He has not forgiven me for something I said in a moment of foolishness."

Meg blinked, but there was still no recognition on her face. "I'm sorry, I had no idea your relationship was so fraught. Is there anything we can do to help?"

Sarah shook her head. The very idea of Kit's friends injecting themselves in their relationship, especially Meg…was terrifying. Kit would see it as a manipulation. He would add it to her list of crimes.

"Thank you, but it is really not your concern," she said. "I'm certain the duke and I will work it out."

Meg stared at her a moment, her brow wrinkling. Then she nodded. "Of course, my dear. If I overstepped my bounds, I do apologize. I'm a fixer, you see. Ask Simon and he will tell you. But I realize that you are a grown woman and well-capable of approaching your own problems."

Sarah bent her head. "It was kindly meant and kindly taken, I assure you."

"Very good." Meg smiled. "Why don't you two come with me? I'd like to discuss some details about tomorrow's picnic with the rest of the ladies. We will have a great many small children to wrangle, even with the assistance of the nannies, and perhaps we can use Phoebe's love of helping as some kind of distraction for her."

Sarah pushed aside her bewilderment. She'd all but forgotten the picnic down by the lake that was planned for the next afternoon. It was a good reminder that she had duties here. Ones she had to take seriously and not just for her own sake.

So she did her best to forget all the difficulties she was facing with Kit and concentrated on Phoebe as she followed the ladies to their friends and all of them began to plan.

CHAPTER FIVE

Sarah couldn't help but feel nervous the next afternoon as she trailed along behind the large group of dukes and duchess and their children. She had not been able to sleep after excusing herself from their party the night before, tossing and turning as she relived every moment of her conversation with Kit. Had she said the right thing? The wrong thing? Would her candor and her attempt at comfort make their relationship better or worse?

When she was honest with herself, she also thought of other things. Like how full Kit's lips were as they moved in conversation. How dark and soulful his eyes were. And those cheekbones. A man should not be blessed with such cheekbones—it really didn't seem fair.

She sighed as Isabel fell back and linked arms with her. "You look tired."

Sarah chose to ignore her sleepless night as the cause and instead focused on her job. "Well, with all the nannies given the morning off so this would be a family event, how could one not be?" Isabel cocked her head and Sarah shrugged because she knew her friend could see right through her. "It was a…trying morning."

Isabel frowned. "I admit I could hear Phoebe when I was across the hall checking on the children in the nursery."

Pursing her lips, Sarah let her attention drift ahead to her charge. Phoebe was walking with James and Emma's oldest daughter, two-year-old Beatrice. She was holding the smaller girl's hand and chatting amicably with Emma as they strolled.

A stark comparison to the morning's collapse. "Phoebe is normally sweet as sugar in the morning," Sarah said with a sigh. "But since her father's death…"

Isabel squeezed her arm. "It is a phase. She's so young, it must be hard for her to process such grief and uncertainty."

"Well, her having a screaming fit cannot reflect well on me," Sarah said.

"On the contrary, I think it reflects beautifully on you. She does not do such a thing to any of the duchesses."

Sarah glared at her from the corner of her eye. "Thank you, that is helpful."

Isabel laughed. "She *trusts* you, Sarah. She knows that she can act out in the worst way without risking the loss of your affection.

Sarah faltered in her steps at that assertion and both women came to a stop on the path. She stared at Phoebe again and her heart swelled with love for the little girl. "I-I suppose I had not thought of it that way."

"At some point, of course it will be required to bring her back in line behaviorally," Isabel said. "But for now, I think your patience and kindness are doing wonders. She adores you."

Sarah shook her head. "Sometimes she does."

"No. I was in the nursery with Adam after her fit and she came in to sit with me. You know how she is obsessed with the little ones."

Sarah nodded.

"Well, she was telling me how much she loves everyone. Ranking those she loves, to be fair."

Sarah laughed. "Oh dear. That seems unkind."

"Well, if it helps, the geese seem to hold most her disdain. One chased her, so she loves him least. But do you know who she loves most?"

"Her brother, I'm certain," Sarah said, unable to hold back her smile as Phoebe released Bibi and raced forward to fall in step beside Kit. Without even looking, he reached for her hand, and she saw the little girl laugh as she snatched it and they began to swing their arms between them.

"It was a tie," Isabel said softly. "Between Kit and you."

Tears leapt to Sarah's eyes. Thanks to her position in the world, she had long ago given up on the idea of being a mother, herself. Despite the short duration of her employment, she had filled some of her maternal desires with her relationship with Phoebe.

"Oh," she whispered.

Isabel laughed. "She even told me she thought you two should wed, then you would be a 'real family'."

Sarah's tears fled, replaced by a lump that seemed to fill her throat immediately. "Gracious, I hope she doesn't say that to the duke. He would be scandalized by the idea, given my position and his strong feelings regarding me."

Isabel tilted her head. "Perhaps at some point he judged you for that day with Meg, but I was watching you two together at the gathering last night and he did not seem upset with you or judgmental."

"A passing moment, likely brought on by grief," Sarah said with a sigh. "Which apparently everyone in that room was watching and judging themselves. And why not? I'm a servant."

"You are not," Isabel said sharply.

The tears Sarah had felt when she thought of her connection to Phoebe returned, but this time they were focused on the loss of her connection to her old life. One she clearly had to address before it spiraled out of control. "Oh, Isabel, I do appreciate your kindness and the fact that you don't treat me as if anything has changed. But the fact is that it has."

Isabel shook her head, but Sarah didn't allow her to interrupt. "*Yes*, it has," she insisted. "My place is far below yours and it will be for the rest of my life. The best thing I can do for myself is to remember that fact. Accept it. And do my best to keep this job so I don't require interference on my behalf again."

"Sarah," Isabel whispered.

"I will always love you very much," Sarah continued. "And I will always remember you as my very best, most devoted friend. But right now I must go to Phoebe and put all my attentions on her. Enjoy your new friends and your lovely new life that I am so happy you get to lead."

She leaned up, kissed Isabel's cheek briefly and then scurried away. But she came down the hill toward the place where the picnic blankets had been laid out for the guests, she couldn't help but feel she had at last walked away from her girlhood dreams.

And into the life she now had to embrace in order to survive.

Kit loved his sister, but at present he was losing patience with the little girl. As his friends sat spread across half a dozen picnic blankets, passing their young children around, eating and drinking, their laughter should have lightened his heavy heart.

Instead, all he could do was watch as Sarah knelt before Phoebe, sternly talking to the little girl. In the hour since they'd come down to the lake, his sister had thrown three tantrums, ranging from a pouting fit to a full-on screaming explosion.

She folded her arms across her chest even now and her lower lip poked out as she shouted, "No!"

Kit let out his breath in a long sigh and got up off the blanket where he'd been sitting. Ignoring everything else around him, he marched across the grass until he reached the pair and bent to look his sister in her face. "Phoebe, that is enough."

Sarah glanced at him and back to his sister. "Please do not trouble yourself, Your Grace. I have matters in hand."

He scowled at her. "Do you? It doesn't seem entirely certain that is true."

The color left her cheeks and she pushed to her feet. Before she could speak, Phoebe huffed out her own breath. "I want to go on the boat."

Kit's head began to throb and he gave his sister a sharp look. "Well, this is not the way to go about it."

Once again, Sarah shook her head slightly and then reached out for Phoebe. Her hand hovered in the air between them and finally his sister took it, her face red with frustration and bright eyes sparkling with tears. In that moment, Kit saw how difficult her emotions were. How pain was driving her bad behavior. He had not been able to see the truth. Sarah had.

And he immediately wished he had not been so sharp with her, or with her governess.

"Phoebe," Sarah said, gently but firmly. "Your brother is right that behaving badly will not give you what you desire. It's a little early in the season for a ride on the boat." Phoebe opened her mouth, the tears beginning to fall. Before she could shriek, Sarah continued, "*But*…if you will take a walk with me, if you will calm down and behave yourself for a few moments, then I will consider your request and we can talk about it like ladies."

Kit held his breath as they both stared at Phoebe. She was shifting now, her mind clearly turning on all her options. Then she drew a long, shuddering breath and said, "Yes, Miss Sarah."

Sarah smiled at her and Kit's heart stuttered. She was lovely when she smiled. He didn't think he'd seen her do it ten times in all the years he'd known her. Circumstance had kept the expression from her face.

Circumstances that included the fact that she didn't like him. That was his doing, of course, but now he regretted not seeing that look before. Not coaxing it in any way possible just because of how it lit her eyes.

He frowned at the paths his mind had taken him on. He reached out to ruffle his sister's hair and she looked up at him with uncertainty. "Good girl, Phoebe. Now run ahead a moment, without going near the boats. I want to speak to Miss Carlton."

Phoebe nodded and raced away, leaving Kit and Sarah alone. He turned toward her, expecting a moment to tell her how much he appreciated her kindness, but he found her glaring at him with what was clearly annoyance.

"Your Grace, I understand that Phoebe is your sister and you are my employer, but I must insist that you do not undermine my authority with her, nor my method in approaching her."

He blinked at the hardness of Sarah's tone. Normally she spoke to him either gently, as she had the previous night, or with hesitation. This was neither of those things.

"I beg your pardon?" he asked.

She folded her arms, which drew his attention to the swell of her breasts, but he dragged his gaze away to focus. She was truly angry. "I did not require your interference. You said it wasn't clear that I had matters in hand, but I did."

"She ought not to act—"

"Like a child?" she interrupted. "She *is* a child, Your Grace. And on top of that, your sister is grieving, just as you are. But she is a little girl, with only a fraction of your self-control, so her emotions show themselves in sometimes unpleasant ways. You would do well to remember that and give her the same space others give you."

"Are you saying that if I had a screaming fit, my friends would not judge me for that?" he asked.

She shrugged. "I think they would understand it. They indulge you if you want to go stand on the terrace away from your own party for half an hour, don't they? Or have an extra drink after supper to soothe your nerves? Doesn't that child deserve the same amount of consideration?"

He scowled as a feeling of shame filled him. Perhaps he had not been patient enough with his sister. And yet Sarah told him he had overstepped his bounds. That she didn't need him. And it still stung.

"You may be right," he said through clenched teeth. "But

do not forget yourself, Miss Carlton. You serve at my pleasure."

The high color left her cheeks at the threat he immediately regretted making. Then her spine straightened and she met his gaze evenly. "Certainly, Your Grace. How could I, or anyone else for that matter, forget that fact when it is lorded over me with such regularity?"

With that, she pivoted on her heel and flounced away, leaving Kit to stare after her in frustration and upset and…other feelings. He felt other feelings as he watched her hips twitch off toward his sister.

He grunted out a sound of displeasure and went back to his blanket. His friends had departed it, gathering on the other blankets or in small groups standing around the area. The only one left was Meg, who still sat on the checkered fabric, her son James sleeping in her arms.

"Everyone else went off to talk to each other?" Kit asked, trying desperately to keep his tone neutral so his emotional outburst would not be so obvious.

Meg had been looking off in the distance, but she jerked her attention back to him. "Er, yes. Perhaps that is good, though. I wonder if you and I need to have a discussion."

She shifted the eighteen-month-old in her arms, laying him across the folds of the blanket gently before she got up and offered Kit an arm. "Come, let us walk, shall we? James will sleep a while, and I see Simon has his eye on the boy."

Kit grunted as he got back to his feet. He did not wish to walk, but there was no polite way to refuse his friend's wife. He took her arm and they strolled to the edge of the water. It gave them a good view of Sarah and Phoebe as they made their own way around the edge. And he watched. He couldn't help himself.

"Hmmm." He glanced down and found Meg was doing the same, her gaze following the pair with a deep frown on her face.

Kit tensed. In all the years that had passed since that night of the ball when Sarah had been so rude, Meg had never brought the topic up. Now he felt that moment coming, Meg's reminder that Sarah had been unpleasant, and he felt irrationally defensive. He had to shake away the odd sensation and breathe deeply to maintain calm.

"You seem troubled," Kit said.

He looked again toward the lake's edge where Sarah stood with Phoebe. From his sister's animated arm movements, it seemed she was perhaps working herself back into another tantrum, though Sarah seemed to be handling it well. Just as she had earlier. She was right that it had not been his place to intrude.

"I am," Meg said, and her voice interrupted his thoughts. He glanced down to find Meg's brow wrinkled. "Though I'm not certain how to even broach the subject."

He pursed his lips, more certain than ever that the past was about to be thrown in his face. "I think we can be honest with each other—we've known each other long enough."

She nodded, and some of the tension left her slender frame. "Of course. Adelaide always says that honesty is the best policy. Kit, I heard something last night and I cannot stop thinking about it."

He tilted his head. Their gathering of friends could not have troubled Meg. Of course, when he came back into the room from the terrace, he'd seen her standing with Sarah. Was it possible she'd been impertinent all over again?

He couldn't picture it, but then again…

"What did you hear?" he asked carefully.

"Where to begin? You see, I saw Diana and Sarah talking, so I joined them. They were discussing…you."

His eyes went wide. Sarah was talking about him with the wives of his best friends? That could not bode well. "Me?" he repeated. "What could they have to say about me?"

"I don't know how their conversation started, but you know Diana. She may be the most insightful of us all…I suppose it is the healer in her. Anyway, she was pressing Sarah about why in the world you would not like her. A subject I have a keen interest in, I admit, as it is not your nature to be so judgmental."

Kit stared at her, uncertain he could have heard that last part correctly. "What?"

Meg gave a smile. "You and Sarah are not entirely unalike. When I asked why your relationship was strained, she gave me rather the same blank, confused look as yours right now and mumbled something about a bad moment in the past."

Kit swallowed. It seemed Sarah recalled that night and what had transpired between them as keenly as he did. The only person who didn't was Meg, herself.

She continued, "Soon after, Sarah excused herself, and I was left with no answers, but a niggling feeling that I ought to know what she was talking about. I racked my brain, trying to recall what it was. I talked to Simon about it, even, and he was just as clueless."

"I…see," Kit said, uncertain if he should jog Meg's memory or not. To do so risked a threat to Sarah and her treatment by the duchesses. That should not have mattered, perhaps, but it did nonetheless.

"And then in the middle of the night I was jolted awake," Meg said. "Bolt upright. I recalled that once upon a very long time ago, Sarah and I had a little…exchange. At a ball at James and Emma's country home around the time of the mess with Simon and Graham."

Kit wasn't certain whether to be relieved she'd come to this conclusion herself or wish she hadn't recalled it at all. But there was no denying it now. It was not in his nature to lie. "Yes," he admitted softly.

All the color bled from Meg's cheeks. "Oh, *Kit*! Please do *not* tell me that you have disliked Sarah Carlton because of some little encounter you interrupted three years ago."

He pressed his lips together. "She was very rude to you, Meg."

Meg rolled her eyes. "As I recall, she was also a little tipsy. James never waters down his punch enough. And at the core of her upset was that she was disappointed. She thought she and

Simon might have made a connection that I frankly ruined by being desperately in love with the man."

"That's exactly right," Kit said, throwing his hands up in the air. "She was impolite at the height of your pain. I interrupted. How was I not to think of that after?"

Meg slapped a hand against her eyes and shook her head slowly. "You idiot."

He blinked. "I beg your pardon?"

"You heard me correctly." She dropped her hand away and stared at him. "Kit! That was a lifetime ago. In the heat of one of the worst moments for me, yes, but clearly in the heat of one of her worst, too."

"Meg," he began, though he had no idea how he would argue his case because the fact was that he knew Meg was correct.

She waved a hand to silence him. "After that night, Sarah *never* had a real chance in Society again. Simon must have felt like her last hope. And while I am very glad she did not succeed in her pursuit, I am certainly sorry that it led her to this."

"This?" he repeated. "Working for me?"

"Her mother dead, her fortune gone, her future uncertain," Meg said gently. "She has been through a great deal in those intervening years. More than enough to pay penance for any rudeness she might have exhibited. Even if she hadn't, I would never have requested, nor required, that you hold that night over her head for the rest of her life."

Kit stared off toward the lake. Sarah and his sister were boarding Phoebe's insisted-upon boat now. Somehow Sarah had gotten her to laugh, and his heart warmed. But also sank. Meg was taking him to task for a behavior he had convinced himself was earned by Sarah's actions. A loyalty to his friends had driven him, after all.

Meg said it was not required.

To assuage the guilt that followed that realization, he set his jaw. "Whether or not you forgave the young lady," he said, "that doesn't change her behavior. I…I was not wrong in believing her to be capable of…bad acts."

Meg stared at him, unblinking for a moment, and then she shook her head. "Oh."

"Oh?" he repeated, not liking the brightness that had entered her dark eyes. "What does *oh* mean?"

"I see it now. How could I have been so blind not to see it before?" she muttered, perhaps more to herself than to Kit.

He lifted both brows. "Would you like to explain yourself or should I go so you can finish the conversation that has nothing to do with me?"

"You weren't angry about what she said to me," Meg said softly. "You never were."

"Of course I was. It was untoward and unacceptable," he said.

"Well, I suppose that her sharpness with me didn't help, but *that* wasn't what drew you to such a prolonged and uncharacteristic reaction."

He shook his head. "You aren't making sense. What are you talking about?"

Meg leaned in. "You didn't like it that Sarah was pursuing *Simon.*"

He let out his breath in a huff. "Don't be ridiculous."

"That's it," Meg said. Her tone had gentled and she reached out to squeeze his arm. "You were jealous."

"You're being absurd." He snatched his arm from her grip and drew back from her, nearly depositing himself into the water to avoid her pointed accusation. The one that didn't feel as absurd as it should.

"*Kit,*" she said, reaching out once more. This time she covered his hand with hers. "Sarah only pursued Simon in desperation, you had to know that. Certainly you must know it now, after watching the terrible consequences to her father's behavior and her mother's death play out."

He stared at her and then let his gaze flit back to Sarah. She and Phoebe had begun to row out to the lake now. Even from a distance, he could hear Phoebe hooting in pleasure as Sarah slowly worked the paddles.

Meg was being ridiculous, of course. He had noticed Sarah before that night at the ball when he heard her nasty words. How could one not? She was pretty and accomplished. But he had noticed many a lady over the years. Sarah had never been anything special.

When he learned she'd been invited to James and Emma's country party, he hadn't been disappointed. And he *had* watched her with Simon, at the party where he and Meg had nearly brought their entire club to its knees with scandal. Had Kit liked seeing her in his handsome friend's arms?

It hadn't mattered. He didn't recall it mattering, at least not much. Meg was wrong. She was just…*wrong*.

He was about to tell her so, too. To set her straight so that this ridiculous notion wouldn't take root in the group of his friends and make them play matchmaker or worse. Only he didn't get the chance. Before he could say a word, he heard a sound that turned his blood to ice.

It was Matthew, and he was screaming. "Don't let her stand up! She's rocking the boat! Stop her!"

Kit pivoted. Out in the middle of the lake, a nightmare scene began to play out in slow motion. Phoebe had risen from her place, off balance in the small boat. As Sarah lunged for her, the entire contraption capsized and both of them disappeared from view.

Kit yelped out a sound of terror, and then he and Matthew were running. Into the water, swimming toward them. And he could only pray they would not be too late.

CHAPTER SIX

Sarah plunged beneath the icy waters of the lake. Despite the warm spring air, the lake was frigid, and it made her body feel even less malleable.

Everything had happened so fast. One moment she and Phoebe were rowing out together, the next the little girl was on her feet and everything was turning upside down.

She sputtered as she managed to get herself above water and reached out to catch Phoebe as the child thrashed wildly.

"No, no! No!" Phoebe cried out as she bobbed under and above the water.

"Calm…down…" Sarah gasped as she struggled to kick her legs and stay at the surface with her charge.

Phoebe was too wild and terrified to hear her. She kicked and twisted, trying to stay afloat. She felt desperately heavy in Sarah's arms as she pushed at the little girl to keep her head above water. Sarah's own skirts tangled around her legs, cumbersome and limiting her ability to kick and stay above water.

She dunked down beneath the surface once more, and panic gripped her. They would drown. Oh God, she didn't want to drown. She gripped Phoebe's hips and pushed her, holding her as high as she could to give her charge the best chance possible.

Sarah kicked and surfaced enough to gasp in a breath, but

she immediately dropped down again. Phoebe's legs flailed and her slippered foot caught Sarah in the temple. Pain exploded and was followed by dizzying stars exploding before her eyes. Everything was starting to feel slow, tired, everything hurt as she fought.

But she couldn't succumb. She couldn't. She had to keep the little girl up. She couldn't let Phoebe drown. She had to stay afloat until rescue came. She'd seen the men running into the water when she last surfaced. They would get here soon and then it would be all right.

Suddenly Phoebe's weight was lifted away from her. Someone had come. She couldn't see who through the dark, dirty water. But she felt the waves hit her as a stronger swimmer drew the child away. Relief filled her, but also fear. She was sinking. Deeper and deeper. She struggled to swim back to the surface, but her lungs burned from lack of air and her skirts felt like weights drawing her to the floor of the lake.

Drawing her to the end of her life.

She sucked in without meaning to and felt water enter her lungs. It was like someone had plopped down on her chest.

There was nothing left to do—she was just too weak. Everything grew dark, the pain began to fade, and she slipped into the cold, wet nothingness at the bottom of the lake.

Kit swam as hard as he could, but he was three body lengths behind Matthew. He saw his friend, who had his own experience with such a terrible scene, moving in the thrashing swirl of Phoebe and Sarah's bodies.

"I have her!" Matthew shouted as he began to swim back toward Kit. "I have Phoebe."

Kit could see his pale, terrified sister clinging to his friend, shaking like a leaf. Relief jolted through him. She was alive. She was breathing.

"Sarah?" he gasped out.

"Still under the water!" Matthew shouted, and began to swim back toward the shore where the others were coming into the water to help. "I'll come back."

But Kit knew that would be too late. Sarah was under the water. She would die. He dove into the murky blackness, but there was nothing to see when the water had been so churned up by the struggle.

Panic gripped him and he reached out in the water for her, praying with all his might that he would touch her. Prayers left unanswered. She was nowhere, nowhere to be found. He surfaced, sucking in a deep breath, and then dove again, deeper this time. God, he had to find her. He had to find her—he couldn't lose her like this.

He swung his arms wildly and was about to come up for air again when he felt his hand bump something. Something soft, fleshy. He jolted and grabbed on. It was Sarah's arm.

He pulled, dragging her against him. He slid his arm beneath her armpits, hating that she was limp, not helping him at all. He pulled her to the surface and looked at her as she flopped against his chest like a lifeless doll. She was blue. Not breathing.

"Oh God," he gasped as he began to swim.

He dragged her toward Simon and Graham, who were coming toward him in the waist-deep water closer to shore. When he reached them, Graham grabbed for Sarah, hauling her onto the shore as Simon tugged Kit to safety.

He flopped down next to her in the dirt. She did not stir. She didn't move.

"Oh God," he whispered again as he realized she was dead. A pain that cut down to his very soul filled every part of him at that horrible realization. Sarah was dead and he would never get to apologize for how he'd treated her over the years. He'd never get to touch her. Coax that smile from her. Keep her safe.

The duchesses were weeping. Matthew was on his knees, tears streaming down his cheeks as Isabel held him, her own sobs wracking her. They had lost someone they both loved to a drowning many years ago. Now that would be something he shared with his friends. A terrible new club born of this awful, unceasing heartbreak.

His bleary gaze shifted, seeking out his sister. He found her with Graham's wife Adelaide. She had wrapped Phoebe in one of the picnic blankets, and she turned the sobbing, exhausted little girl away so she wouldn't see her lifeless governess lying on the shore, lost to them all.

"No," he moaned as he reached out to touch Sarah's cheek.

"Get out of the way." Lucas was pushing his way through the crowd of their friends. He dropped down beside Sarah's body and waved Kit off. He stared as Lucas leaned down and pressed his mouth to hers.

Kit jerked his face toward Diana, but she didn't seem to be troubled or surprised by this…was it a kiss? What was the point now?

"Come on, sweetheart, work with me," Lucas grunted as he lifted his mouth from Sarah's. He jerked his face into the crowd. "Diana!"

She didn't hesitate, but shoved Kit aside none too gently. He got to his feet and stared along with the others as she began to gently press Sarah's chest. Lucas put his mouth back on Sarah's, and it was then that Kit realized his friend wasn't kissing her. He was breathing into her.

Breathing her back to life.

Hope flared. He had no idea if such a thing would work, but he gripped his hands into fists at his sides as he prayed it would.

"Please," he murmured, not caring that the mournful sound was out loud now, heard by all. "Oh, please don't take her. I will do anything."

They continued their work for another moment and then Sarah turned her head and retched water onto the shore. She gasped for air, one breath, two, and Kit went down to his knees as he realized she was alive. She was alive.

The sobs of his friends turned to gasps of relief, joy and disbelief. He hardly heard any of it as he reached out to touch Sarah's hand again. She turned her face, her blue eyes locking with his.

"Ph-ph-phoebe," she managed through the shivers that now wracked her.

"Is fine," he said as he bent and swept her into his arms. "You saved her life." She didn't fight him, but her head lolled into his shoulder. He looked at the group. "We need to get them up to the house and everyone dry."

"Yes, that water was frigid," Diana said. "Everyone needs to change their clothes so none of you catch your deaths. Sarah more than anyone."

Kit was already striding up the hill, retracing the path they had come down with such laughter and happiness what felt like a lifetime ago.

"Y-your Gr-gr-grace," Sarah whispered without lifting her head. He ignored her, though her warm breath on his wet neck was the most beautiful sensation he'd ever felt in his life. "K-Kit! Please, I c-can w-walk—"

He glared down at her. "Please shut up," he snapped, sharper than he should have been but unable to do anything else thanks to the fear that still coursed through his veins. He felt her collapse against him again, her weak protests gone now.

He was almost to the house now. Barrymore must have been doing something in the parlor and seen their approach, because the door flew open and he hurried out to the step.

"Your Grace?" he called out, face lined with deep concern.

"Miss Carlton had an accident," he said. "Is my chamber at the ready?"

Barrymore looked confused but did not comment on the odd request, just said, "Yes, Your Grace. They just finished with it. The fires are still lit."

"Good," Kit said as he carried Sarah up the stairs two by two. He could hear everyone else talking to the butler, explaining to him what Kit had not been able to say out loud for fear of reliving those awful moments in the water and at its edge. He couldn't do that, not when she was still unwell.

"N-n-not your ch-chamber," she murmured.

Once again he ignored her protest and strode through his chamber door. Two maids, Jill and Lydia, were just finishing up their work, and both of them stopped and stared in horror at the soaking wet image before them.

"Your Grace!" Jill cried. "Is that Miss Carlton?"

He moved to rest her on his bed, but Diana and Hugh's wife Amelia raced into the room.

"No!" Diana called out. "You'll make the bed wet. Put her on the settee. Amelia and I will take care of her."

He placed Sarah gently on the settee as they'd asked.

"I'll r-ruin i-it," she said, staring up at him weakly.

"I don't care," he managed through clenched teeth.

"Now get out," Amelia said, grabbing his arm and guiding him to the door. "You need to change out of those wet clothes. Check on your sister."

"Phoebe?" he whispered.

Diana had moved to Sarah and glanced up. "Adelaide, Emma and Meg are tending to her. Now go."

Amelia gave him a short nod and then closed the door in his face. He stared at the barrier now between him and the woman who had nearly died to save his sister's life. And he tipped forward to lean against the door as all the fear hit him at once.

Sarah was aware of the soft, female hands moving over her body. Her sopping wet gown was being stripped away, and they were talking to the maids. Warm air brushed her bare skin and someone was rubbing a towel over her none too gently. Her flesh tingled as heat returned to it and slowly her awareness increased.

"Here, hold up your arms," Amelia, the Duchess of Brighthollow, said softly.

Sarah lifted them as high as they would go, despite how heavy all her limbs felt. A shirt came down over her naked body. A man's shirt. She realized with a start that it was Kit's shirt. It was leagues too big and smelled of him. Leather and sandalwood and something generally masculine.

The women caught her arms and helped her to unsteady feet. She let them draw her to the bed that the maids had turned down and slid between the sheets. Someone had placed a warming brick wrapped in flannel down at the bottom of the bed, and she shuddered as her cold toes hit that warm heaven.

She was coming back to reality now. Memories returned of going under the water. Of the darkness. Of a bright light that followed it. A tunnel of light that had felt so welcoming. She'd seen her mother there and farther back, over her shoulder, Kit's father. Everything had seemed so warm and happy and good.

But her mother had reached out her hand and whispered, "Not yet, love."

Then Sarah had been on the shores of the lake, her lungs burning as she retched up water. She had died. Or almost died? Either way, a wave of emotion rose up in her and she began to weep.

"Oh, dearest," Amelia said as she climbed up beside Sarah on the bed and guided her head into her shoulder.

"My hair is wet, I'll ruin your gown," Sarah said, her shivers finally subsiding enough that she didn't stammer.

"I don't give a whit," Amelia assured her as she smoothed her hand over that damp hair. "You cry now, it's all right."

Diana was bustling on the side of the bed, pressing her thumb to Sarah's wrist, placing a hand on her forehead, checking her eyes.

"I'm sorry," Sarah sobbed.

Diana hesitated and then cupped her cheeks gently. "You have nothing to be sorry about. You were so very brave."

She shook her head against her friend's hands. "No. No, it was my fault."

"How is that true?" Amelia asked.

"I knew Phoebe was in a dudgeon and that it was far too early to go out on the boats. I was trying to give her space and allow her a little extra time. I was responsible for keeping her safe and I-I didn't." Her thoughts spun to Phoebe's terrified expression, to her fearful thrashing. "That little girl has been through so much. Was she truly unharmed?"

Amelia stroked her hair. "Just frightened, I think more over the potential of losing you than anything. You saved her life. And as far as it being your fault, any one of us might have taken her out in that boat. We're all being a little more indulgent with her as she navigates her grief. If you hadn't taken her, Hugh was discussing that he should, himself."

"If he had, I'm sure he wouldn't have let her flip the boat," Sarah said, her tears subsiding as she lifted her head from Amelia's now-damp shoulder.

"Don't be ridiculous," Diana said as she finished with her bustling and perched on the edge of Kit's bed. "As Amelia said, that could have happened to anyone."

Sarah worried her lip. "I doubt the duke will see it that way," she whispered, thinking of Kit's arms around her as he carried her to the house, and of the sharpness with which he had spoken to her. "He shall sack me at last, put me out on the street without a reference."

"No," Amelia reassured her.

"He has been looking for a reason to do so," Sarah said.

Diana shook her head. "If he dared to do something like that after your heroics, he would have a gaggle of duchesses at his throat. The gentlemen have learned over the years, my dear, not to cross the wives. Kit included."

Amelia pushed to her feet. "I should go give the others an

update on your condition."

Diana nodded. "A very good idea. And I know that Adelaide will make certain Phoebe is dry, but also be sure those men changed their clothing. I will not deal with pneumonia because they refused to stop beating their chests."

Amelia laughed as she gave a mock salute. "Yes, Your Grace."

After she'd gone, Diana glanced at Sarah. "You cannot really believe that Kit would dismiss you so cavalierly?"

"I don't know," Sarah whispered. Except that wasn't true. She did know. No matter what anyone said, she knew exactly the hell that would come. And probably sooner rather than later.

CHAPTER SEVEN

Kit walked into the parlor, straightening his waistcoat as he did so. He had not wanted to leave his chamber, but Barrymore had been quite insistent that he change so he didn't fall ill. It had rather reminded him of when he was a child and the old butler had been an authority figure.

As he entered the room, he came to a stop. Matthew and Isabel were sitting on the settee together. Her arms were around him and she was murmuring soft words in his ear. Both looked pale, drawn, and for a moment Kit considered just slipping out to grant them their privacy. But Isabel looked up before he could and got to her feet with a gentle smile.

"Ah, Kit. Are you well?" she asked.

He nodded slowly. "Any word about Miss Carlton?"

"Amelia let us know the young lady will be fine," Isabel reassured him. "Diana is still with her. And your sister is with Adelaide—they're getting her dried off and taken care of. I think they intend to send her here to you in a short while."

She moved closer and glanced at Matthew. He had not risen from the couch, and stared at a spot on the floor with a faraway stare. "Talk to him," she whispered.

Kit jolted. He had been so wrapped up in his own part in the drama of the day that he hadn't been thinking clearly about how it might affect Matthew. After all, he had witnessed a drowning before. It had not had a happy ending like today.

"I will," he said, stepping toward his friend.

"Love," Isabel said.

Matthew jerked his gaze toward her and gave a weak smile. "Yes?"

"I'm going to check on the baby," she said. "And then I will find Lucas so you can have your questions answered."

Matthew pushed to his feet suddenly. "I love you."

Her expression softened. "I never doubt that. Never."

Then she slipped from the room. Matthew all but collapsed back on the settee and Kit took a careful place beside him. "You look like hell."

Matthew managed half a smile at the old form of ribbing the friends had shared for years. Decades. But Kit could see it would take more than a private joke to free Matthew from his dark thoughts.

"You saved my sister," he said.

Matthew nodded. "Christ, Kit, when I saw that boat flip, I swear I was taken back in time."

"To Angelica," Kit said gently. She had been Matthew's fiancée what seemed like a lifetime ago. And she had died in an accident almost identical to today's.

"Everything seemed to slow to half time and all I could do was run."

"When I see you so happy with Isabel, it is easy to forget that you went through such an ordeal," Kit said. "But I understand it better now. God knows I will never forget today until the day I draw my last breath."

"You will not," Matthew said firmly. He glanced toward the door. "Speaking of Isabel, I feel terrible. My reaction was strong, I know it. So was hers…after all, Angelica was her cousin. It is our shared loss. But I hope it doesn't hurt her, or make her think that I still hold Angelica in my heart."

"One only has to spend a moment with you two to see that Isabel holds your whole heart," Kit said softly. "I'm certain she understands that you are reacting to the shock." For a moment the two men were quiet, each lost in thought. "Why is she getting Lucas?"

Matthew bent his head. "He did that thing…breathed into Sarah. Some kind of kiss of life."

Kit shifted. He'd thought it was a kiss, too, when Lucas had begun. "Yes, I've never seen such a thing."

"I want to know what it was," Matthew said, his voice shaking. "And how to do it."

Kit reached out to squeeze his arm. "Of course you do."

Matthew sighed heavily and then shook his head. "What about you? How are you holding up?"

"I'm…*terrible*, honestly. All I can do is think back over and over to my sister's terrified face. And to how blue Sarah was. I thought she was dead, Matthew. I thought she was dead and I—"

Matthew lifted both brows. "You what?"

"It was such a strong reaction," Kit whispered. "Like someone had reached into my chest and was tearing my heart in two. I've spent years telling myself I do not like this woman and yet when I thought I would lose her, I felt only regret."

Matthew's brow wrinkled, but before he could say anything in response, Lucas entered the room. Like Matthew and Kit, he had also changed out of his wet clothing. They rose together, and Kit stepped forward.

"Thank you," he said.

Lucas tilted his head. "Of course. I'm just glad I had the training to be of some assistance."

Matthew gripped his hands at his sides. "What was that?"

Lucas looked at their friend and Kit saw the same concern he felt. The same acknowledgement that when it came to this subject, Matthew was not going to be capable of rational response.

"Matthew—"

"Could I have done the same and saved *her* life?"

Lucas reached out and gripped his arm. "The training is not common. I learned it from a boat captain just a few years ago while on assignment for the War Department. Diana and I have discussed it and altered it over time. There was no way you could have known to try such a thing in your situation. And you've told me about it before. Angelica was much farther away, your lake was larger. Honestly, a few more moments and it is possible I could not have saved Sarah. There was nothing you could have done, Matthew. Look at me."

Matthew was shaking and he met their friend's eyes slowly. "Yes?"

"There was *nothing* you could have done," Lucas repeated.

As Matthew relaxed a fraction, the door to the parlor opened again, and this time it revealed Phoebe and Adelaide. Immediately Kit dropped to his knees and opened his arms. His sister rushed to him, burying her face in his shoulder as he rocked her gently.

"Come," Lucas said, slinging an arm around Matthew gently. "Let the siblings reunite and I'll teach you the method."

"Yes," Matthew said, and the two joined Adelaide in the hallway and closed the door behind themselves.

Kit swept his sister up and carried her over to the settee. He sat down, adjusting her in his lap, and couldn't help but smile. She was getting so big—it seemed like she was all arms and legs now. And he would get to see her grow up, thanks to Sarah and his friends.

"I'm sorry, Kit." Phoebe's voice was muffled against his shoulder and he reached up to smooth her hair. It was still damp, and he shuddered a little at the memories that brought back.

"I know you are, poppin," he said. "It was an accident— you didn't mean to flip the boat."

She lifted her face from his shoulder and stared up at him. Her brown eyes were wide and still filled with unshed tears. "I didn't."

"Shall we discuss what happened?" he asked softly,

fighting to keep his voice firm but kind when all he wanted to do was cuddle her close and forget about what had happened that day.

"I was upset."

"Yes," he said. "You were throwing a tantrum."

She glanced away, a furtive and guilty stare. "I got up in the boat."

"Even though Papa told you many times that you shouldn't do that," Kit said. "Now you see why."

She nodded quickly. "Yes. And then we were in the water. I was scared, Kit. It was cold."

He hadn't recalled that fact, but now it rushed back. The icy grip of the water swirling around him as he raced to his sister and her governess.

"Miss Sarah saved you, along with Matthew," he said.

"She held me up in the water," Phoebe said solemnly. "She wouldn't let me go under like she did." She shifted. "Kit, is Miss Sarah hurt?"

"No, Amelia reported that she was fine. We are very lucky that Lucas knew how to breathe air back into her lungs." He snuggled her closer. "She's resting now. And I think you should do the same after we're done talking."

Her face crumpled, but to his surprise she didn't argue. Apparently the day's events had taken some of the starch from her.

"Phoebe, just because you don't mean for something to happen, just because it was an accident, doesn't mean that you don't have responsibility," he said carefully. "I know it's hard right now. You miss Papa. So do I."

"You do?" she whispered.

He tilted his head. "Of course I do, with all my heart. And when we are sad, sometimes we don't behave well. But we must do better, mustn't we? We must try a little harder so our grief doesn't make things worse."

She seemed to ponder that a moment and then she nodded.

"Yes, Kit."

"If you are sad, instead of getting angry or acting badly, you come to me. We can talk about Papa. We can be sad together."

"And talk to Sarah," Phoebe said, lifting her hand to play with one of his buttons.

"Yes, and talk to Sarah," he said with a soft sigh.

"Can I see her now?" Phoebe asked. He heard the hesitation in her voice. The guilt.

"You shall," he said with a little squeeze for her. "But I need to talk to her first."

And it could no longer wait.

Sarah rested her head back on the fluffy pillows, staring up at the finely carved ceiling above the comfortable bed. She was exhausted and her eyelids drooped, though she tried to stay awake. It felt wrong to sleep in Kit's bed. Wrong to be in his bed at all, no matter how welcoming it felt.

Diana stepped up to look at her. Sarah smiled. "You must stop fussing," she said. "I'm fine."

"You drowned and were brought back to life thanks to my husband's training. I will fuss all I like."

Sarah sighed. "I should get up. Get back to work."

She moved to sit up, but Diana placed a hand on her shoulder and held her steady. "I think not!"

"I cannot stay in the Duke of Kingsacre's bed all day, Diana," Sarah protested, though she didn't fight the hand holding her in place. "It is unseemly!"

Before Diana could answer, there was a light knock on the door from the antechamber. Sarah tensed, fearful of who had come. Diana shot her a hard look and then slipped off to answer. She didn't open the door all the way, but spoke to the person outside for a brief moment. Then she opened the door and Sarah caught her breath.

It was Kit. His gaze slid past Diana and speared her, unreadable. Unmovable. And she was suddenly painfully aware that she was in the man's shirt and nothing else, propped up in his bed, her hair down around her shoulders.

"Diana," he said without removing his gaze from Sarah. "I'd like to speak to Miss Carlton alone."

Diana blanched and glanced back at Sarah. She could see the healer fighting a little war in her head between propriety and the fact that Kit was Sarah's employer and could ask whatever he liked of her.

She arched a brow. "Let her rest," she said, then smiled back at Sarah and slid from the room.

Kit reached back and shut the door behind her, and they were alone. In his bedchamber. Sarah had never felt so exposed, and she lifted the sheets just a little more as he took a long step toward her in the suddenly very quiet room.

She swallowed hard. "Your Grace, I apologize for all the trouble," she squeaked out.

He kept moving forward, though his jaw tensed a fraction. "Hmmm."

She worried her lip at the noncommittal response. Dear God, but he was tall. Had he always been so tall? Perhaps it was just that she'd never seen him from this angle.

She shook the odd thought away and focused. She knew what was coming—there was no use being a ninny about it. It was better just to face it and have it done with.

"I assume you have come here to sack me," she said, happy that her voice was a little stronger than it had been a moment before.

The words stopped him in his tracks and he came to a halt at the foot of the bed. He stared at her, his eyes wide, and his cool demeanor cracked for a moment.

"Do you?" he asked.

"Of course. You've been looking for a reason, haven't

you?" She didn't wait for his response as her high emotions, which had been held inside for so long, suddenly bubbled up. She supposed it didn't matter anymore. She was done for, so she might as well just let it all out. "You don't like me because of what happened all those years ago between me and the Duchess of Crestwood. Which isn't fair! If I owe anyone an apology for that night, it is Meg, not you. And yet you have lorded it over me since that horrible moment when you threatened to destroy me."

His cheek twitched. "Are you finished?"

She shook her head. Now that she'd begun, she realized she *wasn't* finished. She wanted to say all these things. To be honest instead of afraid. She'd almost died today, so the consequences of anything else now paled in comparison.

"No!" she said, and he jolted in surprise. "I realize that I was very wrong with your sister today. She almost..." She blinked violently against the tears that returned to her eyes. "She almost died because of me. And if you sack me for that, it is no less than I deserve."

One eyebrow lifted and he stared at her a long time before he said, "Are you arguing for or against my dismissing you?"

She blinked at the question. Then she shrugged. "I-I don't think my opinion on the matter makes any difference. You shall do as you please. As you said to me earlier today, I serve at your pleasure."

He let out his breath in a long, almost painful sigh, and to her surprise he sat down on the foot of the bed. His weight changed the feel of the mattress, his warmth seemed to seep through the blankets. Her breath was suddenly short and she tried to pretend that was only because of her precarious personal situation, but it wasn't true.

He was just too close to breathe.

"Of course your opinion matters," Kit said softly. "You— you would have died today for my sister, yes or no?"

She bent her head as memories flashed through her mind.

Her terror for Phoebe, for herself. The horrible weight of her gown. The little girl's thrashing. The way the water had felt as it filled her lungs.

"Yes," she whispered as a tear slid down her cheeks.

"You did die," he said slowly. "That means everything to me, Sarah."

She caught her breath. In three years, he had only once called her anything but Miss Carlton. It kept a distance between them. But now her name was a caress. A prayer. And it moved her far more than it should have when he said it.

He got up but didn't back away. He came closer, settling back into a seat next to her. Now she could smell him. A soapy, clean, fresh and masculine smell.

"I pulled you out of the water," he continued. "And my world shattered when you weren't breathing."

She blinked. It was all she could do in the face of this unexpected confession, in the face of all the emotion in his voice and his dark eyes. She watched his hand lift, hesitate, and then he touched her cheek.

It was like someone set her body aflame. He slid his fingers along her cheekbone and tingles flared in their wake, making her aware, once more, of what a precarious position they were in. He ought not to be touching her while she lay in his bed.

But she wasn't about to stop him.

Nor did she stop him as he leaned in, closer, close enough that his breath stirred her lips. And then he kissed her. For a brief moment, it was the lightest of touches. A chaste brush of lips on lips. Then his fingers burrowed into her hair, cupping her scalp as he tilted her head, and the world exploded.

His mouth became insistent. She opened to him without understanding why and tasted his tongue as he breached her lips. She reached for him, trying to find an anchor as she lost all sense of time, of space, of propriety, of everything but the feel of him as he touched her.

She was alive. Back from the dead. And she understood it

now, felt what she had nearly lost under that dark water. This. This pleasure, this wicked bliss, this dark desire that pulsed through her entire body and settled in the most private and inappropriate places.

But she didn't care about appropriateness anymore. Or whether he liked her or judged her. All she cared about was that she didn't want this heated, sparkling moment to end.

All she wanted was more.

CHAPTER EIGHT

Kit knew he had to stop kissing Sarah. He had to stop because the desire that was burning in his blood was too powerful and in a moment it would sweep him away. Then God knew what he would do.

But pulling back felt physically painful, and it took every ounce of control in his shaking, throbbing body to do just that.

He remained close to her, though, their faces inches apart. Their lips so close he could almost still taste her. She stared at him, blue eyes bleary with desire that he'd tasted in her kiss. And confusion, which he understood. Five minutes before they were talking about his dismissing her, about their history…

And then his mouth had been on hers and nothing else in the damned world mattered.

"I didn't mean to do that," he said, his fingers still tracing her impossibly soft skin. He wanted to touch all of it in that moment. Feel her body beneath him as proof that she was safe and whole.

He had never been a libertine, but there it was. The truth in stark terms.

There was a knock on the chamber door and he released her, rising and turning away just as the door opened. Phoebe stood with one of the maids, twisting with discomfort as she peeked into the room.

"Phoebe!" Sarah called out, her voice slightly hoarse.

The moment her name was said, Phoebe seemed to lose all shyness. She bolted into the room at full speed past Kit and launched herself onto the bed and into Sarah's arms. He wondered if she should be so rough, but held his tongue and stepped away a fraction as the two embraced.

She cuddled into Sarah's arms, and they stayed that way for a short while. Silent as they bonded in a way that didn't require words.

Finally Phoebe glanced up into her face and whispered, "I'm glad Lucas saved you."

Sarah's expression softened. "As am I. And that the Duke of Tyndale saved you. We were both very lucky."

Phoebe worried her lip. "It was my fault, Sarah."

Kit kept his gaze on Sarah even as he tried to pretend he was not paying attention. There was no anger on her face, no blame. Just love. Just everything he would ever want for his sister.

"It was an accident," Sarah said gently. "You didn't mean to capsize the boat. I know that."

"We will never go in the boat again," Phoebe said solemnly. "Or the lake."

Kit expected that Sarah would agree to that suggestion. Right now it seemed fine enough to him. He would burn that damned boat if it hadn't already sunk to the bottom of the lake.

But to his surprise, Sarah shook her head. "Oh no, sweetling. We mustn't be afraid of things, that is no way to live. What we must do is to learn from our mistakes. You learned a great deal today, I would think."

Phoebe was nodding. "Oh yes. Not to stand in the boat."

"Exactly right," Sarah said, smoothing a lock of hair away from Phoebe's forehead. "And to listen, yes?"

"And not to have a tantrum when I'm sad." Phoebe glanced at Kit swiftly. "Kit says I can talk to him or to you."

"A very good idea." She glanced over at Kit and her

expression was unreadable. Certainly he couldn't tell what she was thinking about him now that he'd kissed her.

Something he wanted to repeat, especially since she looked so damn fetching in his shirt and in his bed. Just as pretty as she'd looked at any fancy ball over the years.

He swallowed those feelings and stepped up to the bed. "Phoebe, we must let Miss Sarah rest now. And you must rest, too. If you go to your room, I'll come tuck you in for a sleep."

Phoebe's lips pinched, and for a moment he thought she might protest. Then she glanced at Sarah and nodded. "Yes, Kit."

She leaned up to kiss Sarah's cheek, then scuttled down from the bed and out of the room. To his chagrin, she left the door open rather than shut it. Which meant more kissing was out.

Probably for the best, but it didn't change the unexpected desire that still boiled inside of him.

"I shouldn't stay in your bed, Your Grace."

"Kit," he said softly. "And staying in my bed is exactly what you will do, Sarah, until Diana says you are free to get up."

Her lips parted. "Your Grace—"

"Kit. Women who save my sister and who I kiss so thoroughly do not call me Your Grace." He leaned in and brushed her cheek with his thumb, watching how her pupils dilated with pleasure at the touch. "Please."

"Kit," she whispered, like she was trying it out. Testing it. Then she shook her head. "I will stay for a while."

"Good." He backed away from her and headed for the door. There he stopped and turned back. "Oh, and Sarah?"

She glanced over at him. "Yes?"

"I'm not going to sack you. You should put that out of your mind."

Relief flowed over her features instantly and stoked guilt in his belly. She had truly been terrified of that outcome, and obviously for a long time.

"Thank you," she whispered.

"But I do not promise that I won't kiss you again," he added. "Provided you give me permission."

Her mouth dropped open, but he did not allow a reaction. He strolled from the room, his step just a little lighter.

Sarah stared at the closed door from which Kit had just departed. She was…astounded. He had *kissed* her. Thoroughly. Oh, so thoroughly. Her mouth still tingled, her body still burned, and for the first time in her life, she understood why someone would throw everything away for just a taste of such passion.

Not to mention he'd said he wouldn't sack her. The weight that removed from her chest…she felt like she could take a full breath for the first time since she was hired and realized Kit would soon hold the keys to her fate.

But now that both those things had been done, now that he'd left her with a promise of more kissing, she was flummoxed. Where the hell did they stand since the world had been turned on its head?

It seemed they were no longer enemies, but what could they be if not that? That had been her entire definition of what they were for three long years.

She got up slowly, resting her hand on the high edge of his bed to steady herself. She really felt fine, just a little tired and achy, like she'd run a long way. Run from death.

Pushing those thoughts away, she looked around the room. It had been the room of Kit's father until a few weeks ago, when the old duke requested to be moved to a chamber that overlooked the orchard rather than the garden. What a solemn day that move had been, for everyone had known that he would never return to his own bed.

The chamber already felt like Kit's. It was masculine, the

walls in dark colors with wood accents, but understated. It was filled with his personal things. She glanced over her shoulder at the door to be certain no one was going to see her spy. Then she stepped up to a little table near the fire. It was covered with miniatures of his family and his friends.

She leaned in and examined the one of Phoebe. It had been painted a few years ago—the little girl could not have been more than two, but she still had the same wide smile and bright eyes. There was a miniature of his father, as well. A younger man, healthier than the one who had hired her and treated her so kindly. There was a miniature of a woman beside the other two, and she picked it up carefully.

This must have been his mother. Sarah had researched the family over the years. She would have loved to say that her questions were only about taking this position, but it had been long before that. After Kit had caught her speaking so sharply to Meg, she'd looked into his life. Obsessed over it, some would say…if they knew.

She shook the thoughts away. Kit's mother had died when he was just fifteen, and the miniature reflected a younger woman. Beautiful. That was where Kit had inherited those fine cheekbones, clearly.

She set the picture down in just the place where she'd found it and sighed as she glanced at the other pictures, set back from the ones of his immediate family. His friends, pictures old and new.

He loved them like brothers. She'd seen the bonds between the men during the last days of Kit's father's life. She envied that he had so many to love him, to comfort him as he grieved.

She walked away from the pictures and back toward the bed. On the bedside table she spied a stack of books. She hesitated. Looking at his reading material seemed almost more intimate than the portraits of those he loved. One could judge a man by what he read. It said so much about his soul.

There was a book on the history of Kingsacre, well thumbed

through, by the looks of it. But beneath it was a slim volume, *Lyrical Ballads* by Wordsworth and Coleridge. Her heart skipped a beat, for she had brought the same volume of poetry with her in her scant belongings. There was a page marked, and she opened it to find it was the ballad "Strange fits of passion have I known." She read the flowing words, though she already knew them by heart.

> *Strange fits of passion have I known.*
> *And I will dare to tell.*
> *But in the Lover's ear alone,*
> *What once to me befell.*

She set the book aside with a shiver. Kit had always appeared to her to be not a man of passions. He'd always exhibited such coldness toward her…until today.

Today his obvious love of the poem made so much more sense. The idea of Kit with strange fits of passion…well, it made her body tingle as much as his lips had.

He'd said he wanted more of those kinds of passions with her. What could she do about that? Was it truly possible to accept his advances? Accept that he wanted her? Would it one day cause her more grief than she'd already felt? And what about her reputation, such that it was? She'd been trained to protect it, but she was no longer a young lady on the marriage mart. Could a governess give in to desire without destroying her life?

She moved away from his side of the bed and back to the other. The shadows outside were starting to loom and after the day's events, she was ready to rest. To dream. She slid between Kit's sheets and sighed. She still had no idea what to do about any of it. But perhaps tomorrow her next move would be clearer.

Perhaps tomorrow she would have some answers.

Kit stood in the antechamber between his dressing room

and his bedroom, and stared at the door that separated him from Sarah. In the hours since he'd left her, as the evening grew long, she was all he could think about. Her heroics, her near death, and most of all, the sweet surrender of her mouth and body when he claimed her lips in a shocking display.

He should have been ashamed of what he'd done, for it was against his character entirely. He wasn't.

He cracked the door and peered inside. The fire had burned down low, but the dim light still cascaded over Sarah's form in his bed. His body reacted of its own accord, tightening with desire as he looked at her in his shirt, half covered by his sheets, blonde hair wild from sleep.

She looked like a woman who had been well loved. And God, how he wanted to be the one who had put her in that kind of state.

But he wanted other things, too. Dangerous things like to protect her. To keep her close and never let anything bad ever happen to her again. He wanted to see her laugh, be carefree in a way she couldn't when she was a servant employed under the fickle pleasure of a master like him.

He shuddered as he closed the door and left her to sleep. Something had shifted in the moment since Meg had asked him if he'd been jealous of Simon, and this moment when she lay in his bed.

Oh, there had been the fact she'd nearly died to protect his beloved sister. Of course that mattered. But it was more than that. More than he was ready to examine or accept.

He exited his rooms and stepped into the hall, but after he shut the door, he turned to find Isabel standing there, her face pale and her expression lined with worry.

"Is Matthew well?" he asked.

She darted her gaze away and he knew the answer. Of course his friend would struggle to process what had happened today. It fed directly into an experience that had changed him to his core.

"He is better," she said softly. "He's with our little Daniel at present. The baby gives him comfort."

Kit's empathy rose as he looked closer at Isabel's face. Their newborn *would* be a source of comfort to Matthew, but he could see Isabel's pain.

"He loves you deeply. Desperately," he said softly. "It is not like anything I've ever seen before with him, you know. Ever."

He said the words as a way to comfort her, but they were true. Yes, Matthew had loved in the past. Losing his fiancée had devastated his friend. But the love Kit saw him share with Isabel was a deeper thing. More connected and well-suited. Something more mature and passionate and filled with much laughter and connection.

"I know," she said, and reached out to squeeze his hand. "But thank you. I actually came to check on Sarah. I had to help Matthew first, of course, but she was my best friend for years." Her breath caught. "Do you think she despises me for not coming to her right away?"

Kit drew back. "Of course not, Isabel. Diana and Amelia tended well to her, and I'm sure she understands where your first attentions had to lie. She is sleeping now, though."

Isabel's face fell. "Oh. Well, that is good. Diana says it will be helpful for her." She bent her head. "Kit, when I thought she was dead…when she *was* dead…"

His own breath hitched at the horrible memory. "I know. I can scarcely bear to think of it. Thank God for Lucas's knowledge that brought her back to us."

"It makes you appreciate how fleeting everything is, doesn't it?" Isabel asked.

"It does," he agreed. "I've had quite a few reminders of that, as of late."

Isabel nodded. "For me, all I can think about is how Sarah has pulled away since she went into service. She feels we can no longer be such good friends. I've…I've let her distance herself because I thought it would help her transition, but that feels so wrong now. Like I failed her."

"You didn't," he reassured her gently. "If anyone failed her, I have. I know she has feared her position here. I told her today that she wouldn't be sacked."

He didn't add the part about the kissing, but he thought of it. Thought of her body rising against his, her mouth opening beneath his as she opened to him so damned sweetly.

"That's wonderful," Isabel said. "It will take a weight from her. So it seems her life has changed in many ways. I wonder what will happen next."

He stared at Isabel a moment. This was Sarah's best friend, the person who likely knew her best now that her mother was no longer with her. "I would like to do something nice for her," he said. "For what she did, she deserves far more accolades than I could possibly arrange, but something to celebrate her."

Isabel's face lit up, her worries fading slightly. "I love that idea, Kit. She has suffered so much in recent years, I would love to see her given some kind of special day. I can help if you'd like."

He nodded. "I hoped you would say just that. I welcome all your input. And I have a few ideas of my own."

Isabel linked arms with him and began to chatter away as they left the hall and headed for the stairs back to the main house. But as they walked together, he couldn't help but think of the question Isabel had asked.

What would happen next?

He had no idea. And he wanted to know. Desperately.

CHAPTER NINE

Sarah cuddled deeper into warmth and sighed as her dreams began to fade. Odd dreams at that, of darkness and pain, transformed by a man's mouth on hers, of her body lifting beneath him. And when she looked to see who this mysterious lover was she found…Kit. She knew she should pull away, but she didn't. She couldn't.

She didn't want to.

She let her eyes flutter open and tensed. Where was she? This wasn't her bed in the little room next to Phoebe's that was reserved for the governess.

And then everything rushed back to her. The boat, the water, the kiss. None of that had been a dream—the previous day had truly happened. Her world had changed and it could never be the same.

She rolled to her side and froze. There was a vase of flowers on the bedside table that had not been there before. Amongst the bright, happy blooms was a cluster of yellow primrose.

Her heart thudded at the sight. It was possible that someone on the household staff had simply included the bright flower in the bouquet, but she couldn't help but recall her conversation with Kit when she'd mentioned her affinity for the flower that reminded her so much of her late mother.

"Don't be ridiculous," she said as she got up slowly. She

did feel steadier today than she had the prior one. Less tired after a blissful night's sleep in Kit's very comfortable bed. She couldn't help but wonder where he had spent his night.

Well, that wasn't about to be repeated. She would certainly never find herself in his bed again. It would be back to normal now. She had to make certain of it so he wouldn't have any reason to go back on his vow that he wouldn't end her employment.

She looked down at herself. She was still in his shirt. His now very wrinkled shirt, which she had slept in. And her gown was nowhere in sight. One of the maids must have taken it during the blurry time when Amelia and Diana were fussing over her, getting her out of the wet things and into something warm and dry.

But that meant she was trapped here. There would be no efficient readying of herself, which she had perfected in the last few months, and then slipping back into her regular routine.

She glanced at the door. Of course, the duke had a bell. But would it bring his valet? She was a little afraid of Mr. Stone, for he was very proper and very good at what he did. He judged the whole household. But if it didn't bring Mr. Stone, then who?

"Just ring the bell, girl," she muttered. "You almost died—you can't be afraid anymore."

She jerked the cord and then panicked. God, should she get back into his bed to wait for help? No, that seemed very wrong. She wasn't the duchess. So she stepped back, settling herself as demurely as she could onto a chair beside the fire as she waited to see who would come. At least Kit was tall and his shirt came down to mid-thigh. She felt horribly exposed, but not as much as she could.

A few moments passed and the door to the chamber opened to reveal one of the maids who had helped the previous afternoon after the accident. Jill stepped into the chamber with a bright smile. Sarah nearly wept in relief when she saw the young woman also had a gown and underthings draped over her arm and slippers tucked into her hand.

"Good morning, Miss Sarah," she said with a deferential nod of her head.

Sarah wrinkled her brow. She'd been in service for months now. The girls below stairs were friendly in the house, but no one ever acted like anyone, aside from Barrymore and Stone, was higher than anyone else. They were servants, with rank and place, but without pretense.

And now Jill all but curtseyed, and for a moment it was like she'd gone back in time to when her family still had money and her maid, Katie, would help her get ready for balls and parties.

She blinked away the old memories, put herself firmly back in her current position and said, "Good morning, Jill. I must say I'm so devilishly happy it is you who came and not Stone."

The maid giggled and some of the deferential wall came down. "Poor man had enough of an apoplexy when he had to go to the guest wing to help the duke ready himself. You should have heard him go on about needing to sneak into the dressing room while you slept in the adjoining."

Sarah's heart sank. That talk could destroy someone below stairs as easily as it could above.

"Oh, please tell me they all know, including Stone, that I didn't choose to be put in the duke's room yesterday."

Jill drew back with a nod. "Of course, miss! Gracious, your heroics were all the talk last night during our supper and this morning before the dukes and duchesses were up and about. Stone was put in his place right quick when we reminded him you had saved Miss Phoebe. He stopped his grousing then and looked mightily chagrined."

Sarah's eyes went wide, not only at the news that Stone had been shamed into ceasing his talk about her, but also at the fact that the dukes and duchesses were already awake. "What time is it, Jill?"

Jill smiled as she set the gown down on the edge of the bed and the other things beside it. "Half past ten, Miss Sarah."

Sarah jerked her hands to her mouth. She should have been up at dawn to prepare for the day, along with all the other servants. "Oh no! What he must think of me! Thank you for the gown—I will dress right away and ready myself as quickly as possible. Please tell the duke I am sorry, I didn't mean to neglect my duties for so long!"

Jill stared at her in surprise. "No one is angry, miss! On the contrary, we were told by His Grace to be sure not to wake you. And when you rang, I was asked to come help you ready yourself."

Sarah's mouth dropped open. She hadn't had help to ready herself in months. Once she'd sold all her finer gowns, she'd been sure to have her plain, serviceable wardrobe designed so that she could fasten and unfasten herself. Her hairstyle was no longer elaborate, but a loose bun at the nape of her neck.

In truth, she rather liked the simplicity her life contained now, and the independence of caring for herself. She could be dressed and ready for her day in less than half an hour, when before she might have taken an hour or more with a maid fastening and fussing.

"I couldn't!" Sarah insisted.

"I don't want to get in trouble, miss," Jill said, worrying her hands before herself and bringing Sarah's focus back to the room.

She sighed. "Of course." She stepped toward Jill and slid the shirt from her body. "But you must stop addressing me as *miss*. I've been nothing but Sarah since I got here—please don't put me in a position where I belong neither with those above stairs or those below it."

Jill seemed to ponder that a moment, then nodded. "Of course. Though I swear that His Grace does seem to see you differently."

Heat suffused Sarah's cheeks, and she hoped it wasn't too obvious to her friend as she helped her button her plain, black gown. Of course Kit saw her differently. He had kissed her so passionately not twenty-four hours before. She could practically still taste him on her lips. Nothing could be the same after that.

"Sarah?" Jill said.

She blinked and realized the maid was pointing at a chair before the table where Kit's miniatures were set. Sarah took it, and Jill produced a brush from her pocket and began to run it through her hair.

Sarah shivered in pleasure. She brushed her own hair, certainly, but there was something extra special about having someone else do it.

Jill swiftly twisted and pinned her hair, then produced a hand mirror. "What do you think?"

Sarah stared at herself. If she'd felt herself talented at doing her own hair, this moment disabused her of that belief. Jill had done wonders. The style was still simple, but it framed her face better and was more firmly anchored so that it wouldn't fall during the day.

"It's wonderful," she breathed. "I'll have to have you teach me your tricks some night. You ought to be a lady's maid, not a housemaid."

Jill's cheeks filled with color. "Who wouldn't rather be?" she asked. "But there is no position to be filled on that score currently, and when the duke marries, I'm certain his duchess will bring her own maid. But Miss Phoebe will one day require assistance, and I hope I will still be here to provide it."

Sarah pursed her lips. Although this was a kind household and the servants were treated well and compensated fairly, the life amongst their ranks was never easy. She knew a maid like Jill might work from six in the morning to eleven or twelve at night, with few breaks. And here she was, praying that in ten or twelve years' time, she might finally move up to a less taxing position as lady's maid.

She forced a smile. "About the time you are elevated to Lady Phoebe's maid, I shall no longer be needed as governess."

Jill shook her head. "Of course you will. Certainly the duke will be married with his own children by then. You will have a job here for a long time to come."

Sarah ignored the pit that set itself into her stomach. Kit would marry. Of course he would. It was silly to think he wouldn't, given his position and his responsibilities. He would marry some lady of Society and probably have eight children with her, if the passion of his one kiss was to be a guide.

So her position would most definitely be safe. And yet she felt no pleasure in that fact.

She shook her head. "Well, I have dallied enough. I do appreciate your help, but I suppose it is time for me to get back to my work. I assume Phoebe has already had her breakfast and will need to be collected for her studies before she joins the others today?"

"Oh no, miss. Everyone is waiting for you in the breakfast room."

Sarah stared. "I'm sorry?"

"Yes, His Grace's orders were for you to join the party at breakfast as soon as you were ready. Miss Phoebe is with them, I believe. A special treat after yesterday's terrible experience."

Sarah covered her mouth with her hands. "And here I am, taking my time. Thank you again."

She fled the room and hustled down the stairs toward the big breakfast room at the back of the house. But as she went, she couldn't help but wonder what in the world Kit had been thinking asking her to join his friends. She didn't belong there, as Jill's statements had reminded her.

And kisses or no, that wasn't about to change. She needed to remember her place and not get swept up in what had to be a moment brought on by high emotions, nothing more.

She heard the group before she reached the chamber. The door to the breakfast room was open and there was a buzz coming from it. Laughter and talk, chatter that said, once more, that life would come back into these halls. The death of the duke, the near tragedy on the lake, all would be forgotten over time.

Or at least dulled.

She drew in a deep breath to calm herself, then stepped into the chamber. All the dukes and duchesses were gathered there, with their children in their laps. It was clearly a big family gathering, and for a moment Sarah froze.

That was why Kit had asked her to come, not because of any personal reason. He just wanted her to be a buffer for the children. To do her job.

But that was quickly belied when the Duke of Abernathe got to his feet, smiled at her and said, "There she is, the heroine of the hour!"

He began to clap. To her surprise, all the others joined him, applauding her as she bent her head and absorbed their attention and affection. It was unlike anything she'd ever known. After all, she'd never really fit in anywhere she'd gone. She had been the lower level of Society and now she was the kind of servant who didn't really fit either. She'd been mostly alone, but never more so than after her mother's death.

And here she was, being applauded by the most influential group in all of England, save the royal family. It was almost overwhelming, and she found her head swimming with it.

She glanced up to find Kit coming across the room toward her. He had a smile on his face and he held her gaze. She found herself clinging to that, using his easy strength as some kind of buoy.

"I'm sorry I slept so late," she burst out, wringing her hands in front of her.

His brow wrinkled and his expression softened further. "You needed to rest. I'm happy you're here now."

She worried her lip and dared to look up into his eyes once more. "I—we—I—"

He chuckled, and the sound seemed to settle its way into her very blood. "Just say you'll bear the celebration of the others."

She nodded at last, unable to think of anything else to do. He offered her an arm, and before she took it, she whispered,

"There were flowers by my bedside this morning."

"Yes. I thought you would miss the ones in your room, so I picked you more and had Jill bring them to you."

Her lips parted and she couldn't help the ragged catch of her breath. "*You* picked them? Yourself?"

He glanced down and then lifted his hands, wiggling his fingers playfully. "Turns out these don't stop working, even when one becomes duke. Was there enough yellow primrose?"

Tears filled her eyes and she blinked at them before she whispered, "Oh yes, it was perfect."

He offered her an elbow again and she took it this time, shocked by the spark of awareness that seemed to flow between them when she dared to touch him. He led her to the main table in the large room and beckoned her to sit. She blinked. The empty chair was right between him and Phoebe. As she hugged the little girl gently, she couldn't believe that was correct.

That was a place of honor.

But he didn't seem to be teasing or mistaken. He pulled back her chair and she glided into place right in the middle of his friends and their families. Like she belonged there.

Like he wanted her there even though she knew that couldn't be true. Almost before she could shake out her napkin and rest it in her lap, a footman appeared with a towering plate of eggs, sausages and pastries. She shook her head as the fragrant aroma of the food hit her nostrils.

"These are…"

"All your favorites," Isabel said from just down the table with a warm smile for Sarah. "Kit wanted to be certain you would be pleased with your meal, so I passed along all I could remember to the cook."

Sarah worried her lip. "Mrs. Parker must think this is a foolish to-do over a governess."

Phoebe reached out and took her hand, holding it so tightly that it actually tingled. She stared up at her with wide, still apologetic eyes. "I helped."

"You helped in the kitchen?" Sarah repeated in shock. "Has the world turned upside down since I went under the water?"

It was Lucas, Duke of Willowby, and the man who she now vaguely remembered had breathed life back into her lungs, who responded. "A shocking event like what you experienced can seem like it turns the world upside down. But I assure you, it is still turning exactly as it was before."

Kit glanced at her briefly. "Lucas is right. And Mrs. Parker was more than pleased to spoil you, Sarah. You saved Phoebe and that means a great deal to everyone in this household, as she is dearly loved." He smiled at his sister. "And she knows it, I think."

Phoebe didn't respond, but her giggle before she dove back into her food was answer enough to let the world know she liked being so loved by all around her. As the others fell back into conversation, Sarah began to eat. She hadn't had a thing since a late breakfast before the picnic the day before. She realized now that she was famished and ate with gusto, hardly able to contain little moans of pleasure at the fine food.

She remained mostly quiet during the meal. She was still uncertain of her place at this table. These men and women could have at one time been considered her peers, but those days were long gone. And yet they were kind, considerate, welcoming to their happy, loving, loud fray.

The meal was a wonderful gift for her. A moment to relax out of her duties and just…be again. Be herself.

She glanced at Kit, who was talking at length to the Duke of Abernathe on his right, and she couldn't help but admire the strength of him. It felt so much bigger now, so much more real since she'd touched him in a way that would shock the entire table if they knew, she was certain. It would surely become the talk of the below stairs set if the truth came out.

Suddenly her stomach felt a little less settled. She pushed her nearly empty plate aside. The others were also finishing their meals and the group began to move, readying to rise and to part ways for whatever would come in the day ahead.

At last, she tore herself away from the stolen moment and got to her feet. "Thank you all, again, for your kindness. I suppose I should get back to my duties. I have much to review for a return to Phoebe's studies and I'm certain there is a great deal waiting for me after yesterday."

She intended to curtsey away, but before she could step from the table, Diana pushed to her feet. "Absolutely not, my dear! You need to continue to rest, at least one more day."

Sarah caught her breath and glanced at Kit, but he merely shrugged. "It is what the doctor ordered, Sarah. And after your heroics yesterday, I think you've earned far more than a mere breakfast in your honor. We would love for you to join in the party today, not as a governess, but as a friend to our group."

Sarah gripped her hands against the table as those stunning words pierced through a veil of disbelief and confusion. Join the party? He could not mean that. But he looked entirely serious, and even more shocking, not a one of the dukes or duchesses seemed even the tiniest bit taken aback or annoyed by the idea of allowing an untitled interloper into their close gathering.

She knew she should say no. That despite their kindness, she didn't truly belong in their fold anymore. But she didn't. She wanted to pretend, to dream. And she would give herself that gift, just for the day.

"Thank you," she said, smiling at the group as a whole.

Isabel got to her feet. "May we start with a walk in the garden? I haven't had a moment to talk to you since…just since."

Sarah nodded as she, too, got up. Isabel had been a friend to her almost her entire life. Right now she needed her, position be damned.

"Yes," she said. "But first…"

She came around the table to where Diana and Lucas were standing, talking quietly. After a beat of hesitation, Sarah cleared her throat. "Your Grace," she began. "I know it was you who saved my life at the lakeside."

The tall, handsome man looked down at her and then he smiled softly. "It was entirely my pleasure, Miss Carlton. I am eternally grateful that my training, and my wife's, could be of any service to you."

The tears Sarah had been willing away collected again and one slid down her cheek. "If there is ever anything I could ever do to repay you—"

He shook his head. "Live a happy life, Sarah. That is all I would wish."

Sarah blinked at the unfettered kindness of the man who had breathed her back into existence. She nodded slowly. "I'll try." Turning away, she smiled at Isabel. "A walk in the garden, yes?"

Isabel wiped at one of her own tears and then reached out to take her arm. "I cannot wait."

CHAPTER TEN

Kit couldn't help himself. As Sarah swept from the room on Isabel's arm, their heads close together, whispering like the old friends they were, his heart swelled with pleasure. He'd wanted to give her a carefree day of fun after the nightmare of the previous afternoon. He knew the idea created conflicting feelings in her. Sarah was obviously aware of her new place, wanted to stay within its confines. And yet she was acquainted with his friends, clearly missed those old days when her life had been more relaxed.

That she had accepted the offer, even after hesitation, made him happy.

"Kit?"

He glanced down to find Phoebe reaching for his hand. When she took it, she was solemn, indeed. "Yes, what is it?" he asked before he crouched to her level.

"If Sarah is a lady again, does that mean she'll go away?"

Kit tensed at the question and the image his sister had created in her misunderstanding. Sarah gone. He caught his breath. "No, sweetheart, Sarah is still your governess. Because she was so brave yesterday in saving you, we are giving her a special day. Do you understand?"

"So she won't be a lady tomorrow?" Phoebe asked, brow wrinkling.

He shook his head. "Sarah will always be a lady. That cannot be changed by a job she holds or a life she leads. But she will be with you, taking care of you. Today, though, we're going to be extra careful and kind to her."

Phoebe seemed to understand that explanation and nodded slowly. "I'll be extra kind. Do you think she'd like a picture?"

Meg had begun to approach with some of the other duchesses. She said, "I think she would love that. Will you help some of the other children and perhaps we can draw her something together?"

Of course Phoebe's eyes lit up—she never turned down an opportunity to corral and rule the other, smaller children. "Yes!" she said, and let go of Kit's hand to race off with the young children toward the playroom upstairs, their mothers and aunts in tow.

Kit stretched his back as he got to his feet once she was gone. It meant a great deal to him how much Phoebe loved Sarah. In just a few months, Sarah had forged a strong bond with his sister. Strong enough that she would die for her.

He shuddered and glanced toward the door where she and Isabel had departed a few moments before. He could picture every line of her face, every curve of her body, and it was entirely disconcerting.

The other dukes were milling about, talking about billiards or rides on the estate. Ewan was writing furiously in his notebook as Matthew read over his shoulder with a solemn expression. For the first time in a long time, Kit didn't feel he…fit. He was in a very different place than all his friends, after all. And in his grief over his father and his confusion over Sarah, he suddenly didn't feel as comfortable in the knowledge of who he was.

"Kit, you look a man in need of an escape." The Duke of Roseford clapped him on the shoulder as he said the words.

Kit smiled. Although they were almost polar opposites in their attitudes, he had always adored his wild friend. But even

Robert had settled down, marrying his wife Katherine just six months before and then taking off on a whirlwind tour of the continent with her. They had only returned as Kit's father grew closer to death.

"If anyone knows that look, it's you," Kit chuckled as he slung an arm around his old friend.

Robert grinned. "Ah, not so much anymore. I'm becoming more and more accustomed to being still. Or at least settled. I highly recommend it." Kit's smile fell, and as it did, so did Robert's. His friend leaned a little closer. "To the study," he said, grabbing Kit's arm and all but dragging him from the room.

Kit allowed it, following Robert to the big, wood paneled room where his father had ruled over his family and lands until the final weeks of his life. He flinched as Robert shut the door behind them. It still looked like his father. It still smelled like him.

And the grief hit him like a quarter horse that had gotten free of its reins. He gripped the back of the chair in front of the fire and tried to breathe through it.

Robert tilted his head and crossed to pour them each a scotch. As he brought the glasses back and pointed Kit toward the chair he was leaning on, he said, "It's too early for this, but everyone will blame me for that, not you."

Kit took the drink and the seat and stared into the fire without seeing it. "Everyone is too busy tiptoeing around to blame me for anything."

Robert took his own place and set his drink on the table between them without taking a sip. "Your father has not been dead a week, Kit. You deserve a little tiptoeing still. I'm certain one or more of us will make you aware if you become insufferable. I wish I could say I understood your pain."

Kit glanced at his friend to find Robert's expression pulled down. He saw a glimpse of the old Robert in his look, and the pain behind all his bad behavior over the years. Katherine had helped him with that. Helped him overcome the past and now he had a bright future ahead of him.

"I fear I had one of the only good men as father," Kit said. "Matthew's father being the other. Baldwin's insomuch that he didn't *purposefully* harm his family."

Robert pursed his lips. "Just doomed them, at least briefly, thanks to his bad debts."

"It's not the same as Graham's father, though. Or James's. Or yours. Does being here make you think of him?"

Robert stared into the flames for a moment. "I hadn't spoken to him for so long when he died. I had written him out of my life, thought I'd let it go, though I obviously hadn't. I suppose I think of him fleetingly, but I think more about how far we've all come from our bad beginnings. Graham is a perfect example. His father abused him, far more than I think any of us was aware. And yet he is so gentle and loving to Maddie. She lights up his world."

Kit smiled at the images his friend's words conjured. "Yes, the problems of the past do seem to have faded considerably for our friends. And I know that as time passes, I will think of my father with great fondness. Those memories will no longer sting, but make me smile."

"I think that's true. Certainly I can think of ten stories of your father's kindness that make me smile," Robert said. "He was as close to a father as many of us had."

"I do wish he were here to offer me advice." Kit frowned.

Robert leaned farther forward. "Problems? Perhaps I can help. Is it the estate?"

Kit snorted. "No, he ran that like clockwork. It's so well organized that Ewan tells me I could run away for a year and the legacy wouldn't suffer in the slightest."

Robert's brow wrinkled. "Phoebe then?"

"Certainly I would love him to be here to help me with any challenges she'll face. She is a spark and she does love to find dry tinder. I'm sure I will have many a gray hair from her spitfire ways in the years to come. But I know how to love her, I think.

And that's not something I need my father to tell me."

Robert's expression softened. "I'm glad you realize that. I watch you with her, you know. She adores you. She's in her own grief at present, but she has a good heart and I know you will be the best brother and father she could hope for."

Kit drew in a long breath. "I will try."

"So if it isn't your legacy that troubles you, nor your sister…then I can think of only one other thing." Now Robert's eyes sparkled like he knew some secret.

Kit's heart sank. His friend had always been too talented at seeing the wicked where it lived. "And what is that?" he asked weakly.

"When Sarah Carlton came into the breakfast room this morning, I saw you light up like a candelabra. So my deductive skills tell me that perhaps your worries have less to do with serious, important endeavors and more to do with…*feelings* you are trying to avoid. And I don't mean hearts and flowers feelings. I mean *desires*, Kit."

Kit pushed to his feet and slugged back half his untouched scotch before he muttered, "Jesus."

Robert chuckled as he settled back in his chair and crossed one ankle over the other. "This is me, you know. Biggest libertine in London."

"Formerly," Kit added.

"Proud *former* title holder," Robert corrected. "I see all, I know all. So talk."

Kit paced away. His mind was split in two on this subject. Part of him wanted to ignore Robert's pressing, to keep the tangled subject of Sarah and his desires for her to himself. But the other part, the part that felt desperate and confused, knew he needed to speak to someone about it. And Robert was the best choice, given the very past they'd just been teasing each other about.

He cleared his throat, turned to face his friend and leaned back against the edge of the sideboard. "We've had a fraught relationship," he began.

Robert blinked. "Ah yes, the night with…Charlotte?"

"Meg," Kit correct.

Robert nodded. "Oh yes, yes, Sarah was mixed up in that mess with Meg and Simon and Graham what feels like ten lifetimes ago. You've been holding *that* against her?"

Kit pursed his lips. "Yes, that was the same tone of voice Meg used when she confronted me about it right before Phoebe's boat capsized and everything went to hell. She chastised me for my attitude toward Sarah. And she said something else, and I'm going to admit to you now that it has stuck in my head ever since."

"What did she say?"

Kit scrubbed a hand over his face. "I'll regret telling you this, I'm sure. She said…she said that the reason I was so angry over Sarah's impertinence had nothing to do with her being impolite to Meg."

"What does she think it had to do with?" Robert asked.

"She thinks I was jealous that Sarah was hoping for a future with Simon."

Robert's eyes widened and he stared at Kit for a moment. Then he shrugged one shoulder. "Actually, that makes sense."

"What?" Kit burst out. "What are you talking about?"

Robert rolled his eyes. "Come now, don't rewrite history. You noticed Sarah Carlton long before that night. I recall you watching her a year before that mess. Sometimes you would comment on her gown or notice a change in her hair. And after that situation with Meg, you got even worse. Always tracking her around. Meg is probably right, though she always is. Damned annoying of her, and I've told Simon so many a time."

"You court a punch in the face if you cross Simon in regards to Meg," Kit said. "But now you're supporting her theory and I feel like I'm being told I never knew my own mind."

"You've always been serious," Robert said gently. "Focused on taking on your father's title and his responsibility.

And then when he got sick, your focus turned in even more. That you weren't ready to face your own…desires…isn't that surprising."

Kit walked the length of the room, pausing at the window to stare out at the garden. Even from here he could see the bright yellow primrose dotting the landscape. Sarah's flower. It had been there all along, of course, in his father's garden for likely generations. Yet he'd never noticed it, never felt it mean something until now.

Was it the same with Sarah? Could Meg and Robert be right? Or was that just a flight of fantasy created by the terrifying events of the previous day and the weight of grief from losing his father?

"I kissed her," he admitted.

"Did you now?" Robert drawled. "Where?"

Kit turned and stared at his friend. He couldn't help but picture all the ways he could kiss Sarah. All the places that would make her blush and moan and sigh. "The…mouth?" he said slowly.

Robert tilted his head back and laughed. "Ah, I like that your mind takes you on such filthy paths. That bodes well for your future. But I meant where in the house, you great dolt."

"Oh." Kit's cheeks flooded with heat. "My chamber. In…er…my bed."

Robert was silent for a moment. A very long moment. His face was unreadable as he just stared at Kit like he'd grown a second head. "And here I called you a monk."

"What?"

"Behind your back. Kit the Monk. I feel I should apologize, for I clearly misjudged you."

"Thank you," Kit said with a glare. "I appreciate the support."

Robert's teasing demeanor faded. "I'm not opposed to the idea of you being swept away by passion. God knows, it can be a very good thing. But I do wonder what brought it on. Was it just the grief? Just the fear of what happened yesterday? Just the gratitude?"

Kit returned to his seat and flopped there. "I don't know," he admitted. "Yes. To all those things. But…it was more than that. I walked into that room and I just wanted to…to touch her. I wanted to touch her, and it had everything and nothing to do with the fact that she nearly died."

Robert nodded slowly. "And was she responsive?"

"God, yes." Kit flashed back to that kiss in full detail. That kiss that had haunted him all night, all morning. "I felt her melt into me and I lost all sense of propriety. I had to force myself to stop because I knew I would go too far."

"That isn't you," Robert said.

Kit couldn't help but laugh. "No, it's *you*! Or it used to be."

"Still is. I just save it all for my amazing wife," Robert said.

"Well, did you will the rest of your libertine ways to me when you got married?"

Now Robert laughed. "I should have. But this is all you."

"Like you said, though…why now? Why here? Why her?"

"Meg's sharp observation may answer why her," Robert said. "As for the rest, we already talked about it. You've been in mourning not just a few days, but a few *years*. You've constrained your emotions as you tried to do what was right. Perhaps this release, this surrender to what you want, is exactly what you need right now."

Kit shook his head. The very idea of surrendering to his desires made his whole body quake. His desires were more powerful and out of control than he intended to admit. And he had one prevailing fear when he dared consider them.

"I will take advantage," he said softly.

Robert shook his head. "Not unless you go too far. And I know you. You won't."

Kit scrubbed a hand over his face. While he appreciated his friend's deep faith in him, he wasn't as certain as Robert was. Because when he thought of kissing Sarah again, his mind took him down paths that were wild and wanton. And he wasn't sure he would be able to keep himself from going too far after all.

CHAPTER ELEVEN

Sarah let out a contented sigh as she strolled through the garden, clinging to Isabel's arm. It felt like old times in this moment, a return to a friendship she had missed deeply.

"I am so, so glad you are well," Isabel said softly. "I was terrified. And Matthew…"

Sarah glanced at her out of the corner of her eye. Her friend's lips were pinched together in a thin line. "Angelica drowned—there is no doubt there is distress there. It must have brought back such terrible feelings for you both."

"Terrible feelings, yes," Isabel said. "And memories for Matthew. Regrets. He realized that Lucas could bring you back to life with his breath. I think for a while Matthew tortured himself with the idea that he could have done the same for my cousin that terrible night."

Sarah stopped walking and jerked to face her friend. She understood the implication in Isabel's quiet statement. If Matthew had saved Angelica, he and Isabel never would have married.

"Did that hurt you? His reaction?" Sarah asked, shoving aside her own complicated problems to focus on this.

Isabel was quiet for a moment. Then she sighed. "I understood his reaction. I cannot imagine what it was like to watch Angelica die. For him, what happened yesterday was like going back in time. Standing in the boat, it flipping, you not breathing. That's *exactly* what happened with Angelica. We thought you were gone, so it's understandable he would have those thoughts when Lucas was able to revive you."

Sarah caught her hands. "But did it *hurt* you?"

Isabel bent her head. "A little. But I know he loves me. Truly loves me, deeply loves me. And he loves our life together and our baby. Angelica is not a barrier between us, nor has she been for almost a year. I will not let her be now, not when I understand his reaction."

Sarah let out a long sigh. "You, my dear, are too good for this world. Too understanding and kind. He had best appreciate that."

"He does," Isabel reassured her, and it was clear she meant it. This moment between her and her husband was just that...a moment. They were too in love to allow it to be anything else. "And as for being too good, you would know, I suppose, my heroic best friend!"

Sarah knew she was blushing, her face was blazingly hot at present. She dropped her chin. "Do you still consider me that?"

"My best friend?" Isabel repeated, almost sounding confused. "Of course I do. Was that in doubt?"

Sarah sighed. "Perhaps. I mean, you have married into this enormous circle of remarkable women."

"All of whom I love, none of whom are you," Isabel said.

"And I've pushed you away," Sarah said, down to the heart of it at last. "I know I have since my mother's death and my change in situation."

"You couldn't help but struggle," Isabel said gently. "Your world was ripped apart, I know that. But hear this now and know it forever, you are my best friend, Miss Sarah Eugenie Frances Elizabeth Carlton. And you always shall be, no matter what."

It was amazing: the relief that washed over Sarah when she allowed herself to accept what Isabel was saying to her. She'd pushed her so far away, told herself they couldn't still be close with their situations so disparate. It was only now that she fully felt how much she'd hurt herself when she created that barrier between them. Coming so close to death made her never want to put it up again.

She put her arms around Isabel and the two women clung to each other for a moment. Then she pulled away and smiled as she retook Isabel's arm. They moved to a bench before the fountain, and she sighed as they sat.

"Well, then, my dearest best friend, I will admit that I need your advice," she said, unable to keep herself from the discussion she'd been so uncertain of when they began.

Isabel nodded. "Oh yes, I would be happy to help. What is the problem? Still worried about Kit and being sacked?"

"Not let go, no. But Kit? Yes." She ducked her head. "He kissed me."

Isabel jolted and when Sarah dared to look at her, she found her friend's eyes had grown impossibly wide and wild. "I'm sorry, what?"

"He came in to check on me after the drowning," she said. "And we were talking and then his mouth was on mine and…and…he kissed me. It seems like more than one kiss, though. One bled into the others."

Isabel continued to stare at her like she didn't understand what she was saying. "What?"

Sarah stuck her tongue out. "Not helpful, Isabel! You can't just stare at me like I grew a second head and say *what*!"

Isabel blinked several times as she muttered, "What in the world do you want me to do? This is incredibly shocking!"

Sarah's heart sank. "You think ill of me?"

"Not at all. I didn't mean shocking, more stunning." Isabel seemed to gather herself. "Firstly I must ask how it was."

Sarah couldn't help the little smile that twitched across her mouth almost against her will. "Oh, Isabel! Recall when I couldn't understand why you would go to Donville Masquerade and seek out pleasure? I understand now."

"That good?" Isabel said. "Gracious, I never would have guessed."

"And he seemed to like it, too." Sarah covered her face with her hands. "But how in the world is this happening? We've been enemies of a sort for years. He hates me."

"Clearly not," Isabel mused. "And at any rate, hate is often a mask for something else. Ask Katherine if you do not believe me. Or even Amelia. What they thought was hate transformed into love."

Sarah caught her breath. Love? She couldn't think about something like that. She was not in a position to fall in love with Kit, of all people. If she did, that would not end well, especially since he'd only spoken to her of more kissing, not courtship.

There was no good end to that path, and she already knew it.

She pushed it aside and said, "You are talking about relationships, Isabel. He doesn't want that with me."

"Forget him. Men will tie themselves into knots not knowing what they want when it is right in front of them," Isabel said with a wave of her hand. "What do *you* want?"

"I don't know," Sarah admitted. But immediately she knew it was a lie. "I want more of his kiss, actually. I may not be alone in that, for he said he wanted to do it again as well."

Isabel giggled. "He sounds like libertine Robert, not the staid, proper Kit of my husband's childhood. You must bring out the beast in him."

"Oh dear," Sarah said, worrying her hands in her lap.

"No!" Isabel said with another laugh. "That is a good thing. Still waters can run very deep, indeed. I should know. I also married a seemingly proper gentleman who holds a very lovely beast inside."

Her gaze slid past Sarah and toward the path where they had come. Her face lit up, and Sarah glanced over her shoulder to see Matthew on his way toward them. There was no denying the deep connection of their look, nor in the way Isabel sat up a bit straighter when she watched him.

Sarah couldn't help being a bit jealous at what she saw.

"And speaking of which," Isabel said. "Hello, husband."

If Isabel had lit up, there was no denying Matthew burned like a torch as he reached them. If Sarah had held any doubt about his reaction regarding her drowning the day before, she certainly felt none now. This man loved her friend. A dead woman was no competition for what they shared. It gave her some satisfaction in the midst of confusion.

"Hello, wife," he returned. "And hello, Sarah. I'm interrupting, aren't I? You two looked very serious when I approached. Should I leave you to your conversation?"

Sarah got to her feet. She knew the pair needed to reconnect. And her problems weren't going to be solved any time soon, certainly not by Isabel's encouraging her that passion wasn't something to fear. That it could lead to a happiness Sarah knew she would never truly feel.

"I think we've solved the world's problems enough for one day," she said. "I should go back to the house and check on my charge. You two carry on in our walk, though."

Matthew's face was filled with relief as he stepped up and caught Isabel's hand in his. Sarah slipped away, but she turned back farther up the path, in time to see him take Isabel in his arms and kiss her with enough passion that it could have matched the heat of the late spring sun.

She blushed, for the action made her think again of Kit, then headed up the path so the couple could have privacy. She had to be careful now as she went back to the house. There were dangers ahead when it came to Kit. Dangers of the heart, dangers of desire.

She just had to decide which ones to avoid and which ones were worth the risk.

Kit was keenly aware of the moment Sarah entered the house. He was, after all, watching her from his study window as she parted from Isabel and Matthew and made her way down the long path. He'd watched her take her time, watched her pause to smell the yellow primrose. She'd looked toward his window then, making him wonder if she could see him spying. But then she'd carried on her way.

And now she was back in the house and his legs were carrying him through the halls toward the parlor where she'd entered from the terrace. He came to a stop as he watched her step from the parlor and into the dimmer hallway, shutting the door behind herself.

She jolted as she saw him standing there, three stride lengths away. Then she smiled and he forgot to breathe.

"Your Grace," she said, a little breathless herself.

He tilted his head, stepping toward her because he couldn't stop himself from doing so. "Sarah."

"Kit," she whispered, and now it was more than a little breathless. "I was coming to check on Phoebe."

He arched a brow. "And here I had specifically said you were to rest yourself."

She laughed at the playfulness in his tone. "I am notoriously bad at following orders, it seems."

"I shall have to think of a proper punishment," he drawled, and caught himself. He was growling and drawling and it was all very rakish of him.

She blushed. "I—truly I only thought to peek in on Phoebe. She was so upset after yesterday's events. Even this morning, she gripped my hand so tightly."

"I know," he said gently. "But she is not here at present. You see, she helped the duchesses with the babies, drew you what I'm certain is a lovely picture and then managed to convince Charlotte and Ewan to take her for a walk. She is obsessed with Ewan's hand language and learning words from him all the time."

Sarah ducked her head with a secret smile that told him she'd noticed Phoebe's infatuation with his silent friend, as well. "I see. Well, she will glory in all that attention and not need me a whit."

"She'll always need you," he said softly. Then he motioned for the parlor she'd just exited. "Diana did mention you should rest. Will you join me?"

She glanced over her shoulder and he saw her uncertainty. It stopped him in his tracks. She'd liked kissing him last night, but it was possible she'd thought better of it since. Being alone with him might not be what she actually wanted.

He stepped nearer. "You have every right to say no. Always, Sarah."

She worried her lip. "I'm not worried about saying no. Yes seems to be more…likely."

Awareness rushed through him at that simple statement and all the meaning behind it. He wanted nothing more than to back her against the parlor door and kiss her until they were both senseless. He fought the urge and instead opened it for her and motioned her in.

"Sit," he said. "I'll ring for tea."

She did as he'd asked and sat quietly as he arranged the service to be sent in. As they waited for refreshments, he faced her again and found her staring at a painting above the fire. It was of him and his father, done years ago. His father was seated, looking formal in black. Kit stood just behind him, a hand on his shoulder. His father's hand covered his.

"I've always liked that one," she said without looking at him. "The way his hand lays on yours is so loving."

He stepped up beside her and only just kept from resting his hand on her shoulder now, mimicking the painting. "It is. We had just lost my mother. We're both still in black."

She flinched. "I'm sorry. I should have guessed by your age, by the outfits. It was uncouth of me to point it out."

"Why?" he asked. "It is a loving portrait. We were two

bachelors after that."

"Your father never remarried," she said carefully.

He hesitated. There were not many people who he talked to about his father's…*existence* after his mother's death. But he didn't have to decide immediately if Sarah would be one of them, for the door opened and tea was brought. He waved off the maid with a smile and poured Sarah's tea after the girl left. Once she'd taken it, he moved to the door and shut it.

Leaving them completely and inappropriately alone. She watched him as he took his own tea and then sat across from her, holding her gaze evenly.

"He loved my mother," he said, picking up from where they had been interrupted. "She was sick a very short time, and I think he was shocked to lose her. For years he buried himself in this estate, in his work, in me. He didn't look at another woman, not that there wasn't interest. I see now that he was quite the catch."

She laughed. "It's hard to see our parents in those terms. Or think they were ever young and carefree."

"You must wonder about Phoebe's mother." He said the words carefully and hoped his tone remained neutral.

She set her cup down and looked at him. "I heard some of the whispers," she admitted. "Not that he would have a child, but that he would take her in, raise her without hesitation. I always thought it admirable of him, even more so when I saw their deep connection."

"The woman was…an ill-advised foray outside of his exile from romantic life," Kit said, setting his jaw. "She wanted his money. Oh, of course he would have settled on a mistress. She wanted more than that. She wanted far more than was reasonable. When she became with child, there was no easier way to blackmail him into keeping her in lavish comfort all her days. She made threats and a great deal of trouble. He paid her a pretty penny for Phoebe. She was worth every cent."

"I had no idea," she said with a shake of her head. "She took advantage of him. Of her daughter. Not well played."

"Indeed," he said, and leaned in. "Did *I* take advantage?"

Her brow wrinkled and she looked genuinely confused by the question. "What?"

"Last night when I came to you," he said. "Tensions were high, as were emotions. Our positions are so disparate. I need to know if I took advantage when I kissed you."

Her lips parted and she got to her feet slowly. He did the same, trained in the action by years of politeness.

"No," she whispered. "I almost died yesterday, Kit. And I refuse to be missish or coy or dishonest about anything anymore. Life is too short to be so. I will tell you I never expected you to kiss me. But I…I liked it a great deal. I have not stopped thinking about it since you left me in that room."

His breath caught, his heart rate increased, and he took another long step toward her. Close enough to reach out, to touch her. He wanted to so badly, but he needed permission like breath. "Would you like to do it again?"

She was already moving toward him as she gasped, "Yes, please."

Kit caught Sarah in his arms and their mouths collided. Unlike the previous night, when she'd been shocked and confused by his touch, today she was ready. Her mouth opened and she welcomed him in. He drove his tongue inside, dueling with hers as he backed her away from the separate chairs in the parlor and to the settee. He lowered her there, his fingers digging into her arms as he positioned her for better access.

He tasted like scotch, despite the early hour. Intoxicating and masculine and heady. She was drunk on him and gripped her hands against his lapels, then around his neck as he practically dragged her into his lap to get closer.

Need mushroomed in her from some deep place she'd never

felt before. A tingling that seemed to bring all her limbs and nerve endings to life, a heat that burned and soothed all at once. She wanted something. She knew what it was called, but had never felt it. Had been trained to avoid it. Now she didn't give a damn about ruination. Just him.

He dragged his mouth away in that instant with a low growl that seemed to settle in that throbbing place between her legs. He didn't release her, but continued to stare down into her face like he didn't fully recognize her. Or perhaps he didn't recognize himself. Then he sighed.

"I will admit, Sarah, I don't know what to do about this. This wanting that seems to sear my very soul. That doesn't seem to give a damn about propriety or grace or anything but touching you."

She shivered at the nature of his words. Things said in the dark by a lover, not in private between duke and governess, no matter where she'd started off in life.

She swallowed hard, past her worry, past her fear, past her uncertainty, and whispered in a voice that was so low and dark and husky with desire that she could hardly recognize it as her own, "Perhaps we don't have to know, Kit."

He brushed a hand across her cheek, smoothing away an errant curl before he released her and sat back into a position that was at least a little more proper.

He smiled. "It is not in my nature not to know. I always know my next move and all the reasons for it." He sighed. "But then again, it is not in my nature to pin a young woman against a settee arm and revel in her taste."

She shivered again. "So?"

"So we are in uncharted territory. And perhaps that is not the worst thing. When I touch you, it is most definitely far from that."

He stood, and she followed him to her own feet. He caught her by the waist and dragged her closer, brushing her lips with hers. This time it was gentle. But she felt the heat throbbing behind it.

"Hmmm," he murmured as they parted. "I should go before I can't. But you've given me a great deal to consider, Sarah."

She smiled as he backed toward the door, gave her a small salute and then departed the room. She sagged back onto the settee where he'd so thoroughly kissed her.

"So have you," she whispered. "So have you."

CHAPTER TWELVE

When his father died, Kit had had a hard time picturing the moment when life would feel normal again. And yet, two weeks past that fateful afternoon, he did, occasionally, feel himself again. So did the rest of his world. The servants had gone to wearing a simple black band on their arm, his friends the same. His sister laughed more often and played with the other children. Not that she didn't still sometimes weep or act out in her pain, but it felt like an improvement, a move toward the better.

The only thing consistently different from the day before his father's death was his relationship with Sarah. *That* had changed, and it didn't seem to have any ability to return. She worked for him, that was the same, but they'd had many a stolen moment in the hallway or a parlor after everyone else had gone. Kissing her was becoming a favorite pastime and she was his ultimate distraction from pain. He wanted more and more and more.

A fact that left him a bit uncomfortable. Was he being fair?

He shrugged off the thought and entered his father's study. *His* study now, he supposed, though it didn't feel that way yet. He had only gone into the room a handful of times since his father's death. He hadn't changed anything when it came to the décor, and his father's papers and notes were still strewn across the mahogany desk top.

He drew in a long breath as he stared around the room. Even more than the chamber where Kit now slept, this place was truly the domain of the old duke. It had the weight of him and the sense of him still in its walls.

And it was time to sort through it. Any one of his friends would have gladly stepped forward to help him in that endeavor, but he had put them off, at least for now. If it became too overwhelming he would ask for the help. He needed to do it soon, as his friends would soon be leaving. That night was a final party with all of them and some friends from the shire, then the carriages would begin to roll out over the next few days.

He was both mournful of that moment and anticipating it. He would miss his friends—their large group was a comfort—but he also looked forward to figuring out what the new normal of his life would look like.

And who would play a part in it.

He settled into the leather seat behind the desk and looked over the piles of papers. Ledgers, letters, notes were all arranged in neat sections. As he moved them around, he found a message written in Ewan's even hand. It didn't surprise him. Ewan and Matthew had gone over the papers in the first days when Kit's grief was too painful and sharp. Ewan wrote notes constantly, since he could not speak.

Still, Kit drew a deep breath before he read this one.

Your father made things easy. There will be little difficulty in taking over and no nasty surprises Matthew or I could find. He loved you, Kit, and he knew, as we all know, that you will be as fine a duke as you are a man. E.

Kit's eyes stung as he folded the note and tucked it safely away. He'd been raised for all this, of course. Taught by both word and example the importance of being a decent landlord, a decent employer, a decent man. Taught to serve his populace with honor and kindness.

And it still felt overwhelming.

He shook it off and opened the right top drawer of his

father's desk. Quills and ink bottles and other writing accoutrement greeted him. The old duke had been a great writer. Correspondence was important to him. Kit smiled as he looked at the well-worn instruments that spoke of his father's craft.

He opened the second drawer on that side and found a few dogeared books and another ledger. He moved to the opposite side and opened the top drawer, expecting to find more of these utterly mundane and completely moving artifacts of his father's day to day life.

Instead, when he opened the top drawer, he found half a dozen leather-bound books stacked neatly in a pile. Not printed works on farming or management like the ones from the opposite side of the desk.

These looked like…

He opened one and found it filled from edge to edge with his father's familiar scrawling hand. Kit caught his breath. This was his father's diary.

He flipped to the end, where a silken piece of fabric marked its place, and discovered the last entry was dated less than a week before his father's death. The hand was shakier, less sure.

Kit pushed the journal away on the desk and stared at it. The pain, which he had succeeded in keeping at bay during the time since his father's death, rushed back to him now. Washed over him. Became unbearable, a mockery of what he thought he had overcome.

He bent his head, feeling every wave of it and knowing it would now wash him away, out to sea where there was no coming back from it.

There was a light knock on the door, and as he lifted his head to shout at the unknown person to leave him be, it opened and revealed Sarah.

For a moment, time stood still. He stared at her, lovely and soft, and the pain faded just a fraction. But not enough.

"What is it?" he barked, unable to temper his tone.

She jumped at the sharpness of it, yet she still took a hesitant half step into the room. "I-I'm sorry, Kit. Last night we spoke about a new riding habit for Phoebe and—"

He jerked his face away. A riding habit? He vaguely recalled the conversation. Something about increasing his rapidly growing sister's allowance for clothes and other necessities. It was part of what he'd come in here to look at today, compare his father's allowance for that expense to her needs.

And now that duty felt so tiny and unimportant when his father's journal was sitting on the desk, screaming at him in the old duke's voice.

"I will deal with it when I deal with it," he snapped, slamming a hand on the desk and reveling in the fact that the physical pain momentarily erased the emotional. All too momentarily.

Her lips parted a little and then she inclined her head slightly. "Of course, Your Grace."

He flinched. When they were alone, she never called him *Your Grace*, always Kit. But his tantrum had thrown her back to propriety, a wall between them.

"I'm sorry to have pushed the subject," she continued, her voice trembling. "I will leave you. Good day."

He shoved to his feet as she turned. "Wait."

She stopped. He could see from her tight shoulders that she wanted to keep walking like she hadn't heard him, but she didn't. And that meant he had a chance.

"I'm…I'm sorry, Sarah," he said as he came around the desk toward her. She did turn back to him now, and he could see wariness and empathy mixed on her expression. "I should not have spoken to you in such a fashion."

She stared at him a moment, then reached behind herself and closed the door. She folded her hands before her and said, "Why did you?"

He glanced back at the desk, at the journal, and the pain spiked high in his chest again. "It's just…I…he…"

He sighed. It seemed he could not form the words he needed to say. So he turned and swept the journal up. He handed it over to her without explanation.

She looked at the leather-bound volume, then opened it slowly. She stared at his father's words and then up to his face. "Oh, Kit," she whispered. "His diary?"

He nodded and took a deep breath. "Diaries, actually. There are at least six more in the drawer, and I would assume those are only the ones from this year."

Her eyes went wide and she glanced down at the thick book. "Seven books for less than half a year?"

"He was a prodigious writer," he explained with a smile. "He wrote *everything* down. A life of lists is a life well lived, he used to say."

Sarah's face broke into a wide smile. "I like that saying. I have been known to make a list or two in my day."

He wanted to smile with her, but instead he took the journal back and smoothed his fingers over the supple leather surface. She watched him a moment, then stepped closer and reached out to cover his hand.

"Finding these journals troubles you," she said softly. "Do you want to talk about it?"

He nodded. "It is interfering with your day, I know."

She shrugged. "No, it isn't. Phoebe is learning to change nappies and is happy as can be despite the subject matter. I'm happy to focus on you, Kit. Now, what is it? Do you fear you will find something in these pages that you won't like?"

"No," he said swiftly. "My father was an open book with both his successes and his failures. And Matthew and Ewan have gone over his finances—it does not seem there will be any surprises there, as happened to Baldwin when his father died."

Sarah's eyebrows lifted in surprise and Kit realized he had just shared a secret, which he wouldn't normally do. It must have reflected on his face, for she shook her head gently. "I will never repeat anything you tell me, I can assure you."

He stared at her. Not so long ago, her word would have meant very little to him. He would have dragged up the past as proof of how untrustworthy she was. And yet he felt no need to do so anymore. Sarah had said it herself—she owed him no explanation. And she had nothing to prove.

"Thank you," he said as he pulled away and set the journal back on the desk. He sat on the edge and looked across the room at the portrait above the fireplace. A family portrait with his father and mother and Kit as a baby.

"Well, if it is not fear of uncovering what you didn't know that makes you hesitate, what is it?"

"They're his words," he whispered. "The last entry in this book is from a week before his death. They are probably the last words he ever wrote. Just thinking of that—"

He broke off and was shocked when he felt a hot tear slide down his cheek. Sarah caught her breath and then she rushed forward, her arms coming around his neck as she drew him in and held him close.

He knew he should push her away. Keep some distance between them. Protect his heart. And yet he didn't. He buried his face into the warm crook of her shoulder and clung there as all the pain came back. Only it was tempered now, soothed by her comfort as she smoothed her hands over his shoulders and back. He could sit with it, feel it, let it flow like a river and eventually dissipate when it was ready.

A peace came over him when it did. Something he hadn't felt before as he fought to keep the feelings at bay. Just letting them…*be*…had been transformative.

He lifted his face and found her watching him closely. "Better?" she whispered.

He nodded wordlessly.

She smoothed her fingers over his cheeks. "Right now you are shocked by the realization that his words, his voice, are so close to you. But in time, I think you will see what a gift these books are."

"Yes, I know you're right," he said with a sigh. "I'm certain the rest are in this study somewhere, they probably go back years. Decades even. It will be like reading his life's story, in his own words."

"Many would give a great deal to have such a glimpse of those they lost."

His brow wrinkled, for he realized she was talking about herself. She had so little left of her mother. He felt that for the first time, as deeply as he felt the loss of his father.

She smiled at him, then leaned in and brushed her lips against his. It was a gentle action, meant to soothe him, he supposed. And yet it did the opposite. That light touch turned his mind from thoughts of family and loss to thoughts of a far more pleasant vein.

She moved as if to turn away, but he rose from the edge of the desk and caught her arm to keep her in place. He dragged her back, loving how her body fit against his as they collided. Her empathy faded from her face, replaced by unmistakable desire, and he was lost. Utterly and completely lost to her.

He dropped his mouth to hers and claimed it, his tongue gliding inside where he could taste her. And oh, how he wanted to taste her. He never wanted to forget that sweet flavor, he wanted to know if it was everywhere.

And in that moment, he knew what he would do, if she allowed it.

He backed her across the room to the chair in front of the fire. When he eased her into it and dropped to his knees before her, she drew back, confused.

"Kit?" she whispered.

He smiled at her before he tugged her in for another kiss. She melted against him, hands gripping at his lapels, tongue tangling with his with as much drive as he felt. She wanted more. She might not fully understand what more was, but she wanted it.

And he could give it, without taking.

"I want…" he panted as he pulled away. "I want to do something, Sarah. I want…to touch you."

She leaned in and took his mouth, her fingers gliding along his cheeks. "Silly man, you *are* touching me."

He caught her hips and slid her forward on the chair. Her legs were forced to open with the action, and he pushed up between them, blocked by her skirts but still keenly aware of the tightening of her thighs around his hips.

"I am," he whispered, and he let his hands move. He glided them down her throat, her chest, over her breasts—he noted she shivered—across her stomach, and then he pressed one hand between her legs. "But I want to do it here."

Her breath hitched. "You want to…to take me?"

He shut his eyes. Fuck yes, he wanted to take her. Claim her. Burn her essence onto his skin until he felt her in every pore. Until she was a tattoo on his soul.

But that was…he wasn't ready to go so far. If he did, he'd have to go further, and that felt impetuous.

"Not take," he said, shocked by how shaky his voice was. "Give, Sarah. Give to you, give to me. Without claiming what should not be mine. Will you let me?"

CHAPTER THIRTEEN

Sarah blinked up at the man looming over her. The man who weeks ago she would have called an enemy and was now asking to become her lover. She wanted that. Wanted Kit. And what other chance would she ever have to take what he offered? Her life was going to be lived in service, whether here or somewhere else. She knew what little time those in her position had for a life of their own, a future that didn't involve someone else's children, someone else's life.

He offered her a taste of what she had lost when her mother died and her situation changed so drastically.

All those thoughts ripped through her foggy mind, and she nodded. "Yes," she whispered. "Please."

Kit's face twitched at the *please*, as if that tiny word affected him. Then he leaned in and his mouth was on hers again. This time he was slower, gentler as he tasted and took, sucked and soothed. She felt her bones going liquid, her body melting into the chair as she surrendered to the wonderful sensations of…him.

His mouth glided lower, his teeth nipping her jawline, then his lips fastened on her neck. She hissed at the new sensation, her body lifting beneath him as he tasted the column of her throat. As he did so, she felt his hands moving. He smoothed his fingers along her side, his hands cupped her hips, and she felt each digit dig in through the fabric of her skirt. He ground against her and she gasped as she felt the hard length of him through his trousers.

Thanks to Isabel's adventures, she knew a little about what a man wanted, what he did to a lady. Isabel had always acted like it was a pleasure, at least with Matthew, but Sarah had always had a hard time picturing that such a thing would feel nice.

Now it made more sense. When Kit pushed against her, her body answered with a heated twitch and the place between her legs felt hot and achy and wet. She gasped out a moan of pleasure as his hands found their way back to the space between her legs and he settled one there, pressing his palm flat against her.

He pulled his mouth from her throat, watching her as he rippled his hand over her, hard pressure receding and returning like waves on an ocean. She dipped her head back as pleasure unlike anything she'd ever known rushed over her and everything else in the world faded, drilling down to that one place where he touched her with such expert attention.

"I'm going to lift your skirts," he whispered.

Her eyes flew open and she looked at him. "You're going to…look at me? Bare me?"

He shifted, and she could see that her questions moved him. His eyes had almost no brown left, they were so dilated with desire now. She had done this to him, made him so needy. She, a woman he had hated until just a few days ago.

She was almost proud of that fact.

"I promise you, Sarah, there is no shame is what I'm going to do," he said, his gaze never leaving hers. "All there will be is pleasure."

"More than what you're doing with your hand now?"

That hand stilled and he leaned in. He kissed her once more, deep and slow. Then he pulled away. "So much more."

She nodded, silent acquiescence, though she couldn't help

but blush as he lifted her skirts, exposing her calves, her knees, her thighs. She knew he had to see the hole in her stocking. The one she hadn't the chance to darn yet. He didn't seem to care. His hands slid up her legs, firm pressure as he pushed the skirts higher and higher, piling them against her stomach until she was exposed from the waist down.

She blushed. Her drawers were worn out. Certainly not as fine as any lady who might allow him this pleasure. Of course, what lady would? Very few in her acquaintance would stoop so low. She was surrendering to her most base needs now. He might say he would not judge her, but he would.

"You are frowning," he said, glancing up from what he had revealed. "Why?"

"Just torn between wanting this and knowing the cost," she admitted, because honesty seemed to truly be the best policy at present.

His expression softened. "What cost?"

"That you will see me as a wanton," she admitted. "That I'll know I was."

"That is an ugly word," he said softly, "thrown at ladies so that they are ashamed of what they want. It seems unfair. I asked you for this—why would I judge you?"

She turned her face slightly and his hands stilled.

"Because I did just that for so long," he whispered.

She nodded without looking at him.

He reached up and slid a finger beneath her chin. Slowly he tilted her face toward him until she had to look into his eyes. "I was wrong, Sarah," he whispered.

She gasped. "What?"

"I was wrong for treating you so callously that night with Meg. I was wrong for judging you after. Certainly I would not want to be judged by my worst moment, my silliest mistake. I was wrong. And I'm sorry."

Her eyes flooded with unexpected tears and she lifted a hand to her mouth. He let her sit that way for a moment, then his fingers stroked her thighs, gliding beneath the hem of her drawers to find bare skin.

She jolted at the contact and found her hips lifting.

"I won't ever do that again," he continued. "Judge you. I *would* very much like to touch you like that again."

She found her lips tilting in a smile, and she nodded. "I would very much like the same. Please."

"You say please so prettily," he said, his voice becoming dark with promise as he caught the edge of her drawers and began to tug them. She lifted her hips and he pulled them away, drawing them down her legs and setting them aside.

Now her cheeks burned like fire, for she was bared to him. Fully revealed. And his wide eyes told her he liked what he saw. Wanted it.

"I wonder how many ways you will say please if I do this." He pulled her farther forward again, making her slouch on the chair. He pushed her legs wider, making a space between them, and then he placed the flat on his hand on her once more.

Only this time there was no barrier of cloth between them. Just the heat of his rough palm on the heat of her slick sex. He pushed and electric sensation jolted through her from head to toe.

She gripped the edge of the chair, digging her nails into the fabric as she cried out, "Please!"

He smiled up at her. "And this?"

Now his fingers stroked her intimately, gliding along the entrance to her body, parting the sleek curls there. He smoothed and smoothed, and then he breached her just a fraction, parting the outer lips of her sex and pressing a fingertip inside.

"Please, please," she mumbled, incoherent, she knew, but unable to find anything else to say when his touch awoke such wicked needs in her. Sensations she hadn't ever felt before.

Her breasts felt heavy, her nipples were hard and rubbed deliciously against her chemise beneath her dress. Her legs shook a little as ripples of pleasure seemed to pulse out from the place where he touched her.

He parted her fully, opening her with his thumbs, and she squeezed her eyes shut. He was stroking her still, gently at first, but building the pressure, and then she felt something she would never have expected.

The warm of his breath blowing along her slit.

Her eyes flew open and she stared down at him. His dark head was bent between her open legs, his stare focused on her, his lips puckered as he blew air over her. She gasped at the coolness against her heat, dry on wet.

"I'm going to kiss you," he said, glancing up. "Here. And it's going to feel wonderful."

She had no chance to respond to that shocking claim. Before she could, his head lowered farther and then he did exactly as he'd promised. His hot mouth closed over her in a wet kiss, his tongue tracing the same route his fingers had earlier taken.

He hadn't lied. His mouth felt wonderful against her as he tasted and teased and explored her in a way she never would have guessed was possible. Her body was on fire, the flames licked higher and higher by his tongue. There were waves of pleasure that he stoked, the tingles intensifying.

His tongue crested over some hidden part of her, a bundle of nerves, and when he focused his attention there, she gasped. He smiled against her flesh, but did not cease the heavenly torment, instead swirling his tongue around and around that place. The intensity of sensation grew, reaching a point where she felt balanced on the edge of pleasure and pain.

And when he sucked that little part of her, she fell into the sensation fully. Her body began to buck as waves of intense pleasure rocked her. She bent her head back, her body shaking as the sensations went on and on, driven by his relentless attack on her body.

Only when her quaking had begun to subside did he lift his head and smile up at her. He looked satisfied, smug even, with his mouth glittering with her juices and his eyes lit with desire and triumph. He leaned up and kissed her. She tasted herself on his lips, sweet and salty and intoxicating. Her arms came around him and she sank into him, into this. She wanted more.

She wanted everything. She knew it in that moment, and also knew what folly it was. And yet there it was, an itch in the back of her mind that kept calling for her to scratch it. But she couldn't tell him how she felt, because he'd never want that. He'd turned to her in pain, in gratitude for what she'd done in the lake.

She knew that. This tryst, this affair, this whatever it was…it couldn't last. Kit would marry some daughter of an exalted title and he would carry on his father's legacy with her.

Sarah was a passing folly, just as he'd described his own father's affair with Phoebe's mother.

She jolted. God, would he now think her the same as that woman he claimed wanted only money? Who would sell her child without thought?

She pulled away from his kiss and he let her get up, pushing past him as she swept her skirts back down and picked up her discarded drawers from the floor. She felt him watching her as she struggled to right herself. But she had no idea what he would say. No idea what he must think now. Only knowing that despite any promises he made not to judge her, she might have just made the biggest mistake of her life.

Kit watched Sarah fuss with her clothing, touch her unmussed hair over and over again in a nervous flutter of movements. He knew she'd enjoyed what he'd done. He'd felt the fluttering force of her powerful orgasm. He'd wanted nothing more than to bury himself in her twitching body and pound into her until he found his own release.

He'd only barely resisted that urge.

He pushed to his full height from his position on the floor and smiled at her in the hopes it would soothe whatever nervousness she now felt.

"What are you doing to me?" he asked.

She froze at the question and pivoted to face him. The high color that had filled her cheeks at the height of her orgasm had faded now, leaving her pale and worried. Not the result he had wanted from this stolen moment of bliss.

"I-I don't know," she stammered at last. "I'm not trying to do anything to you."

There was a lilt of defensiveness to her tone. Like she was under attack. He wrinkled his brow. "Having regrets?"

She paused and her shoulders rolled forward. "No," she whispered, and that one syllable was so comforting he nearly sagged beneath it. "I have been alone a long time, Kit. And what just happened…I liked it, whether I should admit that or not." Her gaze darted away. "I just hope you know that I understand it cannot last. I have no expectations, Your Grace. I have no desire to trap you or use this against you."

He froze at her words. Here he'd been worried about taking advantage of her, but she was talking about taking advantage of him. It was possible, of course—he'd watched it happen with his father and Phoebe's nightmare of a mother. Obviously Sarah was thinking of the same, trying to push herself out of the category of villain.

One he hadn't thought to put her in, still didn't. And yet her words stung. As did the fact that she was trying to push them so far apart after an act that could have brought them closer.

"I should…" she began. "I should go check on Phoebe now."

She moved toward the door, and Kit felt a swell of need rise up in him. Not need for her body—something else. A desire to have her stay at his side. And that was dangerous, indeed.

"Sarah!" he burst out.

She turned at the door, just as she had earlier, and he could see her anxiousness, her uncertainty. "Yes?"

"The others will begin to leave tomorrow," he said.

She nodded. "Yes, I know the Northfield, Crestwood and Roseford parties are all departing before luncheon. The rest after, save for Willowby. Barrymore told the staff about the schedule."

"And you know there is a small party tonight, with all my houseguests and a few friends from the surrounding area?" he asked.

"Yes," she said. "Do you want Phoebe to make an appearance?"

He frowned. "No, she's too young. No reason to stress her with that sort of thing. I wanted…will you come?"

Her lips parted, and for a moment he saw how much the request meant. How much she'd lost when she lost her place in Society. Then she bent her head and the connection he'd seen there departed.

"I-I do not think that would be best, Kit," she said softly.

Her rejection stung more than it should have, and he turned away from it and from her and retook his place at his father's desk in order to create a barrier between them.

"I see," he said, picking up a quill and dipping it into ink, though he had no idea what he would write. "As you wish, Miss Carlton. Good day."

She took a moment at the door, watching him as he pretended to do something official. Then she inclined her head. "Good day, Your Grace."

And she was gone, leaving him alone in his office, alone with his thoughts. Exactly where he didn't want to be.

CHAPTER FOURTEEN

Sarah was distracted as she hurried down the hall away from Kit's study. Her body still tingled from his touch. And she also still stung from his attitude. When she'd refused his request about her coming to the gathering, it was like a wall had slammed down between them, closing off whatever progress they'd made.

But why? He couldn't truly want her there, in a place she didn't belong. And yet it was like she'd hurt him.

She turned a corner toward the stairs and, in her upset, slammed straight into another person. Not just any person. Margaret, Duchess of Crestwood, staggered back from their collision, then righted herself with a laugh.

One Sarah didn't share. She covered her mouth in horror. "Oh, Your Grace, I'm so dreadfully sorry. I was not paying attention. Are you injured?"

"Of course not," Meg laughed. "And I was distracted, as well—it was just as much my fault as yours."

Sarah ducked her head. Meg had been nothing but friendly to her this entire trip, but that didn't change their history.

The duchess wrinkled her brow. "Are *you* well?"

Sarah lifted her gaze and nodded. "Of course."

"Of course," Meg repeated slowly. Then she shook her head. "I think you and I must finally have a discussion that has been years in the making. Come with me, won't you?"

Sarah caught her breath. Oh dear God, here it was. The moment when Meg would confront her with her bad behavior all those years ago. The moment everything would crash around her once more.

But there was no way to deny the woman who was now striding away from her into the closest parlor. All she could do was obey and follow her into the room.

Meg closed the door behind them and took a seat on the settee. She patted the cushion beside her, and Sarah held back a sigh as she joined her.

She was very much not in the right state of mind for this. Not when everything with Kit was already so confused.

"I-I owe you an apology," she began. "I know I do. I'm sure you have been waiting for it for years."

Meg's brow wrinkled. "Don't be silly. Of course you don't. To be honest, I didn't even recall that night until you reminded me just after the death of Kit's father. I certainly have not been waiting around, looking at the clock, for some kind of request for forgiveness."

Sarah bent her head. "But Kit is right in one thing. I was abominably rude to you that night. I'd had too much punch, just as you said then, and things were getting so bad when it came to my future. But I had no right to speak to you that way. No right to accuse you of doing something wrong. The Duke of Crestwood was nothing to me. And as you said, you cannot steal a person."

"You do recall every detail," Meg said softly. "And here I only remember just the barest of facts. My dear Sarah, know this…whatever was said or done, it was a lifetime ago. And I understood, even then, that you lashed out over fear for your own position, it had very little to do with me."

"Yes." Sarah flashed back to that horrible time. "My father's death put us in a dreadful position and I was making no headway in landing a match that could save us."

"Simon's attention gave you hope." Meg was nodding now. "He would feel terrible if he knew, so perhaps it is *he* who owes you the apology."

"Oh no!" Sarah clasped her hands. "I would never think that or ask for such a thing. You two were clearly made for each other. I can see now that it would have been a bad match."

"And then there is Kit," Meg said. "He isn't still troubling you about what he witnessed, is he? I gave him a stern talking to on the subject."

Sarah blinked. She'd had no idea Meg had spoken to Kit about her. He'd never said anything about it. "No, Your Grace."

"Meg."

"Meg," Sarah repeated. "He has even apologized to me for holding that moment against me all these years. And he…"

Meg leaned in. "It's obvious there is some connection between you two. Something that goes beyond duty or gratitude or shared love of Phoebe."

Sarah covered her mouth. She was certainly mucking everything up if her connection to Kit was obvious. It could destroy her in this position and keep her from ever having another.

"I don't know what to say," she whispered when it felt like a lifetime had passed.

"You don't have to say anything," Meg said, her tone gentle. "But I know you have been…very alone for a long time. I know you'd probably rather speak to Isabel, but I'm the one who nearly mowed you down in the hallway and saw that you were upset. Since you were coming from the direction of Kit's study, I must deduce your reaction has something to do with him. And since that connection I mentioned does exist, I think it is a personal matter. Is there any way I can help? I do have experience in fraught relationships to recommend me for the duty."

Sarah stared, unblinking, for a moment. If someone had told her three years ago that she would be sitting with Margaret,

Duchess of Crestwood, with the lady offering to be her friend, her confidante…she would have fallen over laughing. And yet here it was. And the offer was more tempting than it should have been. Everything felt upside down and she needed help in righting it.

"I don't know what to think," she admitted softly. "We have not…defined…whatever is between us. He's made no promises and I would never ask for any."

"Never?" Meg asked.

Sarah shifted in her place. "My situation is very different than it was back when I lashed out at you. I realize I no longer belong in the kind of Society you or Isabel or…or Kit inhabit."

"That's nonsense," Meg said. "Your circumstances may have changed, but you are still a gentleman's daughter. Kit knows that as well as anyone. If he is conflicted, I would wager it has *nothing* to do with your standing."

"He asked me to attend the party tonight," Sarah admitted.

Meg's grin was instant and wide. "Did he now?"

Sarah nodded. "Of course, I said no."

"Why?"

"I've nothing to wear," she said swiftly, though that wasn't why. At least not the only reason.

Meg lifted her brows. "That is the second time you've given me that excuse."

Sarah flinched, for she had forgotten she'd told Meg that earlier in the party. It felt like a lifetime ago. "Well, earlier it was only the other dukes and duchesses at the gathering. This is a party. It may be solemn thanks to the recent loss of the duke, but I will stand out in my serviceable clothing."

Meg leaned back and looked her up and down, like she was sizing her up. Then she nodded as if she were satisfied. "That will work."

"Work?"

"Come with me," Meg ordered. "I can fix this problem and I shall."

Sarah blushed as she stood in the middle of Meg's chamber an hour later. All the duchesses surrounded her, holding up one gown or the next, clucking over jewelry and hairstyles in a loud cacophony of kindness and fun. When Meg had brought her here and surrounded her with the other women, she'd felt awkward. She'd even tried to escape by making an excuse to see Phoebe. That had been squashed by Charlotte's explanation that her charge was taking a nap. Their kindness had quickly made her discomfort fade. Now she was actually having fun.

Isabel approached, holding up a robin's-egg blue gown. "That color matches your eyes perfectly," she cooed. "But I think my bust is a little too small for it to fit you right."

Katherine, Duchess of Roseford, clapped her hands. "I have a gown in the same color. Robert bought it for me in Spain, and it is exquisite!"

"I am so very envious of your adventures with Robert," Emma said as Katherine rushed to the pile of gowns on Meg's bed and dug through them looking for the one she wanted.

"You should tell James to take you," Katherine said. "Traveling together is wonderfully romantic. You truly get to know each other in a new way."

The women sighed almost en masse, and Sarah couldn't help but do the same. "You and Roseford are recently married, are you not?"

Katherine nodded. "Yes, just half a year ago. We had a great deal to overcome, but I cannot deny that I have never been happier."

"You earned all that happiness," Adelaide said as she slid up and squeezed Katherine gently. "Both of you."

Katherine smiled and then grabbed for the gown. "Ah, here it is."

Sarah caught her breath. The silk on the gown was

incredibly fine, the cut was amazing, and the detailing of braided silk and scalloped edging was impeccable.

"Oh, no," she breathed. "I couldn't wear that, Your Grace."

Katherine shook her head. "Why ever not? You will look stunning in it."

"You should wear it."

Katherine stepped forward and held the dress up, then turned her toward the mirror. "No, I think you should. Please."

It was clear there was no arguing, and in truth Sarah wanted to wear the fine dress. She wanted her hair done by Meg's maid. She wanted to wear Isabel's jewelry. She wanted to pretend that she would be the kind of woman Kit could have a future with. Just for one night.

She nodded, and the room let out a collective murmur of approval. Meg glanced at the clock and gasped. "Oh my, we shall all be late. Ladies, you should go get ready. Isabel, will you stay here with Sarah and me? We can share our maids."

Isabel stepped up to squeeze Sarah. "Of course."

"Thank you all so much for your kindness," Sarah said softly. "I do appreciate it more than you could know."

Each of the women squeezed her hand or said something kind as they trailed out. Emma was last and rang the bell by the door so Meg's maid would come.

Within a few moments all three women were readying themselves. Sarah reveled in this time where she could almost forget all she'd lost. When everything was finished, she stepped up to the mirror.

"I look like…" She trailed off as tears filled her eyes. "I look like me. The old me. Only a much finer me."

Isabel shook her head. "No, my dear. Just you. You could not be finer. Are you ready? I believe it's time to join the party."

Sarah drew a breath. She wasn't exactly ready. She'd refused Kit's invitation, and now she would just arrive at his gathering. Given his cool response earlier, she had no idea how he would react. And what about the others? The dukes and duchesses might be welcoming, but there would be strangers amongst their ranks tonight.

"You'll be fine," Meg said gently. "And you look wonderful."

Sarah nodded and followed the ladies into the hallway. She was surprised to find that it was not empty. Phoebe stood with Adelaide, waiting for her to come out of the room. When she did, the little girl's face lit up.

"You're a princess," she cooed, reaching out to stroke her fingers over the silky skirt of Sarah's gown.

She crouched down to be closer to Phoebe and kissed her cheek. "No, lovie, I'm just me. I think you were going to help with the babies tonight, werren't you?"

Phoebe nodded solemnly, as if she took this as a sacred duty. As she leaned in to kiss Sarah's cheek, she whispered, "I wish you were my mama, Sarah. I don't have a mama."

Sarah caught her breath as she leaned away from the little girl. It was clear Adelaide had also heard the tiny declaration, for she turned her face with tears in her eyes.

Sarah caught Phoebe's hands gently. "One day Kit will marry and you will have a lovely lady who will act as your mama, just as Kit acts as your papa now."

Phoebe looked worried. "I want you."

She could see the little girl was tired and anxious. So instead of arguing, she brushed her cheek and said, "Well, we'll talk about it later. Now go and join the other children. I'm sure their nannies are looking forward to your help."

Phoebe smiled and then skipped off in the direction of the nursery. As Sarah straightened, she shook her head at Isabel, Adelaide and Meg. "How do I explain to her that what she wants isn't possible?"

Isabel shrugged. "Stop believing that it is. You never know what could happen. Now come on."

Isabel linked arms with her, and the four women went down the long stairs together. At the bottom, Matthew, Graham and

Simon waited together. Sarah saw their faces light up when they saw their wives. Felt the woman ripple with electric connection to the men they loved.

She understood that connection now, better than ever before. And she also mourned it more. No matter what Isabel said or what Phoebe wanted, her situation with Kit could only be a temporary one for them both. He would never feel for her the way these men felt for their wives.

And she didn't want him to. Only that was a lie.

The duchesses stepped away to their husbands, and now the small group of them all stared at her.

"You look a vision," Matthew said gently.

"It is all Katherine's dress, I assure you," Sarah said with a blush as she darted her gaze away.

"I think the world would beg to differ," Simon said. "Now, shall we enter? Who goes first in these situations? I can never recall when we're forced to be proper."

"Distance to the throne, I believe," Graham said. "So Matthew, me and then you."

"I think you made that up so that we would go last," Simon said with a teasing glare for Graham.

"You two," Matthew chuckled, then led Isabel into the ballroom. Sarah heard them announced and her heart leapt to her throat. She hadn't thought about the announcement. How would Barrymore, who knew her from below stairs, react to her? What would he say?

Her heart thudded as the next couple entered. Then Simon and Meg were all that was left between her and the room of buzzing, judging people who she had once strode to make her peers. Who all knew, she was certain, that she had gone into service for Kit. They would whisper.

"The Duke and Duchesses of Crestwood," Barrymore intoned as Simon and Meg stepped into the room. When Sarah stepped up, Barrymore jolted to see her and then glanced down at his notes.

"Er, the Duke of Kingsacre requested I join the party," she said softly.

"Of course. Hero of the hour and all that," Barrymore said.

Sarah worried her lip. Of course that was why, but it certainly burst the princessy bubble she'd allowed herself to float in.

"Miss Sarah Carlton," he announced, his booming voice interrupting her trailing thoughts.

She caught her breath and stepped into the room. All around her, people turned to look at her. She felt their eyes on her, their judgments, and then none of it mattered. Because she caught sight of Kit across the room.

His expression was surprised, but then his gaze flowed over her from head to toe and his face lit up. It lit up just as the other dukes' faces had done when they saw their wives.

He left behind whoever it was he was talking to before she came into the room and then he was gliding toward her, that gaze never leaving her face. Her heart was throbbing and she fought the urge to fidget as he reached her at last and caught her hand.

"You came," he murmured.

She nodded. "You asked."

He arched a brow playfully. "And you refused. But I am glad you changed your mind. You look…stunning, Sarah. Absolutely beautiful."

"Thank you," she whispered, unable to raise her voice any further when he was looking at her like that. Like she was his. Like he didn't give a damn if anyone knew it. "Meg and the other duchesses were a great help after they convinced me to take your invitation. Katherine's gown, Isabel's jewelry, and Meg's maid did magic of some kind on my hair."

He shook his head. "And none of that is why you outshine every other person in this room."

Her lips parted. "Kit," she whispered.

He stepped in, and for a moment his expression said he wanted to kiss her. And God, how she wanted that, too, despite standing in the middle of the ballroom. Despite the fact that the world was watching.

He blinked and looked around, as if he had remembered himself. Then he stepped back again. "I will not be dancing tonight, for obvious reasons," he said. "But I am glad you're here. I must see to my guests now, though. I think I may have utterly abandoned Lord Middleton and his wife mid-sentence."

"Of course. Perhaps we'll have a moment later."

He squeezed her hand and finally released it. "I can guarantee I will find a moment with you, Sarah."

He turned and left her, and she watched him go. But when she was alone, she let out a sigh. When Kit was with her, nothing else mattered. But now, standing in the middle of the room, all those eyes flitting over her, she felt a little lost.

Because her place in the world was no longer clear. And she had no idea how to find it.

CHAPTER FIFTEEN

Kit forced yet another smile as one of his guests told a story about the late duke. It wasn't that he didn't appreciate the tales of his father's kindness or strength or friendship—he very much did. He also knew they were kindly meant. And yet each word about the man he'd lost felt like a dagger to his heart. But he was not allowed to demonstrate his grief. Men were expected to stiffen their lips and never let it show. He would have to hold it in until he was alone...or with Sarah.

She never judged him for letting that grief flow.

He'd been thinking a great deal about Sarah tonight. It was impossible not to watch her, a goddess in blue, as she glided across the floor, chatted with his friends or sipped her drink along the wall.

As his companion droned on, he found her in the crowd again, but this time his heart sank a fraction. She was standing with Lord Geoffrey, heir to the Earl of Edencross. The man was young, handsome, and he seemed enamored with Sarah at present, if the way he leaned forward to attend to her conversation was any indication.

He frowned just as his companion, Mr. Jonas Kline, said, "Wouldn't you say, Your Grace?"

He blinked and forced himself to attend. "I'm sorry?"

"I was just saying that you must be thrilled to finally take on the title of Duke of Kingsacre," he said, his expression one of annoyance. "You've been waiting many a year. It must have been difficult as your father dragged out his end."

Kit's eyes went wide at the hideous, vulgar implication. But his expression didn't slow his companion's awful words. "And now you have all that was his," he continued with a tipsy chuckle. "Money, lands, even that comely governess. What's his is now yours, in every sense, eh?"

Kit might have been able to simply dismiss this man in disgust on a normal night. Mark him off as a person he would never interact with again and leave it at that. He'd never been one to have a loud, public altercation, not like some of his friends.

But tonight was not a normal night. It was too close to his father's death, too close to the near tragedy at the lake days before, too close to the fact that Sarah was smiling at Lord Geoffrey, and it made Kit want to scream. He reached out and caught Mr. Kline by the lapels, yanking him forward.

"What the hell did you just say to me?" he growled right in the bastard's face.

"I—just—I meant—" Kline stammered.

Before he could finish, before Kit could go too far, Ewan, Hugh and Lucas were suddenly at his side. As Ewan gently put a hand on his, meeting his gaze and telling him everything he needed to hear without words, the other two pulled Kline away.

"Enough, Kit," Hugh said gently as he glared at Kline.

Kit shook his head and looked around the room. Everyone was staring now. Even the orchestra had stopped playing. Sarah was watching, too, her lips slightly parted as she stepped forward, away from her companion, and just…watched him.

"Get him out of my house," he muttered, and then turned on his heel and strode across the ballroom and out the door onto the terrace.

He yanked the doors shut behind himself and paced away down the long veranda that stretched all the way along the back of the house. He moved away from the ballroom, past the parlors adjacent, far away toward a darkened corner where he prayed he wouldn't be found when—not if, *when*—one of his friends or five of his friends came looking for him. He had no idea what to say when they did.

He stared up at the sky. The moon was only a sliver, providing little light. He was reminded of nights he'd stood out here with his father when he was just a boy, almost the same age as Phoebe was now. His father had taught him constellations on this terrace. Told him the stories that went along with the stars.

He didn't remember them now, at least not all of them.

"What am I doing?" he asked the night, longing for his father's voice to answer. To advise. To comfort or to command. Wouldn't that make life easier?

"It's a very good question, Your Grace."

He froze and turned to find someone had indeed followed him out to his hiding place. But it wasn't a friend, it wasn't a gawker. It was Sarah.

She shouldn't have come here. It wasn't her place to follow Kit from the ballroom as the others buzzed about his attack on his guest. And yet when she saw his face, crumpled with pain, she had no other choice. She needed to go after him, needed to ensure he was well.

She *needed* that. So did he.

His expression now told her she'd been right. He looked relieved to see her and his shoulders relaxed a fraction as he returned his attention to the sky.

"It's just…hard," he said. "Tonight was difficult."

She stepped up beside him and rested her hands beside his on the stone wall. "Yes, I think I understand. It wasn't easy for me, either."

He jerked his face toward hers. "No? When I saw you, you always seemed to be having a good time. Especially with Lord Geoffrey."

There was a hint of jealousy in his tone, and she wondered at it. Liked it, if truth be told. Even if it was entirely unfounded.

"Lord Geoffrey is a nice enough person, I suppose, but he might be the greatest bore in all the empire."

To her great joy, Kit chuckled and even more of the tension dissipated from his frame. "The eligible ladies in Town vying for his attention might disagree."

She wrinkled her nose. "He talked to me for ten minutes about the difference between Trevithick's first steam engine and the one he used just last year."

Kit shifted. "Huh. Well, it is a leap in technology to be certain."

"I understand the science is fascinating." She rolled her eyes. "But...*ten minutes* on every exhaustive detail of the engines, Kit."

He laughed. "I'd forgotten how pedantic the man could be on those subjects. But you were smiling while he spoke. I never would have guessed you weren't enjoying yourself."

"It was a grimace," she said, and now she couldn't help but smile genuinely. "Perhaps I'm being unfair. Lord Geoffrey is certainly not the worst company I kept tonight."

There must have been something telling in her tone, for Kit turned and faced her. "Did something happen? Was someone unkind to you?" When she didn't answer straight away, his lips thinned. "Tell me."

His anger, which he normally controlled but had bubbled over twice tonight, showed the tangle of his heart quite clearly. She reached out and caught his hand, joining her fingers with his.

"The duchesses are accepting," she explained softly. "But there are more than just the duchesses here. And those others know my story."

"They *think* they know," he spat, his tone still laced with frustration that she doubted was entirely about her.

"Whether it's truth or not, they have something to say when they see me in the middle of your ballroom in a borrowed gown."

He let out his breath gently. "There were whispers."

She shrugged, trying not to let the reality of that sting her too greatly. She'd known it would happen. It didn't make the moments any easier.

"I'm sorry," he said, the pepper gone from his tone as he looked out over the dark garden.

"It's not your fault, Kit," she said, and leaned up to touch his cheek. She turned his face and he looked down into her eyes. Her breath caught at how beautiful he was. How much she cared about his well being.

How much she was coming to love him.

That reality slammed into her and she could hardly breathe.

"It feels like my responsibility," he said. "Even if it's not my fault."

She pushed away the realization that had just changed her world and focused on this man and what he needed. "What brought on your anger in there? It was out of character to say the least."

"Kline said something terrible. About my father, about my taking on the title. Something I won't repeat."

"And that was all there was to it?"

He looked again into the darkness, his gaze unfocused and faraway. She felt the weight on his shoulders. She understood it.

At last he sighed. "I'm not…ready for this, Sarah. Taking his place."

"Kit, look at me." He did so, his dark stare glittering in the starlight. "You aren't meant to take his place."

"Of course I am," he said, his tone now strained with pain. "It is what I was raised to do."

"You were raised to take *your* place. And I have watched you for years and know you will do that with great honor."

His lips thinned. "You know that after feeling my misplaced judgement of you for years? I would not think that would bode well for my future as a good duke."

"You could have damaged me," she said. "I feared you would, but you never did, despite what you thought of me. And aside from that one mar on your character, I know you have intense loyalty to your friends. You are intelligent, you study subjects in order to truly understand them. You are kind to your household staff, I'm certain just as kind to your tenants. Those are things you learned from your father, certainly, but that does not mean you will take his place or rule like he did. You will break your own path, make your own way, with his words as guidance."

His expression softened and he stared into her eyes for a moment, almost like he was seeing her for the first time. Like he understood something that had been a riddle before. Then he bent his head and his mouth found hers.

She lifted into him, winding her arms around his neck as his lips brushed gently, then firmly, against hers. Her mouth opened and he took, just as she'd known he would. She tasted his pain, his desperation, but as they kissed those darker emotions seemed to fade, replaced by desire.

Only then did he part from her and trace her cheek with one fingertip. "I'm glad you're here, Sarah."

She nodded. "So am I."

"I need you," he continued. "That is a little terrifying, honestly, considering where we began and what is ahead of me. But I do. Will you—"

He broke off and shook his head, a self-admonishment she didn't fully understand. "Will I what?" she asked.

"Come to me tonight," he finished. "It's unfair to you to ask. I expect you to refuse."

"Yes," she whispered, feeling no hesitation in that answer even though she should have. But this is what she wanted, to comfort this man she had grown to love. And she wasn't about to deny either of them what they needed.

Kit was practically bouncing in anticipation when there was finally a knock on his chamber door hours later. The party, despite the difficult moments, had ended up a success, but he'd been waiting for its end. Waiting for Sarah, because right now Sarah was all that mattered.

He crossed to the door and opened it wide to reveal her standing in his doorway, still in that fetching blue gown, her hair piled high on her head, like a goddess called down from Olympus. And here he was just a mortal who wanted to worship at her feet.

She entered the antechamber and looked toward the door to his bedroom with a smile. "The last time I was here…"

"Don't remind me," he said with a shake of his head. "You do not know how many times I wake crying out as I drag you to the shore of the lake in my dreams. Only no one can make you breathe in my nightmares."

Her expression softened and she took his hands in hers. "But I did not die," she said gently. "I'm here with you. And so is Phoebe."

She made it seem like everything could be so easy. But nothing felt easy at present, it just felt heavy.

"When everyone is gone, I think you and I should take Phoebe out in the boat," she added.

He tensed. "I don't think it's a good idea."

"You know what I said to her that day," she said. "And you know I'm right. The longer we avoid it, the more fearful it will become. Neither one of us wants her to grow up terrified of what might be."

Kit bent his head. She *was* right, of course. She knew what was best for his sister, she could see past the momentary terror in a way that was difficult for him at present. He wondered at her ability to have so much clarity considering what she had endured herself.

"And I don't want that fear for you either," she said as she stepped closer. "Please."

He shook his head at that last word. "I think I am learning that you are impossible to argue with. You will use all my weaknesses against me to win your way."

She laughed, and the sound was like music. "Only when I'm right. And you know, what I was going to say is the last time I was in this room, you came to that bed and you kissed me."

He glanced at the bed and thought of the same. "You looked so fragile in my shirt. And so damned delectable. I couldn't fight what I wanted. And right now I just want to…"

He trailed off and finished the sentence by catching her cheeks gently and bringing his mouth to hers. Unlike on the terrace a few hours before, there was nothing to temper his passions and he dove into the safe haven of her mouth. Of her sigh. Of her surrender as her arms came around him and she drew him even closer.

The heat between them built, just as it had done in his office earlier that day when he had pleasured her with his mouth. His body had been screaming for release since then. A release he knew he couldn't ask for. A release he knew wasn't fair, and yet his cock throbbed as it rubbed against the front fold of his trousers.

Her hand reached up to settle on his chest as she parted her mouth from his. She stared up at him in wonder, in desire. And then she cleared her throat.

"Since we were talking about when I almost died—" she began.

He frowned and stepped away. "That's a mood killer," he muttered.

"Not if you listen to what I'm going to say," she said. "Kit, that day has made me want to be more bold, more honest, more daring than I've let myself be. Life is so short—I understand that better than I ever did. And if I don't ask for what I want…then I may never get it."

He blinked, uncertain of where she was going with this conversation. Wanting to know.

He tilted his head. "What do you want, Sarah?"

Her cheeks darkened in color and her gaze darted away from a moment. But then he saw her steel herself, steady herself, and she met his eyes once more.

"I want to go to your bed, Kit. I want you to make love to me. And I want to give you my innocence. *That's* what I want."

CHAPTER SIXTEEN

She had shocked Kit. Sarah could see that in the way his mouth dropped open and he stared in stunned silence at her for what seemed like forever. She had no idea if she had gone too far. If he would call her a wanton, a proper label at present, and turn her out onto the street.

What she did know was that she had to take the risk. She didn't want regrets. Not asking for this stolen night with him would surely become one of those.

"Please say something," she whispered at last.

He took a step closer. "Sarah, what you're asking—"

"Is bold, I know. Unorthodox. But think of my position, Kit. I am no longer in Society. My virginity is not a commodity to be purchased by a husband. I will never have the future I once protected my innocence for."

"You don't know that. Someone like Lord Geoffrey—"

She held up her hands. "Despite your focus on the man, he would never be interested in me. Perhaps as a lover, but he would see me as any other man of his level would. I have nothing to recommend me, and now I am a governess. Besides, I don't want Lord Geoffrey or any other man I spoke to tonight." She took a deep breath and dared to move toward him. She traced her hand down his chest, starting at the collarbone, pressing down to his stomach, feeling the hardness of him beneath his proper party attire. "I want you."

He grumbled something incoherent under his breath. "You would grant me such a gift."

"Knowing you would honor it? That you would take care not to hurt me? Yes." She held her breath as she awaited his response. She could see him waging a battle in his mind. Desire versus duty. Propriety versus passion.

"You don't know how much I want you," he whispered as he edged closer, caught her hand, drew her flush against him once more.

"Then show me, Your Grace. Please."

His mouth moved to hers, but this time there was no desperation to his kiss. He had decided and now he had all night to take his time. To take her. She knew he would do both. And it would be a night to remember with a man she loved and couldn't have.

But she pushed that thought aside and melted into him instead. His kiss burned slow, but burn it did. As he tasted her, teased her, sucked her tongue, her body started to throb. Thanks to his intimate games in the study earlier that day, she understood the throb more now. Understood why her body called to him and how it would answer if he touched her.

And she wanted that so badly that she almost couldn't think of anything else.

Luckily it didn't seem she had to. He turned her as they kissed, backing her through the door to his bedchamber. He kicked the door shut behind them and maneuvered her to his bed. There he stopped. There he stepped away, and the panic rose in her.

"Please don't tell me no," she whispered.

"I'm not," he promised. "But you are giving up something of significance. It isn't fair not to let you have something in return."

She shook her head. "What is that?"

"Control." He lifted his hands to his cravat, untying it,

unlooping it. She watched, mesmerized, as he shrugged out of his jacket. Then he unbuttoned his shirt and tugged it over his head.

Her heart all but stopped. She'd never seen a man in any state of undress before, and this man was…beautiful. He had a lean, muscular body with taut shoulders and a narrow waist. There was a smattering of chest hair across his pectorals and then it trailed into a most interesting line that disappeared into his trousers.

"Kit?" she whispered, her voice almost not carrying.

"Touch me," he said. "Explore. This is for you, Sarah. Tonight is for you."

She swallowed at that idea. Then she reached out a trembling hand and brushed just her fingertips along the muscular plane of his chest. The fibers bunched beneath her fingers, and he smiled as she flattened her palm over his heart and felt it pounding against her hand, matching the heavy rhythm of her own.

Somehow that helped her, eased her nervousness and gave her enough bold drive to lean closer and press her mouth against his shoulder. He hissed in a breath and his hands came into her hair, tangling amongst the curls. The pressure against her skull, the way his pulse quickened, drove her on. Her fingers clenched against his skin and she glided her tongue lower, tasting the clean maleness of his skin. It was the most potent aphrodisiac, and she groaned as she licked his nipple.

He jolted against her and tugged, bringing her up straight as he kissed her once more. His hands slid down her body and he cupped her backside, grinding against her. She felt the hard length of him pressing into her stomach, and the erotic electricity of their bodies colliding was unexpected and powerful.

"Please," she whispered, mimicking her needy words from earlier in the day.

He pulled away, smiling down at her, and then he turned her so her back was to him. He slid his fingers up and down her arms, across her shoulders, and then he unfastened the first button of her gown.

"You looked like a queen tonight," he whispered, pressing a kiss to the triangle of skin he had revealed. "Like a goddess."

She shivered as the next few buttons slid free and he parted the back of her gown gently. She leaned into him, feeling his bare skin touch hers and his heat suffuse her skin. His fingers looped beneath the satin fabric of the gown and he glided it forward, down her arms until it bunched at her waist and left her only in her chemise. Her undergarments were the only thing she hadn't received from the duchesses that night, so she blushed as he saw the truth beneath the borrowed lie.

Slowly she turned and shifted the skirt to the floor. She stepped out, picked up the gown and carefully draped it over a chair next to his bed.

"You see that I'm not a goddess, though," she said. "Certainly not a queen. I'm a woman in a worn-out chemise whose friends pitied her enough to let her play dress up. A woman who pretended she belonged when she didn't. So if you're expecting a goddess or a queen in your bed tonight, Kit, then you will be disappointed."

His gaze held hers for what felt like forever. Then it slid over her, his pupils dilating. "The dress you wore tonight was very pretty. The jewels were lovely. Your hair was beautiful." He stepped forward and placed his hands on her shoulders, stroking his thumbs across her worn chemise straps gently. "None of that is why I saw a queen before me."

She shook her head. "But—"

"You would be a goddess if you were in a scullery maid's gown or an empress's. It's you, Sarah. You I saw, and you I want in my bed."

His mouth covered hers and she let out a sigh against his lips. Suddenly she didn't care about her worn undergarments or the future or the imprudence of what she was about to do. She just wanted to do it. She slid her hands up his arms, clenching the hard muscle of his biceps as they flexed beneath her fingers.

He drew back and caught her hands, flattening her palms against his chest and drawing them down until they reached his waistband. She bit her lip as she struggled with the buttons along his fall front and finally managed to open them. It fell forward and she caught her breath.

There it was. This thing she had been told to avoid, to fear, to never have a curiosity about. She'd been a very good girl for a long time, behaving as a lady should. But now she looked at the hard cock between them and all thoughts of being a lady fled.

Yes, it was intimidating, for he was so very different from herself. But it was also tempting beyond measure. She looked up at him, and he smiled as he pushed the trousers away and stood before her naked, a study in muscle and sinew.

"What do you want to do?" he asked, his voice rough in the quiet.

"Touch you," she admitted on a blush. "I want to touch you."

He nodded, silent permission, and she slid her hand around his length. The skin was so soft over that steely evidence of desire and potency. She stroked her thumb over the mushroom head and then down the vein that strained along the shaft. He grunted as she did so and his eyes fluttered shut.

"Did it hurt?" she asked, tempted to jerk her hand away.

"No. Not hurt," he gasped, his tone garbled.

She had given him pleasure, seemingly just as intense as what he'd done to her in the study earlier in the day when his mouth had covered her sex and awoken every desire she'd pretended away.

She stroked her hand over him, watching with curiosity to see how he would react. He jerked against her, his abdominal muscles tightening as he grunted in pleasure once more. She smiled. This was power. He was a duke, her employer, a man who could crush her like a bug any time he wanted.

And she held power over him that she could wield

whenever she…

She stroked her hand again, and he cursed. "You will kill me," he grunted. "And I don't want to die like this. I want to be inside of you, watching you shatter."

Her eyes went wide, but she didn't resist as he put his hands beneath her chemise straps and glided them down her arms. It was all she wore beneath the fancy gown, so when the thin scrap of worn cotton fell at her feet, she was naked. With him.

She blushed, turning away as she lifted her hands to cover herself.

"Please don't," he whispered as he caught her hands. "I want to look at you."

"No one has ever looked at me," she said.

"I realize it's strange. But you are so beautiful, Sarah. And looking at you is almost as much of a pleasure to me as touching you." He slid a finger beneath her chin and tilted her face up so that she looked into his eyes. "Please grant me that boon."

It was impossible to deny him when his seduction was so gentle, so in tune with her fears and her worries. He didn't judge, which was strange given their past. He just…was. And she wanted to give him everything he desired and trust she would get something in return.

She faced him straight on and dropped her hands, letting him see her. And he looked. God, did he look. His eyes caressed her, sweeping over every naked inch like she was the goddess he had pretended she was earlier. His to worship. As he stared, her discomfort began to fade, replaced with something else. Something warm and wonderful that spread through her, awakening the same nerves he did when he touched her.

"I would very much like you back in my bed, Sarah," he growled, his tone suddenly low and possessive.

She nodded as he backed her toward that very bed. Her backside hit the edge and he crowded in, his hands closing over her bare hips as his mouth crushed to hers. She opened, swept away by the increasing passion of his kiss, and then she felt him lift her onto the high edge of the bed. Her legs came open and he pushed into the space. She felt his cock at her entrance and shivered at the feel of hard on soft. She braced for his entry, but he didn't make a move to take her.

In fact, instead, he stepped away and helped her settle onto the pillows before he joined her, lying on his side as he returned to those kisses that set her on fire and made her want more and more.

His hands roamed her body, fingertips skating over her hot skin, cupping her breast, stroking her sensitive nipple so that she broke her mouth from his with a harsh gasp of pleasure. He smiled and his dark head bent as he covered that same place with his mouth. His tongue was rough as he stroked it along the peak, nipping and sucking as she writhed beneath him in a pleasure she had never dared imagine. It pulsed through her very blood, settling between her legs, teasing her with the release he'd shown her earlier in the day.

While he switched his tongue from one breast to the other, his hands roved down her body, fingers brushing her ribcage, her stomach, her hip, his nails gently raking her thighs, and she arched beneath him helplessly. Finally, he settled his hand between her legs and her sigh turned to one of relief. Now he was touching her. Now she would be free.

He opened her gently, massaging the sensitive folds of her sex, teasing the nub of her clitoris as he smoothed her own juices over her shaking body.

"I want to help ready you," he gasped as he broke from her breast. "It will feel strange. Let me know if there's pain."

She nodded. Her mother had vaguely spoken of what happened between a man and woman. Not particularly kindly, mostly of bearing a husband's touch, but no details. Isabel had been more open, but there was nothing to prepare Sarah for the exquisite feeling of Kit's index finger gently breaching her trembling body.

When she gasped, he slowed his entry and looked up at her

face. "Pain?"

"No," she breathed. "I don't know what it is, but it isn't pain."

He smiled. "I'll teach you what it is, Sarah." He pushed a little farther, always gentle as he stretched the untried channel. She felt a twinge of discomfort, but it wasn't pain. Just a strangeness that another person was inside her body, a fullness as he stroked inside of her, a shocking pleasure at the wickedness of this act.

He pressed a thumb to her clitoris as he fully seated his finger inside her. She gasped at the electric sensation that sizzled through her. He stroked, thrusting as he circled her clitoris, slowly, gently. Until she was gasping in pleasure, until the same explosion of release that had happened earlier in the day overtook her and she gripped the coverlet with both hands and called out his name in a long groan.

When he withdrew his finger from her body, she saw the streak of blood and blushed. "I'm…sorry," she gasped.

He wrinkled his brow. "Why? My purpose was to ease the way. Of course we would encounter your maidenhead. But now it should be easier for you."

She swallowed as he rolled over her, his big body covering her, but not crushing her as he braced himself away. She opened her legs out of pure instinct, giving him a place to rest between them, and he moaned softly as he settled there so that his cock nudged where his fingers had just departed.

"I can't keep this from hurting," he whispered. "I wish I could. Do you still want this? Because you don't have to do anything else. We could lay together, I could—"

She shook her head, shocked at how easily he could give without expecting a damned thing in return. After all those years she'd thought him cold and judgmental, he was so far from that. That man she'd thought she knew did not exist.

Just this one who she loved.

"I want you," she whispered, cupping his cheeks and

drawing him down for a kiss. "I want this."

His mouth took hers gently, probing and claiming with an almost lazy rhythm that mesmerized her. Enough so that when she felt him shift, felt the head of him at her entrance, she no longer feared what would happen. He slid forward, taking just an inch, and she gasped at the invasion, parting their mouths.

He watched her, careful, caring as he thrust a little more. His finger had been nothing compared to this, this claiming that was a mix of utter magic and unexpected sensation. He continued, claiming more and more. When she squirmed with a twinge of pain, he slowed, stopped, let her grow accustomed to his girth stretching her. When she gasped in pleasure, he took more, until finally he was fully seated inside of her and he rested his forehead on hers.

"How does it feel?"

She laughed. "Odd."

He lifted his head to grin at her. "You will make me blush."

"Well, I've never had a person inside me," she teased. "Give me a moment to adjust. How does it feel to you?"

He grunted a sound of pleasure. "Like a hot, wet glove was made to fit me perfectly. Your body grips mine and if I died in this moment, I would be completely content."

She leaned up and kissed him. "Please don't die, I have a feeling we aren't finished."

"Not by any stretch of your wonderful imagination," he whispered. Then he ground his hips against hers.

She barked out in surprise, pleasure. His pelvis hit her in the most amazing way and it was like someone had jolted her entire body with sensation.

"Do it again," she gasped.

He obliged, not once but over and over. His body ground inside of her, against her, in shallow thrusts. Her fingers dug into his bare shoulders as he took her, her body adjusting to his feel, accepting his claiming and finally, finding pleasure. It built inside of her, different than before because her body had something hard to brace against as the flutters of release began.

"Kit," she mumbled, burying her head into his shoulder as her hips ground of their own accord, her body jolting against his.

He thrust harder in response, his brow sparkling with sweat, his neck straining. He was waiting for her, drawing all her pleasure from her. It was only when her orgasm at last subsided that he let out a long cry, withdrew and spent. Then he collapsed against her, his arms coming around her, holding her like she was a treasure and he didn't want to let her go.

Kit smoothed his fingers through Sarah's tangled hair and she snuggled against his shoulder with a contented sigh. He had no idea how much time had passed since he claimed her and she surrendered with such sweet, passionate responsiveness. Time seemed to have slowed as they lay in the silence of the growing dark.

She sighed and then sat up, dragging his sheets with her as she smiled down at him.

"Thank you," she whispered.

He frowned. Her thanking him felt like he'd done her some kind of favor. Or that she owed him a debt. Neither of which was true. He'd asked her here because he wanted her here. He'd wanted what they shared.

She moved to slide from the bed and he caught her hand. "Where are you going?"

She looked back over her shoulder, utterly unaware of how sensual she looked with her blonde hair love-mussed and her naked body just hidden by the sheets and the angle of her position.

"Come, Kit," she whispered. "We both know this is a night stolen from time. And it was wonderful—I'm so glad I came here and risked what I was told to protect. But I have to go back to my room, my life, my reality."

She pulled her hand from his and walked away, now totally naked as she gathered her chemise off the floor and pulled it over her head.

He watched her as she held up the gown, examining it closely before she stepped into it. Then she turned her back to him. "Would you help me?"

He wanted to refuse, to ask her to stay, but her body language made it clear that she wanted to go. Or felt she had to. Perhaps both.

He got up, standing behind her just as he had when he removed the beautiful gown, then slowly buttoned it as he breathed in the lilac scent of her hair and tried to permanently mark it on his mind.

She faced him. "I hope this isn't going to make things…awkward between us."

He shook his head. "No, I see no reason why it should. We were two adults who agreed to what we shared. But Sarah…"

She worried her lip and he saw the anxiety she'd been trying to mask. "Yes?"

"You act like you want this to end. That you don't want to do this again. Is that true?"

She swallowed hard and reached out to catch his hands. "You don't know how much I want to come here to you every single night and surrender to what we just shared. How much I want to pretend that I can straddle my world as your servant and this fantasy where I'm your lover in her beautiful gown. But you must know that isn't possible."

"Why?" he whispered.

"Because no one can balance on that kind of precipice forever." She bent her head. "And we both know Phoebe needs me as governess more than you need me as your mistress. So that's what I must be."

He frowned. He'd spent his life being careful and prudent, and he knew that what she said was exactly the right thing. But he didn't want it to be. Didn't want her to walk away from him and know that it would be forever.

"This was an odd set of circumstances," she continued as she glanced over her shoulder toward the door. "Your father's death, our bonding over grief, that horrible day at the lake. And it led to this, and I'm not sorry. But I have to walk away, Kit. Or else I risk so much pain in my future."

Pain. Yes, he felt that pain right now, low in his gut. The pain of losing her, losing this thing that had built between them, this connection he'd never allowed himself to acknowledge even though perhaps it had always been there.

She lifted up to her tiptoes and brushed her lips over his. When he caught her arms and deepened the kiss, she smiled against his mouth and gently extracted herself from his grip.

"I have to go," she whispered, then turned and left the room without another word.

He watched her leave, filled with an emptiness like nothing he'd ever felt before. And he wished he knew how to keep things just as they were, and knew he couldn't because the world didn't work that way. And now his world was a darker, lonelier one.

Without her, he feared it always would be.

CHAPTER SEVENTEEN

Kit sat at the desk in his study, leaning back in his chair as he pored over the book in his hand. His father's journal.

There was a light knock on his door and he started as he glanced up to watch Hugh, Duke of Brighthollow, enter the room. Kit glanced at the clock and shook his head when he realized it was after nine in the morning.

He wiped the tears that had collected in his eyes as he read and stood to greet his friend. "Good morning. Up early, aren't we?"

Hugh smiled. "I've never been one to be idle," he said. "Drives Amelia mad, and I admit it is much harder to leave a bed when she is in it."

Kit turned his face, for his friend's words couldn't help but remind him of his night with Sarah. That was why he was in his study, after all. He couldn't sleep after she left and had come down to distract himself from his desire to chase after her and try to convince her to change her mind.

Only he couldn't do that. It felt impossible.

"Are those your father's journals?" Hugh asked as he craned his neck to look at the pile of books.

"Yes," Kit said. He motioned Hugh into the chair across from the desk and returned to his own place behind it. "I've been reading for hours. This is the last one I found in his drawer." He tapped the cover of the one book he hadn't opened. "Though I'm not certain it belongs in here. Barrymore said my father would file the journals on a special shelf in the library once a year had finished, but what I've read filled up this entire year until shortly before his death. So it must be a leftover from last year."

"Hmmm," Hugh said, then smiled at him gently. "And what have you discovered by reading all his words?"

"That Sarah was right," Kit said as he rubbed his tired eyes. "These books are a gift. His last to me, I suppose."

Hugh's brow wrinkled. "Sarah?"

Kit jolted. Had he just casually mentioned the woman like that? To his friend who was now looking at him far too closely. Reading him, as Hugh was wont to do. Kit shrugged like it didn't matter. "She was here in the study discussing some household matter with me just after I found the journals."

Hugh nodded slowly. "I see. And so the subject came up."

"Mmmm," Kit murmured, he hoped noncommittally. He'd had too many conversations about Sarah as of late—he didn't want to start another when he was so raw about the subject.

Not that Hugh cared. He leaned back in his seat. "It seems you and Miss Carlton are becoming quite close recently."

Kit bent his head as images of his night with Sarah flooded his mind. Her body lifting beneath him, her sighs of pleasure echoing in his mind. Her expression when she claimed it was a night that could never be repeated. That she could not straddle two worlds and had no expectation that he would offer her more than passion.

"Kit?"

He shook away the thoughts. "I suppose," he said. "But it is hard to imagine there could be a future there. Look at our past."

"The past can only destroy if you allow it to do so," Hugh said, and his lips thinned. "Christ, I tricked Amelia into marrying me. I lied to her for weeks. It isn't exactly an auspicious beginning, but we chose to overcome it. Thank God she could forgive me."

There was no doubting his friend's passion when it came to his wife. Nor his true belief that the past could be overcome. And when Kit thought of it in those terms, certainly his coldness toward Sarah was not so bad when compared to what Hugh and Amelia had gone through. Or Robert and Katherine. Graham and Adelaide. Hell, all his friends had endured their own troubled paths toward the women they loved.

But that was love. Worth any risk. Kit didn't…*love* Sarah. Did he? He wanted her. He liked her. He thought of her a great deal. But love her?

That seemed so fast to him. That a few weeks of comfort after his father's death could lead to such a powerful connection.

He fiddled with the cover of his father's final journal as he considered it. "It feels different," he said.

Hugh shrugged. "That's how you know."

To avoid the subject, Kit flipped open the journal absently. He expected it to have a date on the first page, a launch into minute details of his father's day, anecdotes about his life that almost made him seem alive again.

But instead, there was something else scrawled across the top of the first page in his father's familiar handwriting. Something that made Kit straighten up and stare.

Hugh cocked his head. "What is it? You look troubled."

"This…" Kit blinked a few times. "This isn't a journal."

"Then what is it?"

"A list," Kit breathed, and slid the book closer.

Hugh laughed. "What did he always say? *A life of lists is a life well lived.*"

Kit shook his head. "Told you that, too, did he?"

"He did. I took it to heart. Amelia is always teasing me about my never-ending lists that she stumbles over on my desk and in the bedroom and in my pockets." Hugh's smile widened. "So what is this particular list about?"

Kit pointed. "It is titled 'Kit's Foolishness.'"

Hugh leaned forward. "It is not! What did he feel you were

being foolish over?"

"*He likes the girl*," Kit read from the scrawl beneath the title. "*Whether he admits it or not. I am compiling this list of each time he mentions her to prove it to him when the time is right.*"

"The girl?" Hugh repeated. "Who did he mean?"

"Sarah," Kit choked as he looked over the list of detailed recounting of his interactions with her. "And the date of the first mention is in 1809, a year before the nastiness with Meg."

"*Mr. Smith was a very...w-wor—wort—*"

"Worthy," Sarah encouraged absently as she listened to Phoebe read along in her copy of *The History of Little Goody Two-Shoes*. It was part of her lesson for the morning. Normally Sarah would have enjoyed this time together.

Today, she couldn't stop thinking. Just a few hours ago, she had been in Kit's bed. In his arms. The soreness of her muscles reminded her of that every time she moved, but it was a delicious pain that made her recall every moment.

There had been passion there. Pleasure. She had given him something that no other man could ever take, even if she did find someone else she ever wanted to share herself with. She couldn't regret that. She wouldn't.

Even if she knew it wouldn't last. Couldn't. And that ending things as she had was better for everyone involved.

"What is this word, Sarah?" Phoebe asked, holding up the book.

Sarah blinked and pushed away her inappropriate thoughts as she leaned in and looked where her charge was pointing.

"Charitable," she said. "That one is difficult. Remember that *c* and *h* together make the *ch* sound, yes?"

"Ch-ch-ch," Phoebe repeated with a wide smile.

"And we should end there this morning—you did a wonderful job. But it's time for us to get ready to say goodbye to your houseguests. Some of them are leaving this morning and the rest this afternoon. Except for the Duke and Duchess of Willowby."

Phoebe's expression fell and she set her book aside with a thud. "I don't want them all to go."

Sarah nodded. "I understand. It's been lovely having so many friends here during such a sad time. For you and for your brother."

Phoebe sighed. "And I'll miss the babies."

Sarah edged closer and gently swept an auburn curl from Phoebe's forehead. "You like having the little ones around. You're such a good help with them, I know they will miss you, too."

"It's not so lonesome when they're here," Phoebe sighed.

Sarah frowned. Of course the little girl would be lonely. The estate was filled with adults who up until recently had been dealing with the passing of her beloved father. The fact that she was alone here, with no one her age to play with, would weigh heavily on her.

"Perhaps they'll come back again soon. Or you'll see them in London," Sarah said. "And there are children in the village. I'll speak to His Grace about allowing us more trips there to meet some girls your age."

Phoebe shrugged. "That would be nice." Her eyes lit up. "And the maids were saying Kit would marry soon. That he has to because he's duke now and all dukes get married. Maybe he'll have babies, too. Then I won't be so alone and I'll be an auntie."

Sarah bent her head at the sharp reminder that Phoebe was exactly right. She'd said it herself, multiple times. Kit was duty-bound to carry on his father's legacy. He would do that with a woman of quality. Someone who would bring more prestige to the line of Kingsacre. And Phoebe wasn't wrong that it would likely happen sooner rather than later.

"Shall we go down?" Sarah asked, rising to her feet and blinking hard at the tears those facts had brought to her eyes.

Phoebe grabbed for her hand, grounding her back where she was meant to be, and smiled up at her. "Yes."

They walked from the room together and down into the foyer. Already Sarah could see the carriages gathered outside. After luncheon, the departing guests would include Matthew and Isabel. Her heart hurt as she thought of her dearest friend riding away. Sarah had felt reconnected with her these last few days and would miss her advice and laughter. They would write, but...but it would never be as it was before Sarah's fall. No matter what Isabel said.

Of course, Kit was there, too, standing in the midst of his friends, talking to them, smiling as they said their farewells. When he saw Sarah, he nodded to her, his gaze held on her, but then he was back to being duke.

And that was how it was supposed to be. She accepted it.

Phoebe ran forward to cuddle with the children, Sarah sidled up to Isabel. Her friend slid an arm around her and drew her away from the fray gently. "You look pale," she said. "Are you well?"

Sarah managed a delicate shrug because she couldn't lie. Not to Isabel. "It's a long story. One that is not appropriate to tell at present."

Isabel's brows lifted. "Then perhaps once the carriages are on their way, you and I should take Phoebe for a walk. While she picks wildflowers, you can tell me all about it."

"I would like a few moments with you," Sarah said, resting her head on Isabel's shoulder. "Before you leave me."

"I'll come back," Isabel said with a smile.

"It won't be the same." Sarah found her gaze sliding to Kit again. He looked at her again, then stepped away, turning his back. Her brow wrinkled. It seemed her conversation with him after they made love had been accepted. He would hardly look at her now. She was back to being his servant.

And that meant she had done the right thing. Now she just had to convince her aching heart. The one that loved the man and the one that knew it didn't make a difference.

Kit stood on the terrace, watching as Isabel, Sarah and Phoebe walked along the garden path away from the house. His sister was skipping ahead, her auburn curls bobbing in the sun, while Isabel and Sarah had their heads together in what looked to be a serious talk.

About him?

He could only guess. And only guess what Sarah would say about him after last night. He knew he had been standoffish with her in the foyer. He had to be. He was still too shocked by what he'd read from his father's journals to be anything but.

It turned out he'd mentioned Sarah a great deal over the years. Enough to fill half his father's Foolishness journal.

"Why were you so cool to Sarah today?" Kit turned toward Matthew as his friend stepped up beside him on the terrace and looked out at the departing women together. "Especially if you're going to immediately moon after her as she walks away."

"I'm not mooning," Kit muttered. "And I wasn't cool. I was simply focusing on my departing friends."

Matthew arched a brow and Kit sighed. There was no use lying to his friend. Matthew would just wheedle until he had it out. And right now Kit needed advice.

"It's everything," he admitted. "I was trying to convince myself that the connection I've built with Sarah these last few weeks has been one born of grief and gratitude, nothing more. But evidence keeps mounting that I'm wrong."

"Such as what Meg said to you," Matthew said.

Kit rolled his eyes. "Of course that information has circulated."

"It's *us*," Matthew laughed. "I know she offered a theory that you liked Sarah and that's why you were so angry about the situation with her and Simon and Meg."

"I tried to push that off, tried to pretend it couldn't be true, but it's needled me. And this morning I discovered…"

Matthew turned toward him in concern when he trailed off. "Discovered?"

"My father believed I cared for Sarah for four years. He kept a damned list of every time I mentioned her."

Matthew smiled slightly. "That sounds like him. A life of lists…"

"Oh, don't—I've had that saying of his slapping my face too much recently," Kit said with a shake of his head. "Matthew, there are dozens of times I mentioned her either to him or around him. Dozens and dozens. And I know I spoke to all of you about her, too, in the years since I overheard her talking to Meg."

"I wouldn't have called you fixated," Matthew said gently. "But interested, yes."

"So let us guess that I talked about her hundreds of times." Kit stared out at her figure in the distance. Even from this far he recognized the twitch of her hips, the bounce of her gait. Because he'd been observing her, not just in judgment, but something more.

And he'd been too blind to see it. Or too afraid?

"What are you saying?" Matthew asked.

"That everything I believed, everything in my world, has been turned upside down, including whatever I thought was true about this woman."

Matthew nodded slowly and then said, "I understand that, you know. I almost made the same mistake."

"Mistake?" Kit repeated, glancing at him.

"You have realized that maybe you always cared, yes?" Kit couldn't deny it, so he nodded and Matthew continued, "And that terrifies you because you thought you knew your mind and your heart. So now you're putting up a wall. Like you did this morning.”

Kit couldn’t argue that. In his heart, he knew there was truth to it. Once again, he nodded.

Matthew held up his hands. “There’s the mistake. When I realized I cared for Isabel, despite everything I believed about her motives, I grew colder, too. I almost convinced her to give up on me. Can you imagine if she had? The woman saved my life. If I didn’t have her I would be…” He shook his head. “I’d be lost. Still lost.”

Kit sighed. “But my situation is different, isn’t it?”

“How? You are also dealing with grief and confusion and responsibility, and there she is…right in the middle of it all. Lighting up your world with just a glance.”

“How do you know that?” Kit asked, trying to sound nonchalant.

Matthew arched a brow. “Because anyone who sees you together can see it. This connection growing between you, that is a *life*. *Your* life, Kit. And if you throw that away because it scares you or confuses you or seems too intense for you, I can promise you’ll be sorry.”

Kit thought of Sarah’s terror that she would be dismissed, her desperation that he had allowed to thrive. He thought of taking what she offered and giving nothing back in return. He thought of how she believed that her life was already set out in front of her, so she had to be grateful for whatever scraps he gave her.

“I’m already sorry,” he whispered. “I’ve bungled this entire thing.”

“Good thing there’s still time to fix it,” Matthew said.

“Is there?”

Matthew’s expression grew distant. Sad in a way it rarely was anymore. “She’s still alive,” he murmured. “And as long as there is life, there’s a way to make up for what we’ve done. Tomorrow this house will be almost empty. Only Diana and Lucas will remain, and if there’s anything two spies can do, it’s disappear when asked. They'd probably even take Phoebe along with them if you asked them very sweetly."

Kit chuckled. "Of course they would."

"And you can fix it," Matthew said, the smile fading from his face. "You can be honest with this woman, and with yourself, perhaps for the first time in years. Risk something. Offer something."

"You mean marriage," Kit said. And when those words passed his lips, they didn't feel wrong. Or off. Or too fast. They fit. Just as he and Sarah fit.

"I mean that life you deserve, and so does she, after everything both of you have been through." Matthew clapped a hand on his shoulder. "You have a life filled with friends who are all happily married. Give in to the herd, Kit. Make a life with this woman who lifts your spirits with just a glance over her shoulder. You'll never be sorry for that, just sorry if you walk away out of some foolishness."

Kit flinched at the same word his father had used to describe his infatuation with Sarah. Or perhaps it was about Kit's denial of their connection all those years. Either way, it fit.

"I'll think about it," he said. "And how to approach her."

"Good," Matthew said, and wrapped an arm around him. "Now come on. The rest are in the billiard room and I want to watch you trounce James in a game before we all depart. You know he hates being dethroned as master of the table."

Kit laughed as he followed his friend inside. But in truth, he wasn't certain he would be able to beat James as easily as he sometimes did. His mind was spinning right now. And there were decisions to be made.

Or perhaps they had already been made, years ago, and now it was just about taking the future he'd secretly wanted all along.

CHAPTER EIGHTEEN

Sarah stepped into the parlor and looked around with a frown. She had been searching the house for Phoebe for the last twenty minutes, but had not been able to locate her anywhere. She wasn't nervous about that. After all, Phoebe was a curious little girl, and she liked to play and hide. Plus, Diana and Lucas were still at the house for another day after everyone else's departures the prior afternoon. She could very well be with them.

Yet she still felt uncomfortable that she had somehow lost track of her charge. Especially since she might soon be forced to ask Kit about it. He had been so strange toward her since they parted in his bedroom what felt like a lifetime ago, though it wasn't.

She was trying hard not to take that personally or let it hurt her. But oh, how much she missed the unexpected connection they'd formed. She missed his kiss and his touch. She missed *him*, even though they were living in the same home. In some ways, that made it all worse. He was so close, and yet so out of reach.

She sighed and shook her head. She needed to focus on her work. That was what she did when everything went wrong. This would be no different.

Thrusting back her shoulders, she stepped into the next parlor. It was as empty as the previous one, and she pivoted to go but nearly ran straight into Barrymore.

The butler straightened his jacket and nodded at her. "Miss Carlton, I have been looking for you."

"Ah, well, I've been looking all over the house for Phoebe," she admitted. "I don't suppose you know where she's hiding."

A small smile turned up just the corners of Barrymore's lips as he said, "I believe she and the Duke and Duchess of Willowby were going to take a long walk and a picnic."

"Oh, thank goodness," Sarah breathed. "Though I do wonder how I missed that information."

Barrymore inclined his head. "Perhaps the Duke of Kingsacre intended to tell you about it. He is asking to see you in his study."

Sarah's heart thudded so loudly in her chest that she was afraid the butler would hear it. She forced a smile. "I will join His Grace there right away. Thank you, Barrymore."

He exited the room with a slight nod, and when he was gone, Sarah gripped the doorjamb with one hand. She would be alone with Kit, the first time since she'd given him her innocence and her farewell. What would he say? What would he do? How would she keep herself from launching into his arms and declaring her love for him like a ninny?

"No," she said to herself as she straightened up and smoothed her gown carefully. "You can do this. One step at a time, that is all."

So she took that step, then another, all the way down the hall and to the closed door of Kit's study. She hesitated, thinking of all the times she had come in here and found him. When he'd talked to her about his grief, when he'd touched her and awoken things in her she hadn't ever allowed herself to feel.

And now she would have to look at him with the cool detachment of a servant and forget that this was one of her favorite rooms in his house because they'd shared so much in it.

She knocked, and Kit's voice responded immediately. "Enter."

As she did so, she caught her breath. She hadn't seen Kit at breakfast, and now she drank in the sight of him. He was standing at the fireplace, half-facing the door. He must have a meeting later in the day, for he was dressed very formally, in a brocaded waistcoat, a perfectly tied cravat, trousers that fit his backside just a tad too seductively. He was even wearing gloves. He looked every inch the duke in that moment, and her heart was throbbing wildly now as she struggled to remember how to breathe around him.

"Barrymore said you were asking for me," she said as she stepped into his study. "I hope I didn't keep you waiting long."

"You didn't," he said, his tone as formal as his appearance. "Will you close the door, please?"

Her hands shook as she turned and did as he asked. For a moment her hand lingered on the finely carved wooden surface as she tried to collect herself. Then she faced him with what she hoped was a benign expression. "How can I be of service, Your Grace?"

He worried his hands in front of himself for a moment, and his cheek twitched, almost like he was…nervous. Which made her own nervousness multiply, as well. Oh God, were they back to this? Would he sack her? She couldn't let herself believe he would do so, but perhaps he had reconsidered the prudence of their affair and—

"I'm not going to dismiss you, Sarah," he said at last.

She blinked. "I—how did you—"

"I think I know you by now," he said, and the flutter of a smile crossed his lips that lifted some of the tension. "Please don't think so low of me."

She let out a sigh of relief. "It is habit to think you are always ready to let me go," she said. "And I apologize that it is where my mind takes me when I'm uncertain. It will fade with time, I'm sure."

He shook his head. "It is my fault, you ought not apologize. I was…I was difficult to you, to say the least, over the years. It will take more than a few weeks of doing the right thing to make you forget the past. I deserve your doubt—I earned it with my actions. I hope I will earn your faith the same way."

She took half a step closer. It was all she could allow herself. It she came any nearer, she would touch him and she'd already declared that she couldn't do that again. No matter what she wanted.

"Let us start again," she said gently.

"Would that we could," he mused.

"Barrymore said you were asking for me to join you. How can I be of service, Your Grace?"

"Sarah, a great many things have become clear to me in the past few weeks," he said, pacing a few steps closer. "My father's death focused a great many facts for me. As did your brush with death. Things I hadn't let myself see. Let myself believe. And now they are right in front of me and I know what I must do."

She blinked. "I…see? No, I don't see. To what are you referring?"

"Your father was Mr. Seth Carlton. Third son of a second son to the Viscount Carlton."

"Yes," she said slowly. "Though my father had very little relationship with the Lord Carlton. They had a falling out before I was born. And of course my father had his troubles, so that is probably why the proper part of our family cut us away."

He nodded. "You had a chance at a good match thanks to those family ties, severed or not. I realize it was circumstances out of your control that kept you from that match."

She shook her head slowly. "I'm sorry, I'm confused as to what you are trying to say to me. My past means little now, my connections mean nothing. I am your sister's governess. That is the path to my future and I see no other, if you are worried I would somehow seek a union."

"You would be happy if you never wed?" he asked, and there was a sadness that entered his eyes.

"I have not the privilege to make a decision on that score. It is what it is, Kit." She tried to keep her affect flat, so he wouldn't see how painful it was to discuss this subject and most especially with him.

He moved closer, and now he reached out to take her hand. "I didn't have Barrymore send you here to have you be of some service to me. It's because I wanted to speak to you about…about…I wanted to ask you…to tell you…"

He shook his head in frustration and she had no idea how to help, but before she could try there was a knock on the door. Kit released her hand and shoved his fingers through his hair, mussing that image of perfection he had presented when she first entered the room.

"Yes, what is it?" he snapped.

Barrymore entered, his face red and his hands unsteady. "I'm sorry, Your Grace. I know what you asked, what you required, but…but there has been a development."

Kit threw up his hands. "A development. Is my sister well?"

"I assume so—she is still out with the Willowby party."

"Then this could not have waited?" Kit asked. "I was in the middle of something."

Sarah stared at his upset, his anger, which he so rarely showed. She wasn't exactly certain what he had been in the middle of in his mind. She was still confused as to why he'd called her. Their entire exchange had been…odd.

"Miss Hannah Beckett is here, Your Grace," Barrymore said.

Kit froze and his gaze became focused entirely on the butler. "What?"

Sarah stared between the men. It was clear the woman's name meant something to them both, though she didn't recognize it. Still, she was seized with an irrational fear. Was this a former lover of Kit's? Someone he loved? Was that what he was trying to tell her when he babbled about her future, that he already had his set in stone?

"Where is she?" Kit growled. Sarah shook her head. He

didn't sound happy, that was certain. Not like he had heard that someone he cared about had come to call.

"In the blue parlor, Your Grace," Barrymore said. He lifted his chin in defiance. "And there is a guard standing by with the door open to be sure she doesn't take anything of value."

"Is she alone?"

"Yes."

"Good," Kit said. "Good. Don't let her leave and don't let her near Phoebe, do you understand? If God forbid their group returns before this is dealt with, tell Lucas to take Phoebe somewhere else."

"I shall, Your Grace."

"I'll be there in a moment to…" His face pinched in disgust. "To *handle* her."

Barrymore nodded and backed out, leaving Kit and Sarah alone again. She moved forward now that they had some privacy. "Kit?"

He jumped, almost like he'd forgotten she was there. His face had gone deathly pale and his dark eyes were filled with tangled emotion. Her heart leapt, but this time it wasn't from desire at being near to him. It was fear for whatever had put him in this state.

"Who is Hannah Beckett?" she asked. "Who is she to make you and Barrymore react so strongly?"

He let out his breath in a scoffing snort. "She is a demon disguised as a woman," he said, but there was no heat to his words, only worry. "She is someone who agreed never to come here again. She was, in fact, paid a huge sum of money so she would stay away."

Sarah caught his hand and tugged it against her chest, holding tight and feeling him tremble. "Phoebe's mother?"

His expression crumpled slightly and his voice broke as he whispered, "Yes. Phoebe's mother."

Sarah caught her breath, but she didn't release Kit's hand, and for that he was grateful. Right now it felt like she was the only thing anchoring him in this horror.

It was so unfair. He'd been trying, badly perhaps, but trying nonetheless, to tell this woman how deeply he cared for her. To ask her to marry him. And then…this.

And now all he could focus on was Hannah Beckett and the danger she meant to his sister. Everything else had to wait.

"Her mother," Sarah repeated. "You told me a little about her."

"I could write books about her," he grunted. "And how she used my father, seduced him when he was lonely. Phoebe has been a bargaining chip for her from the moment Hannah knew that a child was growing inside her."

Anger overwhelmed him. Pain. He remembered how upset his father had been when he had to admit that his affair with the woman had gone wrong. How foolish he'd felt when her cruelty was let loose and how fearful for the baby they had produced together.

"That bad?" Sarah whispered.

He nodded. "Worse. I…I was worse, too. I told my father to walk away at the time. To just surrender the baby, told him that she might not even be his. Cruel words, they feel like now, when Phoebe was such a light to his life, is such a joy to my own." He bent his head, self-loathing overcoming him.

"It sounds like this Beckett woman was not someone you wanted to have holding something over you," Sarah said gently. "And you wanted to protect your father. He ignored that advice."

"I'm glad he did. But the fight that ensued was painful to say the least. She hid from him. She lied and said she'd lost the baby. Then she showed up again and demanded he take care of her. Marry her. He almost did it."

"He was a man of honor," Sarah said. "What stopped him?"

Kit turned his face. "He found out she was with some new man. That they had a plan to get her married to my father and then take him for even more. They even stole some of my mother's jewelry. *That* ended any warm feelings my father might have been nursing. Hannah had the baby, he offered her five thousand pounds to just…go away. Never see Phoebe again."

"She took it?" Sarah whispered, her disbelief thick in her voice.

Kit walked away. "She laughed and told him he could have offered her a thousand and she would have done it. She never wanted her daughter. She walked away without so much as a letter to inquire after her in five years. And now she's here and I can damned well promise you she doesn't want to hold Phoebe close and form a real connection."

His fear was obvious in his tone, and Sarah moved forward, her hands coming up to cup his cheeks. The touch was soothing and he was once again sorry he hadn't been able to complete his ill-said proposal.

But she was here. And that was enough for now.

"Kit, you know what she is," she said softly. "And Phoebe is safe with Diana and Lucas—there is no one aside from yourself that would protect her more."

"You," he said.

"Aside from the two of us," she corrected. "You aren't alone. We will face this woman and whatever she's come for together."

He stared at her. He knew he should refuse. Protect her from the ugliness that would surely transpire once they entered that room. But he couldn't. He needed Sarah at his side, her strength at his back. Her advice once he'd heard Hannah's demands.

"I would like to have you with me," he said softly.

"Of course," she whispered, and her fingers traced his cheeks gently before she released him and straightened her shoulders. She was ready for battle, it seemed. And he had to be too.

"Come on," he said, taking her hand. "We've a dragon to slay."

CHAPTER NINETEEN

It wasn't a guard at the door so much as one of the footmen, and the young man looked nervous as Kit and Sarah came down the hall together. He glanced into the open room and nodded to them. "She's just been sitting, Your Grace. Having tea."

"Barrymore brought her tea?" Kit muttered. But of course he would. Kit's father had been the kind of man who would serve tea to his enemy because it was the polite thing to do. One didn't behave according to the actions of others, but by their own moral compass.

Something Kit was struggling with as he nodded to the boy. "You may go, Carver. Find Barrymore, he will tell you what to do." The footman scurried off and Kit exchanged a look with Sarah. "She can be charming when she wishes," he said softly. "Don't be fooled."

Sarah squeezed his hand with a nod and then let him step into the room with her a pace behind him. When he did, Hannah looked up from her tea without rising and smirked at him.

He stared. The woman had always been voluptuous and attractive—there had been no doubt why his father had been seduced. But she'd lost what looked to be almost two stone since he'd last seen her in his father's parlor in London as she handed over Phoebe. She looked tired, sallow, unkept. Her red hair was piled on her head in a sloppy bun. Her bright blue eyes, however, had not lost any of their sharp and manipulative intelligence.

"Christopher, Christopher," she murmured as she set her cup aside and folded her hands on her lap. "Duke at last."

Kit set his jaw. "Have a care, Miss Beckett," he growled.

She arched a brow and looked past him to Sarah. He found himself wanting to step in front of her, shield her from Hannah's watchful stare. "And who is your friend?" she drawled.

"Miss Sarah Carlton," he said. "She is my—"

"Governess." Sarah stepped forward.

"Do you still need a governess?" Hannah chuckled. "I suppose any man needs one so comely. Good afternoon, Miss Carlton. And how is my daughter?"

Sarah caught her breath and he felt her stiffen at the reference to Phoebe. Then she inclined her head. "Very well. Intelligent and kind."

There was a tiny twitch to Hannah's cheek. Otherwise, she didn't react at all to the report on her daughter's health. Not that Kit was surprised. She had not made any attempt to find out about her over the years. It was a blessing, of course, but one that made him doubt her motives today.

"Why are you here, Hannah?"

She stood up at last. "Adam is dead."

Kit flinched. "Do not dare call him by his given name."

She smiled. "It's what he had me call him when he took me to his bed, dearest boy. Why should it be different now that he is in a grave? Took him long enough, didn't it? I heard he drew it out a long time."

Kit stepped toward her, but Sarah caught his arm and gently held him in place. "Don't give her the satisfaction," she said softly.

He bent his head and took a long breath. Sarah was right, of course. His anger would only please Hannah. She fed on that sort of emotion. Lived for it.

"Whether my father is dead or alive," he said through clenched teeth, "I have no idea why it would matter to you. You settled with him years ago. You've no business here."

"Settled with *him*," she said. "But there is a new duke now. So it's time that you and I settled. I'm here for a renegotiation of my bargain with Adam for Phoebe."

Kit's stomach turned as he stared at her. She could not have looked more disinterested. Like she was bartering over the price of coal, not a most beloved child.

"What the hell do you mean, renegotiation?" he snapped. "You don't want Phoebe now any more than you did when she was born."

She smiled. "No. But you do. And you should pay for that desire."

Sarah stepped forward when Kit's rage kept him from answering right away. "What exactly do you think His Grace would be paying for? From my understanding, you have not seen the girl for half a decade. Do you really think you would have any kind of standing to take her from a man of Kit's stature? His wealth? He could crush you like a gnat if he desired to do so."

"Could he now?" Hannah asked with another of those smiles for Sarah. "Fucking him, are you? The Kingsacre men are quite good in bed, aren't they? But be careful, my dear. The snake has quite a bite when it's done. Though it can be a lucrative endeavor if you manage it right."

Sarah let out a sound of disgust and turned away, but Kit saw the brightness of embarrassment to her cheeks.

"Miss Carlton is correct," Kit said, unwilling to put up with Hannah's presence a moment longer. "You have no power over Phoebe anymore and no right to her. You surrendered it years ago. There is nothing to negotiate and you need to get out."

"I can whisper," she said. "Talk. I've been silent a long time about her. But if I did not remain so, it could make her future a little darker."

"You would do that to your daughter?" Sarah cried, and now it was she who moved toward Hannah and Kit who reached out to catch her arm and steady her.

"Only if I'm forced to do so."

"She is five," Kit growled. "So whisper all you like and I will make sure that there will be consequences long before your words will matter to her. Now get out of my house. If you come back, I will not see you. If you ever approach my sister, I will make sure you regret it. Get out."

Hannah let out a long sigh as she headed past them toward the door. "Well, I tried to do this the easy way. You won't like the harder way. Good day, Christopher. And Miss Carlton…" Hannah smiled back at her over her narrow shoulder. "Good luck, my dear. Spread your legs enough and you might land him yet."

Sarah could feel Kit's rage all but pulsing from him, but he somehow managed to hold his tongue as the horrid Hannah Beckett walked away. She called impertinently for Barrymore to get her rig brought around, and Sarah's stomach turned. She stumbled to the door and swung it shut as hard as she could to block out Hannah's voice.

Then she came toward Kit, wishing her eyes were not brimming with tears. "Great God, *that* is Phoebe's mother?"

Kit nodded, his expression tight and sour. "Yes. Unfortunately."

"You said she could be charming, I saw no evidence of that," she said, marching to the window to watch Hannah's departure from the drive and be sure she'd gone.

Kit shook his head. "She was when she met my father. She was a chameleon, and I suppose she became what he desired. I didn't even oppose the affair when he told me he'd taken a mistress. He had been alone so long and she seemed to be good for him. He was happy with her for a time. She required a great deal of…upkeep. Not general upkeep, not something reasonable that a man might give to support a lover. Outrageous upkeep."

"Money?" Sarah said. "More than money?"

"Yes. And time. I spoke to him about it and saw he was as troubled as I was by her growing demands. He was going to break it off when she declared herself with child. And then it spiraled into the mess it is now. I suppose she no longer feels it necessary to keep up the mask. She's desperate, though." He scowled at the door she'd left through. "I sensed that and I don't like it. Desperation is dangerous in a person like that."

Sarah frowned, for she heard the same desperation in Kit's voice. Anger, desperation and fear. The fear pulsed beneath his surface, like a heartbeat. She moved toward him. "Oh, Kit."

He clenched his fists at his sides. "How dare she? How dare she come into my home and threaten me? Threaten…" His voice broke. "Threaten *her*?"

Sarah couldn't help herself. She cupped his cheeks, smoothing her fingers over them as if she could soothe away this hurt that went so deep. How she wanted to.

"I've lost too much, Sarah," he gasped out, his voice trembling with the depth of his emotion.

"You will not lose your sister," she promised. "Everything I said and you said to that horrible woman was true. She has no power in this situation. And we will protect Phoebe…*together*."

He nodded against her hands and she felt some of the terror leave his body. Like saying it out loud and having her hear it had helped somehow. She hoped it had.

He caught one of her hands as she lowered them from his face, and lifted it to his lips. He brushed a kiss over her knuckles absently and then he stared off toward the window.

"I need to see Phoebe," he whispered. "I just need to see her now."

Sarah glanced at the clock. "They should be back momentarily," she said, "if Barrymore was correct that they intended to return just after their picnic."

Kit tensed a fraction. "Yes."

As if on cue, there was a knock on the parlor door, and it opened to reveal Diana, Lucas and Phoebe together. They were all smiling and Lucas was laughing at something—it made his serious face all the lighter and younger.

Kit transformed in that moment. All his dark emotion was pushed aside and he dropped to his knees, his arms open as he cried out, "There she is!"

Phoebe let out a little giggle and then rushed across the room to him and into his arms. He hugged her for a moment, then stood up with her feet dangling around his hips as she squealed and laughed with glee.

Sarah glanced at Lucas and Diana and found them exchanging a look. From the sudden change in their expressions, it was obvious they sensed something was wrong, even if Kit showed very little of it. Sarah had heard whispers from the other duchesses that Lucas had once been a spy, so she supposed if anyone would be good at reading people, it would be him.

They both glanced at her. Not in question, but in concern. Sarah forced a smile and gave a tiny nod, even though she didn't understand why they thought she would be involved in Kit's upset.

"Did you have the best day, my love?" Kit asked as he swung Phoebe around to balance her on his hip.

She nodded with gusto. "Oh yes. Diana showed me all the plants that can heal a person. And a few that I am never to taste ever, ever."

"Goodness," Kit said with a wink for Diana. "Is she going to make you a healer yet?"

Phoebe grinned. "I want to be a healer, Kit. So I can save people like Lucas saved Sarah at the lake."

A little color left Kit's cheeks and he shot a side glance at Sarah. Then he smiled at his sister. "I think it's a fine idea. But healers, I've heard told, need lots of rest. So I am going to take you upstairs and tell you a very soothing story and help tuck you in for a little sleep."

Phoebe shook her head. "You are? Not Sarah?"

"Do any of them tell stories as well as I do?" Kit asked.

She seemed to ponder it for a moment. "Sarah's stories are almost as good."

Sarah smiled at the concession. "Thank you very much."

"Well, I shall have to do better." He glanced at his guests and Sarah. "Excuse me." He sent Sarah a meaningful look, then exited the room with a loud, "Once upon a time there was a dragon…"

"Kit!" they could hear Phoebe squealing. "The dragon cannot be the hero of a story!"

Their voices faded away, and Sarah leaned against the back of the chair as emotion overtook her. Kit loved his sister and Phoebe adored him in return. If she was harmed, even in the slightest, he would never forgive himself. And who knew what a woman like Hannah Beckett could do?

Would do.

"What happened?" Lucas asked softly, his gaze never leaving Sarah's face.

"Yes, did the afternoon not go…well?" Diana asked.

Sarah blinked. "It was fine. Kit and I were having a talk, a very odd talk, quite honestly, and then…"

She glanced toward the door. It was not her place to tell Kit's friends about what had happened, but it felt like it was. And he would need their help, wouldn't he? Perhaps not having to repeat the awfulness of that day would be a help to him.

"And then?"

She let out her breath in a long sigh. "Do you know who Hannah Beckett is?" she asked.

Lucas exchanged a glance with Diana and then shrugged. "I went into the War Department in 1803. I was out of the loop with most of my friends for a long time, until Diana brought me home to them. I don't recognize the name."

"Sit down," Sarah said. "It's a long story, I think."

They all sat, and Sarah told them what she knew about the

past and what had happened that day before their return. Both of them sat silent through her recitation, not even asking for clarification. Once she had sunk back on the settee in emotional exhaustion, they looked at each other.

"She's come back now," Lucas said to Diana, not to Sarah. "You think it truly is just because of the duke's death?"

"No," Diana responded softly. "Kit said desperation. She's out of money or in trouble, I would wager. Something else is driving her."

They faced Sarah together and Lucas said, "Does Kit truly think she would harm Phoebe?"

"I don't know," she admitted. "But after just spending a quarter of an hour with the woman, my skin crawled from her cruelty and disregard for her own child. I don't know how far she would go, but I also don't think she cares about creating damage on some level if it gets her what she wants."

Lucas frowned. "Stalwood?" he said softly.

Sarah didn't know what that name meant, but Diana seemed to, for she nodded. "He could bring resources to bear. Investigate. Should we head for London now instead of wait until tomorrow as we planned?"

"I'm not sure," Lucas said. "I'd want to talk to Kit. He might need us here instead. I could send fast riders to London before we could reach there with a carriage, at any rate. Get Stalwood started for us."

Before Sarah could ask for clarification, the door opened again and Kit reentered the room. His face was drawn, pale. Sarah stood up and came toward him.

"She's asleep?" she asked softly.

He nodded. "Despite telling me five times that she was not tired, too old for naps and that she needed a higher fire, then a lower fire."

Sarah laughed. "That sounds familiar." She took his hand and held it a moment, wishing she could transfer any strength she had to him. "I-I told Diana and Lucas," she said, glancing over at the couple, who smiled gently at them. "And now I think I shall let you talk to them yourself. I'll go…I'll just go make sure she's…safe."

He held her gaze for a long moment before he said, "Thank you."

She nodded and slipped away, feeling utterly helpless and completely unsure of her place with him.

Kit sank into the settee Sarah had abandoned when he entered the room and stared across at his two friends. He was just as happy not to have to retell the terrible exchange with Hannah Beckett. He only wished he could stop reliving it in his own mind.

"What is the danger?" Lucas asked. "How far is this woman willing to go?"

Kit scrubbed a hand over his face. His gut reaction was to focus entirely on the deepest terror. But that would serve no one. He had to be clearer. More rational if he expected his friends to help.

He sighed. "I don't think she would hurt Phoebe physically," he admitted. "But Hannah Beckett will protect herself at all costs."

Diana nodded slowly. "Sarah explained some of it, but you've seen it before, yes? When she broke with your father?"

Kit pursed his lips. "It was an utter nightmare. She was willing to hide her child from him, to threaten to give Phoebe away where she'd never be found to get what she wanted."

"Which was money," Lucas said as he got up and paced away restlessly.

"Yes. And she sees this as a way to get more," Kit said. "It's an opportunity and she is an opportunist."

Diana leaned forward, and her beautiful face was soft with

empathy. "You're afraid," she said. "I see that and I understand that. But you must know you aren't alone in this. We're all going to protect her."

"You two had plans to depart tomorrow," Kit said. "You cannot take this on."

"Like hell we can't," Lucas said sharply. "There may be a physical threat, so Diana and I will do better to stay here and help you face that. In the meantime, I'll send a message to my old contacts in London to begin an investigation into this woman."

Kit's lips parted as he stared in wonder at his friends. "You would use your War Department resources for me?"

"Of course," Diana said with a wave of her hand that made it feel like this wasn't the extraordinary act of friendship that it was.

Relief rushed through Kit at the idea that they would make such an offer. "Thank you," he whispered. Then he leaned back and looked from one to the other. "Tell me something. Are you two still spies?"

Diana grinned and winked at Lucas. He also smiled. "I'm sorry, Kit. That's a classified matter."

Kit shook his head. "Let me know what you need from me. I can provide all the information I have. And my father's journals are in the library. We can find the ones from the years surrounding his affair with Hannah."

"Good," Lucas said. "We'll start there. I'm sure there will be information to mine from those. And I'll let you know what else we need."

Diana pushed to her feet and Kit followed. She stepped toward him. "May I offer you some advice?"

He nodded. "Of course. I welcome anything you have to say, considering your experience."

She glanced over her shoulder at Lucas before she said, "Let Sarah help," she said softly. "She loves that child. And she cares deeply about you."

He frowned. He hadn't talked to Diana and Lucas about his intentions that morning, just that he needed time alone with Sarah.

"Protect each other," Lucas added.

Kit sighed and then nodded. "I know you're right. And I know what I have to do."

"Good," Diana said before she turned to Lucas. "Now come along, my love. We have some journals to find."

The two of them linked arms and left the parlor together. Kit followed them out, and turned toward the stairs that led to the family quarters above. When he moved to his sister's room, he was surprised to find Sarah sitting on the floor in the hallway at the nursery door. Her teary stare was faraway and troubled, and she worried her hands in her lap mindlessly.

He moved toward her, keenly aware of when she snapped out of her reverie and noticed him. Her eyes went wide, but she didn't get up. So he sat down beside her, placed his back against the wall and let out his breath gently.

"It's been a long day," he said.

She nodded and wiped at her tears swiftly. "And it's not even tea time."

They were quiet for a moment. Not an uncomfortable silence, or one where he felt separated from her. On the contrary, it was as if they needed no words. That he knew her emotions because they mirrored his own. And that was more reassuring than anything she could have said or done.

All his nervousness from earlier faded, replaced by a calm that allowed him to know exactly what to do and say next.

He turned toward her. "She needs us both."

"Yes," she said. "She does."

"Marry me."

CHAPTER TWENTY

If Sarah hadn't already been sitting on the floor, she would have fallen over as that simple statement fell from Kit's lips. Not a question, but a statement. *Marry me*. Two words, and yet she felt like they had flipped her over on her head.

"You…I…" She shook her head. "I don't understand, Kit."

He reached out and took her hand. His fingers traced over the webbing between her forefinger and thumb as he said, "Marry me. Please. This situation with Hannah could stretch on for a very long time. She dragged it out with my father for months, hiding my sister from him. We can protect her better if we are man and wife. We'll have more options."

She nodded slowly, to indicate she understood, for he seemed to need her to show him that she did.

"Phoebe loves you, Sarah. And you can't deny that we have a…" He hesitated, and she found herself leaning forward, praying for him to say the words she so needed to hear in this charged moment. "We have a connection."

She fell back against the wall, trying not to allow disappointment to overtake her. Yes, they had a connection. And they would use it for Phoebe. That's what he wanted, not anything more. It wasn't what she hoped for when she'd dreamed of a proposal in those girlish days before she had experienced loss and disappointment.

Before she'd wanted love from this man so much that it rocked her to her very core.

She pushed it aside. What he offered was the life she wanted. Not perfect, perhaps, but she would be with him. She would be with Phoebe. No one could take either one of them away from her.

"Yes," she said softly.

Relief flowed over his features and he rested his head against the wall for a moment before he nodded. "Good. Very good. I'll arrange a special license as soon as possible. And we'll want to tell Phoebe."

He got to his feet, then held out a hand for her. She took it, her skin tingling as he tugged her to her feet. She stumbled forward, into his arms, and they stood together in the hallway, bodies locked. His smile widened and she returned it.

He dipped his head and his mouth was on hers. She opened to him, pushing aside her doubts, her fears, her disappointments. She would marry him. They would be together.

And that would be enough. It had to be.

Kit smiled as Phoebe came into the parlor, her hand in Sarah's. She looked rested after her nap and completely oblivious to both the drama about her mother and the news about to be shared with her and with Diana and Lucas.

Sarah brought Phoebe to the settee, where she settled herself in next to Kit. Then Sarah took a place beside her and he drew in a deep breath. "Did you sleep well, poppin? All happy dreams?"

Phoebe nodded.

"Good," he said, and glanced toward his friends. Diana's brow was wrinkled and she was staring between Kit and Sarah with concern lighting her pretty face.

He ignored it. "I have some news, Phoebe, that I think will make you very happy."

"News?" Lucas repeated. "What news?"

Kit glanced over at Sarah and she nodded slowly. He cleared his throat. "Sarah has agreed to marry me."

There was a stunned silence from all parties in the room. Diana's lips parted in shock and Lucas flinched. As for Phoebe, she stared up at Kit and then she smiled. A wide, happy grin that lit up her face before she spun to Sarah.

"Marry Kit?" she squealed.

Sarah laughed, though Kit noted her eyes were not quite so happy. "Yes, darling. I hope that is all right with you."

Phoebe had begun to dance and she squealed again. "Yes, oh yes!" She turned back to Kit. "I knew it. I knew you would love her. And now we will be a proper family. She like the mama, and you the papa."

Kit stomach rolled. "You know I would never try to take the place of Papa."

She nodded. "A different kind, though. Oh, Sarah, I'm so excited!"

Phoebe flung herself at Sarah, who caught her with a laugh. She cuddled the little girl into her arms, and Phoebe sank her head onto Sarah's shoulder. As Sarah held her, her gaze slipped to Kit and they held eyes.

This wasn't how he'd imagined asking her to marry him. Not that he'd done a better job at his first attempt earlier in the day. But here they were. And once this threat to Phoebe had been dealt with, he could focus some time on growing closer to the woman who would now be his wife.

On nurturing their bond in the hopes that it could deepen and grow. That was what he wanted, after all. What she deserved.

"When is this happening?" Lucas said, his tone tight.

Kit glared at him. "Considering the changes to our circumstances today, I thought it would be best to marry right away. I intend to visit the magistrate immediately. I had hoped you would accompany me."

"If the magistrate can be...convinced," Lucas said softly. "It would be, what? A day or two?"

"Yes," he said, glancing at Sarah. Her·cheeks were bright with color and she seemed to be intently focused on a strand of auburn hair that had come loose from Phoebe's ribbon.

Lucas nodded slowly, then got up. "Certainly I will be happy to join you," he said. "Shall we call for the horses?"

He leaned in and pressed a brief kiss to Diana's mouth, then began to exit the room, but not before he placed a hand on Sarah's shoulder. "We are very pleased for you, Sarah," he said. "I hope it will be a happy union."

"Thank you, Your Grace," Sarah said, her voice barely carrying.

Lucas stepped from the room with Kit behind him. Kit held his tongue as they waited for the horses to be brought round. It was only when they were headed down the long drive toward the gate that he glared at his friend.

"What was that?" he snapped.

"I could ask you the same thing," Lucas retorted without looking at him. "What the hell do you think you're doing?"

"The right thing for everyone," Kit explained in exasperation. "You said to let Sarah help. Well, if we are married, she will be in the best position to do so. And my sister is overjoyed."

Lucas shook his head. "You could have left her as governess if those are your reasons to wed her. You should have, for this cannot end well."

Kit gripped the reins harder and stared straight ahead. "I had already intended to ask her to be my wife," he admitted. "Today before this mess with Hannah began."

Lucas jerked his gaze toward him. "That was why you asked Diana and I to take your sister for a walk and a picnic?"

Kit nodded. "I wanted time alone to propose. I had no

thought to rush the time table like this, but it was my intention to marry her then."

"For what reasons?" Lucas asked.

Kit shifted in his saddle. "Because I am attracted to her," he said. "Enough that I have behaved imprudently. Because it seems I have wanted her for far longer than I even knew. And I…I like her. I like being around her. I like having her to lean on and I hope that I can offer the same support to her."

"And did you tell her all that when you spoke to her this morning? Or when you asked her to be your wife some point between when we parted ways and when you made your announcement?"

Kit opened his mouth and then shut it again. "This morning I admit I struggled. I couldn't find the right words—she didn't even know what I was trying to say."

"That's an auspicious beginning," Lucas muttered.

"As for later—" Kit shifted again as more and more discomfort washed over him. "Well, I must think of my sister right now. Things with Sarah will work themselves out. We'll be married and have all our lives to explain what we want and how we feel."

Lucas shook his head. "You know that isn't true. Even more now than before, since you watched that young woman die already."

Kit recoiled at the harsh fact, thrown in his face by one of his best friends. A man who had given Sarah back to him with the breath of life.

"I'm just starting to understand my heart myself," he said. "And it's a distraction right now that could endanger Phoebe. I *will* talk to Sarah. I will give her everything she deserves. But not right now. Not when I will only be half-present. Only half hers."

Lucas was quiet, and Kit could see he was mulling over that statement. Then he nodded. "Just don't let your fears destroy the happiness it's clear you could share with her."

Kit sighed. "I'm trying, my friend. I'm trying."

"It seems I am destined to be borrowing dresses from the duchesses forever," Sarah said as she stood in front of the mirror in the gown Diana had insisted she try on. It was a lovely pale gray silk, suitable for a wedding performed during a mourning period, but with a few pretty pink highlights that gave it a joyful burst of color.

And yet, as Sarah stared at herself, she did not feel joyful. She felt…numb.

"First, you shall soon be a duchess yourself, and as soon as this nonsense with Phoebe's…" Diana glanced over her shoulder into her dressing room, where Phoebe had become distracted performing a wedding with her dolls. She whispered, "*Phoebe's mother* is resolved, you will not have to borrow anything. I'm sure Kit will provide well for you."

Sarah had no doubt that would be true. Kit was too honorable a man to do anything but provide well for his wife and any family they had in the future. Only as time went by, as the threat to Phoebe was finally resolved, she feared he would resent this decision made in desperation. When passions faded, both those emotional and physical, he might not want her anymore.

"He doesn't love me," she said out loud, though quietly so Phoebe wouldn't hear.

Diana stopped fussing with her hem and straightened to look at her in the reflection of the mirror. "Kit?"

Sarah nodded, and the tears filled her eyes for what seemed like the hundredth time in this emotional, difficult day.

Diana hugged her gently. "It must hurt to believe that is true."

Sarah wiped her tears with a shake of her head. "It *is* true. He wants me, there is no doubt about that. He likes me, despite the person I am or he once believed me to be. But he doesn't love me."

Diana was quiet a moment, then motioned Sarah to the chairs before the fire. When she sat, there was a quiet sadness to her that Sarah had never seen in her before. Diana's own eyes filled with tears. "You know, I once thought that of Lucas, too. That he didn't love me. That he couldn't. It was one of the worst times of my life. I almost gave up on him entirely."

Sarah's lips parted. "But it is evident that he *does* love you."

"To distraction," Diana agreed with a tiny smile. "But I couldn't see it at the time. Others sensed it more. The same is true with you, though I know my saying that won't change your feelings."

Sarah sat there a moment, digesting Diana's suggestion that she merely couldn't see the truth. There was a hope that flared in her chest at the thought. Dangerous hope that could only lead to more pain if it was proven unfounded in the future.

"You think he…cares?" she asked, unable to ask for more.

"I do," Diana said gently. "I see him watch you. I see him come to you for comfort in his fear or his grief, even when he has his brothers around him. It's still you he seeks in those worst moments."

Sarah considered that. She'd thought that Kit had begun turning to her because they shared the loss of a parent they'd loved. But she knew several of his friends had loved their fathers, their mothers.

"I suppose it is…*something* that he would want my advice or solace," she said.

Diana nodded. "Is this ideal, this marriage in haste to protect Phoebe? Of course not. But it is not the end of the story. It is only the beginning."

"I hope so," Sarah breathed as some of her anxiety dissipated and it felt like she could draw a full breath again. "I truly do."

Diana tilted her head. "Because you love him."

Sarah ducked her gaze away. She hadn't said those words out loud, not even to Isabel, who she loved like a sister. It had felt too dangerous. But now she couldn't deny her heart.

"Yes. I do love him."

Diana smiled. "Then the best advice I can give you is to keep fighting for that love. It is worth it in the end. So don't give up."

Diana squeezed her hand, then got up and moved toward the adjoining room. "Phoebe, come and look at how pretty Sarah looks. Do you think this will make a lovely wedding dress?"

Sarah stood and smiled as Phoebe set aside her dolls and came in to look at her with wide, excited eyes. But even as the two cooed and giggled over her, she couldn't help but think about what Diana had said.

It was time to fight for what she wanted. Fight for Kit. Fight for Phoebe. Fight for the family she wanted and the life she deserved when the drama had passed.

CHAPTER TWENTY-ONE

Sarah had no idea what Kit had said to the magistrate or how much he'd paid the man, but when he'd returned the night before, he had come with a special license. And now as late morning of the next day spread surprisingly warm sunshine across the long path leading from the garden, Sarah had to adjust to the idea that tomorrow she would be Duchess of Kingsacre.

Kit's wife.

It wasn't that much had changed otherwise. She was still sleeping in the governess's chamber, mostly because she had her things there and it seemed silly to make someone move all of it not once, but twice in such short order.

So life remained much the same. Except that Kit stared at her far more intently, and when he'd kissed her goodnight it had contained so much more promise than ever before.

She smiled at the thought and then forced herself to focus on the matters at hand. She and Phoebe were taking a walk around the property, given permission to do so after Lucas had reported it appeared Hannah Beckett had departed the shire directly after their unpleasant encounter the day before. Sarah was under no illusion that the woman was finished with whatever her plans required, but at least she could breathe easier knowing Hannah was no longer around at present.

"How many butterflies are there, Sarah?" Phoebe called out as she leapt ahead of Sarah on the path and chased one of said butterflies.

"Types or total number?"

"Both!" Phoebe squealed, and bounded after the fluttering bug as it dipped and swirled out of her grasp.

Sarah laughed, troubles and worries fading as she trailed behind her charge a few steps. They rounded the path toward the woods at the edge of the maintained part of the estate, and suddenly a man was in their path.

Sarah's heart was immediately in her throat as Phoebe came up short in front of him. He was huge, more than six and a half feet tall, and thickly built. His shoulders seemed impossibly wide and he had a scar across his lip that disappeared into the folds of his stout neck.

She didn't recognize him. He wasn't one of Kit's servants, nor was he a tenant or a resident of Kingsacre Village two miles from the estate.

"Phoebe, come here," she called out.

Phoebe was still frozen, staring up into the man's harsh face. She took a step back from him and he lunged, catching her by her waist and smiling back at Sarah before he pivoted and started lumbering away toward the tree line.

Phoebe screeched in his arms, twisting and kicking at him. Of course, that was like a gnat nipping at a horse. He didn't even seem to notice it as he continued on his way.

Sarah let out a cry and hurtled after them. She leapt up, catching the man around the neck from behind. She stuck her fingers into his nostrils and yanked, hauling his head back as she screamed, "Let her go! You let her go right now!"

He yelped in pain and dropped Phoebe. The little girl bounced on her backside and then scurried up and away from Sarah and the stranger.

"Run!" Sarah screamed as their attacker clawed to get her off his back. "Run to Kit now! Run!"

For a moment, Phoebe hesitated, her blue dark eyes wide and filled with tears. Then she did as she'd been told and raced toward the house in the distance, screaming her brother's name the whole way.

The stranger grunted in displeasure as he tossed Sarah away from him. She hit the ground hard, her wind knocked out of her lungs. For a moment, she stared up at him, dazed, and watched as he turned toward where Phoebe had gone. He was going to chase her. And if Sarah didn't stop him, he would catch her.

She flung herself forward, catching his ankles with both arms and hanging on tight. He staggered and went down, his big body jostling her.

He glared down at her and then back down the path. Phoebe had disappeared around the bend in the road, and neither could see her anymore.

"Stupid bitch," he grunted, then pulled one leg free and kicked Sarah hard in the face.

She blinked as stars appeared before her eyes and the world began to swim. The blurry image of her attacker got to his feet. He stared down at her a moment, though he was anything but clear with her mind turning. Then she felt herself being lifted. He slung her over his shoulder and carried her toward the trees, just as he'd done with Phoebe.

Her slipper fell from her foot as he carried her, but he ignored it. She watched it as it got farther and farther away. Kit would find it there later. He would see where she was taken. Her bleary mind screamed at her to think. To think of that slipper. And to leave a trail.

So she kicked off her other slipper to do just that, as she did her best to stay awake.

Kit stood at his study window, staring out at the garden

behind the house. Diana and Lucas were behind him, going over the journals they'd brought in from the library.

"Hannah was truly a master manipulator," Diana breathed as she glanced over Lucas's shoulder. "I would not doubt that the woman is up to her neck in other crimes."

Kit grunted. "Nor would I, though that gives me no pleasure. Her mind is twisted and right now it is focused on my sister. How can I—"

He broke off, for in the distance, he saw something. He leaned closer to the glass and squinted. That looked like…Phoebe. Phoebe running toward the house. Alone.

"No," he murmured, and turned to race out of the room.

"What is it?" Lucas asked as he and Diana followed. Kit ignored them as he burst from the first room that connected to the terrace and then along the rock parapet to the stairs to the garden.

"What is it?" Diana repeated.

"My sister," Kit panted as they ran together through the garden. As they cleared the fancifully trimmed bushes onto the wide lawn beyond, Phoebe saw them.

"Kit!" she screamed, her voice weak from running and her face red from exertion.

"Phoebe!" he called back, and they collided in the middle. He fell to the ground with her panting in his lap. She looked petrified and exhausted. "What is it? What happened? Where is Sarah?"

"A man," Phoebe sobbed. "He was in the path. He tried to take me. Sarah jumped on him."

Kit shook his head. "Sarah…"

"She told me to run," Phoebe choked, her sobs hitching her breath. "I ran as fast as I could."

"You did wonderfully, sweetling," Diana soothed, taking her from Kit's arms gently. "You must have been so afraid."

As Kit got up, Lucas exchanged a look with him. "Hannah left. All my sources said so."

"Well, all your sources were obviously wrong," Kit barked. "There is no way this isn't related. We have to go now. We have to find Sarah."

"I agree," Diana said. "I will take Phoebe up to the house, make sure she isn't harmed. And I'll send for the magistrate and as many men as the village and household can spare."

"Thank you," Kit called over his shoulder before he and Lucas started down the path from where his sister had appeared. "I don't even have a weapon."

"I do," Lucas said, pulling a small pistol from his boot.

Kit shot him a side glance as they ran. "Always?"

"Always," Lucas said. "Now, you must listen. We have no idea what we are walking into. You cannot let your emotions overtake you. You must remain calm, do you understand me? It's the best thing you can do for Sarah."

Kit's stomach turned. The kind of man who would attack and try to abduct a child was the kind of man who could do anything. And Sarah was in terrible danger. He'd already nearly lost her once at the lake. The very idea that he could lose her again, this time permanently, made his blood run cold. She was his future. His life.

He loved her. And he knew that and he hated himself for not telling her earlier. For not listening to Lucas and Diana's advice and not letting the confusion of recent events keep him from giving Sarah everything she deserved, including his heart.

Why had he waited so damned long?

"Stop thinking of regrets," Lucas snapped. "You must focus. For her."

"For her," Kit repeated.

They ran for what felt like an eternity, then careened around the corner in the path, and he stopped. In the distance, there was a slipper in the middle of the road.

"Sarah!" he screamed out.

He and Lucas rushed to the shoe and Kit snatched it from the ground. "It's hers," Kit breathed as he clutched it.

Lucas pursed his lips and took it from him. He turned it over looking at it closely. "There's a little blood on it," he said. "Hers or the attacker's, I don't know. But since she isn't here, we must assume she was taken. It took us a quarter of an hour to get here. It could have taken Phoebe half an hour to get back. So this man, whoever he was and whatever his purpose, might have as much as a forty-five-minute head start. He could have gone anywhere."

Lucas looked around, and as he did so, Kit jolted. "There's another shoe," he said, pointing to the edge of the woods. They rushed to it together, and Lucas smiled.

"Clever girl," he said. "She's making a path for us. And there are footprints here, too. Big and fresh." He knelt and looked at the imprint in the soil. "Very big. We must be prepared."

He pulled out a handful of bright ribbon from his pocket and tied one to a branch. Kit shifted, ready to go, and stared. "What is that?"

"Diana will bring the men once Phoebe is settled and they can be roused. This is how she will find us. Now let's go."

Kit shook his head as he followed Lucas along the trail the kidnapper had unwittingly created. "So you just carry that around?"

Lucas glanced at him over his shoulder. "You asked if we're still spies. There's your answer. Focus, Kit. Sarah may need you."

His stomach dropped as his mind trailed off on stories of what horrors Sarah might be experiencing at the hands of her attacker. He could only hope she would reveal that she was engaged quickly. If the bastard thought she had value to Kit, as much as his sister, he might not hurt her.

Kit could only pray that would be true. And that he would reach her in time to tell her everything that was in his heart.

Sarah's mind was finally beginning to clear as the ogre who had taken her stepped into a clearing at the far end of the property and unceremoniously dropped her into the clover. She winced as she hit the ground and glared up at him.

He paced away and she scrambled to get up and run, but found herself staring down the barrel of a rifle that was being held by Hannah Beckett. The woman glared at her, then at her attacker.

"Damn it, Tooney, where's the girl? You were supposed to take the girl, not this one."

"I knew it," Sarah breathed with a shake of her head. "I knew this was your doing. You would really send this monster after your own child?"

"Shut up," Hannah ordered, pressing the rifle closer to her face. "You don't want to cross me—it's not a good day. Tooney, tie her up."

The big man grunted and then swept up a rope that was in the middle of the clearing. He bent and wrapped it around Sarah's wrists, pulling it so tight that she almost immediately lost feeling in her fingers.

"What was your plan?" Sarah said, ignoring the order for silence. "To tie up a five-year-old little girl? Do you know how terrified she was when this bastard grabbed her?"

"So you did follow orders," Hannah barked at her partner. "Idiot. Why did you let her go?"

"This one jumped on me," he grunted. "Stupid bitch grabbed me and the little one got away. So I took her."

Hannah let out a long sigh. "She's the governess, so it's possible Kit won't trade anything of value for her." She leaned a little closer. "Though I think we both know there's more you're *serving* to His Grace than help with my daughter. So maybe he'll want to bring her back whole."

"So same plan then?" Tooney asked.

Hannah shrugged. "Same plan. Go ready the rig and I'll stay with her."

Sarah's head throbbed as she stared up at Hannah. She hated this woman down to her very core, but that dark emotion was not going to be of any help in her current circumstances. Phoebe had run for Kit, and Kit would bring help to search for her. She knew that. So her best bet was to try to stall Hannah. To keep her from following through with whatever she had in mind, or taking Sarah to another place where she couldn't leave a trace so Kit could find her.

"Your daughter is brilliant," she said softly, watching Hannah's face for any reaction.

There was only the barest twitch to her cheek, but it was enough to let Sarah know that Phoebe did mean something to her. Not enough, but there was a tiny piece of her that gave a damn.

"She reads very well," Sarah continued, "and is curious about the world. Do you really want to separate her from the only family she's known?"

Hannah pivoted on her, the gun shaking slightly. Sarah flinched, for one wrong move and it would fire and this would be over. *Everything* would be over.

"I don't want the girl," Hannah snapped. "She'd only be in my way, and if you think I'd let a child around that one—" She jerked her thumb over her shoulder toward where Tooney had left. "—you're mistaken. I just want my money. And if I get it from Kit wanting you or his wanting her, doesn't matter one bit to me."

Sarah shook her head in disbelief at the dismissiveness, her heart hurting for Phoebe. This woman was her mother. "Do you really not care about her at all?"

Hannah shrugged. "I don't know what brought you to service, but it's clear you didn't start there. You don't know what it's like to lose everything. You don't know what you'd be willing to do and say and trade to survive. I don't have time to care about Penelope."

Sarah blinked. "Phoebe," she corrected softly. "Her name is Phoebe."

Hannah's face remained stone. "Doesn't matter. She isn't mine, is she? Never has been. But if you stay good, if you do what I say, you'll get to go back to her." She looked away. "You seem like a better mother for her, anyway."

Sarah stared at her. She had no idea what to think of this dreadful person, the kind of woman who could suppress all her love for her own daughter.

And yet that was her only bartering chip.

"She lost her father less than a month ago," Sarah said softly. "And was upset by an accident soon after. Please, don't take me away. Not for myself, not for Kit. For her. She would be devastated if she suffered that kind of loss."

Hannah walked away, seemingly unmoved, and Sarah wiggled her fingers to try to get feeling back into them. It was a test of the knot at her wrists, too, but it didn't budge. She was helpless here, locked in the trap of two mercenaries whose intentions and limits she couldn't begin to guess.

She could only hope Kit came. And soon.

CHAPTER TWENTY-TWO

Whatever preparations the lumbering Mr. Tooney was making, it was another quarter of an hour before he reappeared at the edge of the clearing. He was running, his round face sweaty and upset.

"They're coming," he grunted. "I saw 'em from the ridge. Two men, one of 'em that duke. I dunnow t'other."

Hannah had taken a seat on the grass and she staggered to her feet, rifle in hand. "What? No! Not so soon."

"They must have found our trail," Tooney said with a shrug. "What am I supposed to do?"

The two stared at each other a moment, then Tooney pivoted toward Sarah as he pulled a pistol from the inside pocket of his worn jacket. "I say we kill her."

Sarah dug her heels into the ground and pushed back, as if moving away would help. There was no way to stop this man from shooting her, and that realization made her blood pump into her ears as time slowed to a horrifying length.

Hannah swatted at the muzzle of his gun and turned it away from Sarah. "Are you mad? Then we get nothing except a price on our heads. Let's take her and go."

He shook his head. "Even if we load up the rig now, they're gonna make chase. I'm not goin' back to that cell, Hannah. Not even for you. We kill her and it slows 'em down. We can escape. Get on a boat, go to America like you always wanted."

"Please don't," Sarah pleaded. "Please don't do this. Think of the consequences to Phoebe. Think of them to yourselves. You aren't murderers."

Tooney turned the gun back on her. "I am."

"No," Sarah whispered as she looked at Hannah for help. For something. The woman stared back, unreadable, unmovable, and Sarah knew that she would die here.

She braced herself, closing her eyes and thinking of her mother. She'd seen her in her vision when she drowned. She would see her again soon. And she thought of Kit. Loving him, loving Phoebe—she would never regret that, despite what was about to happen.

There was a blast of a gun firing and she tensed, but there was no pain that roared through her. She opened her eyes and found Tooney now lying dead on the ground and Hannah standing over him, smoke curling out of the barrel of her gun.

"I'm the brains, you overgrown bully," she muttered. She turned to Sarah, and Sarah flinched again. Hannah swallowed hard and then said, "You tell the duke that I'm going to America. You hear? He doesn't need to chase me—I won't be back. I come back now and I hang."

Sarah's lips parted as she stared at the woman she saw as a monster. The same one who had just been her savior. "Why?" she whispered.

Hannah shrugged. "Because I may not want that girl, but I don't want to hurt her. I never wanted to hurt her. Tell her that maybe, when she's grown enough to know. Now I've got to run."

She did so then, sprinting into the woods. As soon as she was gone, Sarah began to scream, hoping her voice would bring the men to her.

The echo of a gun firing brought Kit up short on the path they were following. His chest hurt like he'd been the one shot, and he stared at Lucas, unable to speak, unable to move, unable to think anything but one word: *Sarah*. It echoed in every part of him, vibrated to his very soul.

"We don't know," Lucas said.

And then the most beautiful sound he had ever heard in this world echoed from the same direction as the gunfire. Sarah's voice, strong and clear, crying out his name. "Kit! Please! Kit!"

Kit shoved past Lucas, not caring that his friend was the only one of them armed, not caring that he was trained. All Kit cared about was getting to Sarah. She was all that mattered. All that would ever matter for the rest of his days. It was her, it was him, it was them and the family they would create with Phoebe and their own children.

And that was what drove him the last few feet, out of the trees and into the clearing. Kit saw her and it was like his world had light again. Sarah was sitting in the middle of the clearing, hands bound behind her back. A huge brute of man lay just a few feet away, blood pooling beneath his head.

As Kit rushed to her, Lucas ran to the man, checking his pulse and then shaking his head. "Dead."

Kit was untying Sarah's bindings, his hands shaking so hard he could hardly do it. She was weeping now, tears streaming down her face, and as soon as her hands were free, she gripped his cheeks, his shoulders, his arms, like she was testing if he was whole.

"I love you, I love you," she whispered. "Phoebe?"

"Is fine," he said. "She's unharmed and with Diana."

"Was there another assailant?" Lucas asked, gun still drawn.

"It was Hannah Beckett," Sarah said, looking away from Kit for the first time and at his friend. "She was behind it. She ran off less than five minutes ago. That way."

She pointed to the edge of the clearing and Lucas sprinted

forward, leaving them alone, at least for a moment. Kit had so much he wanted to say, to do, to reveal, but only one thing that mattered.

He caught her cheeks and kissed her, breathing in that she was alive, that she was whole, that she was his and he would never let her go again. She clung to him, returning the kiss with the same fearful fever he felt, and their tears mingled before he finally pulled away and stroked her face. She had a bruise beneath her eye, and as she removed her hands, he saw the raw marks the ropes had left on her wrists.

"He hurt you," Kit whispered.

"A little," she admitted. "But not as badly as he wanted to. She…she stopped him."

He drew back in surprise. "Hannah stopped him?"

"She's the one who shot him, when he threatened to kill me in order to slow your chase."

He rocked back, collapsing on his backside beside her. "My God, I'm sorry, Sarah. I didn't know she was capable of so much."

"There was no way to know," Sarah soothed him gently. "She wanted us to think she'd left the village, just so we would let our guards down and she could snatch Phoebe."

His heart felt sick and he bowed his head. Before he could say anything more, Lucas came back into the clearing, his gun put away and his face long and frustrated.

"She's gone," he said. "There was a rig on the ridge that she left behind, but she took one of the mounts. I'll never catch up to her on foot. Did she give any indication as to where she'd go?"

"She said America," Sarah said as Kit rose and helped her to her feet. "She wanted Kit to know, wanted him to let her go and told me she'd never come back now that she'll have a price on her head for kidnapping and murder."

Kit turned away with a groan. "That woman. She is…a demon." Lucas sent him a hard look, and Kit turned back to

Sarah. "But she saved you. Come, are you up to walking back to the house? We'll likely meet the rescue party Diana is putting together along the way, and we can ride back from there."

Sarah let out her breath in a ragged sigh. "Yes," she said. "I'm ready to go home."

Kit took her arm, and they followed as Lucas led them back through the woods toward the main path. He felt Sarah's trembling as he helped her through the brambles. And he also felt her uncertainty. But now was not the time for confession. No, he wanted to do that when they were alone and he could truly reveal his heart to her. And hope she would accept what he had to say now that the danger had passed.

Diana stepped into the little room Sarah had been keeping as governess and smiled at her. "Phoebe is asleep?"

Sarah nodded. "At last. It took a great deal to calm her. We will have to be extra attentive for a while. But she's such a sweet child, with so much love. Strange that her mother has so little."

"Just enough," Diana said with a solemn glance at the bandages around Sarah's wrists and what she knew was a terrible bruise on her face. "Did the salve help at all?"

Sarah lifted her hand to the spot. "Yes, the pain is much better, thank you."

"I'll stay until the bandages no longer need changing," Diana said. "Lucas has already written to have the docks and ports watched for that dreadful Beckett woman."

"But we both know she'll be long gone before anyone can do that," Sarah sighed.

Diana shrugged. "If she truly means to exile herself to another continent, then I think you can feel safe."

"I'm sure I will, with time."

"And love," Diana said. "I was sent here not just to check

on you, but because Kit wants to see you."

Sarah bent her head. She had been waiting for this moment. Dreading it, really, because she already knew what would happen. What she had to say to him and what his reaction would probably be.

But now the moment was here. She got up and trudged to the door. "Is he in his study?"

"No," Diana said quietly. "He's in his chamber. *Our* chamber, I believe is what he actually said to me, meaning yours and his."

Heat filled Sarah's cheeks and she peeked up at her friend. "So he still intends to marry me."

"I would say so, if he's calling his bedroom your chamber." Diana smiled. "And yet you love him and you don't look happy."

"Obligation is not a great aphrodisiac, is it?"

"It's more than that, and I think you know it. Maybe it frightens you a little." Diana patted her cheek. "But that's up to you and him to work out. I'm just the messenger. Good night, my dear. And good luck."

She left and Sarah got up. She looked at herself in the narrow full-length mirror. She was bruised and a little battered, marked from her brush with danger. But Kit wanted to see her and there was no avoiding that.

No matter how long she wished to do so.

She stepped from her chamber and made the long walk down the hall to Kit's room. Outside his door, she paused, gathering herself, and then she knocked. He answered it, his jacket, cravat and boots gone. His shirt was half undone and his normally impeccable hair mussed. He looked like Kit, not the Duke of Kingsacre, as he had that morning. He stepped back to allow her inside the chamber wordlessly. She noted the door to his bedroom was closed and her heart sank a little.

It might be that what she'd come to say would be received more with relief than an argument. And perhaps that was for the best.

Once he'd shut the door, he stepped up and looked closer at the damage to her face. "Oh, Sarah," he whispered, his voice shaking.

She shook her head. "The bruises will fade. There is nothing permanent to any of it."

"Except the memories," he said. "Would you like a drink?"

She nodded. Liquid courage wasn't the worst idea in truth. He handed over a scotch and she sipped it as he cleared his throat.

"That is the second time you have risked your life to save my sister," he said softly.

She set the drink aside and worried her hands before her. "Well, I would do it ten more times. A hundred."

He nodded. "I know you would."

She took a long breath. "But Kit, that gratitude you feel, it is…it's not a reason for us to marry."

He drew back and his expression crumpled, so she rushed to continue before he could interrupt. "Kit, you asked me to be your wife because your sister was in danger. We both know Lucas's reports will come back saying that Hannah boarded a ship, headed to America. I don't like that any more than you do, but it solves your problem just the same. She won't be able to hurt Phoebe. And so your reason for marrying me goes away."

"*That's* what you think?" he said softly.

"Yes," she said, and heard the strain in her voice. The pain in it.

"You said you loved me," he said. "When we found you in the clearing this afternoon."

She flinched, for she hadn't meant to bare her heart to him that way. Not in that moment. But she refused to deny it, either. "I-I do love you, Kit. I didn't mean to fall in love. I tried not to, even. But I do. I love you, and that is a greater reason for us not to wed than any other."

"Your loving me is a reason *not* to wed," he said. "Explain that."

She shook her head. "I could never hold you to a bargain you made under duress is one reason. That wouldn't be love. And the second…"

She trailed off. Finding the courage for this was harder than she'd thought. Harder than jumping on the back of that behemoth who had threatened Phoebe, certainly.

"The second?" Kit encouraged gently.

"I know you don't feel the way I do," she said, ducking her head. "I realize you want me, but wanting fades. And I realize you may even like me, despite your previous thoughts on my character. But those are not love. And I think that I couldn't be happy, at least not in the long term, knowing that you held my heart, but I couldn't touch yours. It wouldn't be fair to me, or to you, or to any children we had in the future."

He nodded slowly, as if he were taking that in. "Yes, I agree," he said at last.

The breath went out of her lungs at that statement. It hadn't been cruelly said, but it felt like he'd reached into her chest and pulled her heart away.

"Then we have nothing else to say," she said, turning to leave.

He reached out, pressing his palm flat against the door so she couldn't depart the room. "I agree that *if* I didn't return your feelings, then it would be best to part. A one-sided love would be desperate, indeed, and I would never ask someone to suffer it."

"If?" she repeated, daring to look up at him. He was staring at her in a way she'd never seen before. Not just with desire, but with tenderness. Not just with gratitude, but with something deeper.

Something that called to her heart and made her cling to a wild hope even though she couldn't dare have faith in it. Faith in him.

"Come with me," he whispered. "Please."

She swallowed as he motioned to that closed door in the distance. The one that would take her to his bed. She wanted so much to be there, but he still hadn't told her how he felt. Still hadn't given her anything beyond hope to cling to.

But he was a flame, she was a moth, and so when he offered his hand, she took it. He led her to the door, opened it and stepped aside to let her enter.

She caught her breath. His chamber was filled with flowers. So many flowers that she was overwhelmed by the heavenly scent wafting toward her.

"Kit?" she asked, glancing at him.

He smiled. "I picked you some flowers."

"You picked the whole garden!" she gasped. "What in the world?"

"I started with yellow primrose, of course," he said. "But as I gathered it I realized that it only represents part of you. That part that was connected to your mother and all you lost once, so long ago."

Her eyes burned with tears, but she didn't interrupt him.

"So I began to look for other flowers in my garden that represent you. Daisies mean loyalty, and you have so much of that you would die to protect those lucky enough to have earned your love," he said.

She found the happy daisy in the magnificent bouquets.

"Hyacinth," he continued, "for the playfulness you show with my sister. Lilies for your exquisite beauty. And of course, daffodils, because they represent a new beginning, which is what I desperately hope you will make with me tonight."

She faced him, overwhelmed by the thought he had put into every flower that surrounded her. And by the patience he was displaying when she could see he wanted to kiss her. But it was more than a kiss in his stare. It was so much more.

"I have cocked this up," he said with a shake of his head. "From the beginning to the end. I realize that. I was cowardly and even cruel in my dealings with you over the years. And then

Meg said that perhaps I was jealous of what you were hoping to build with Simon and that blew my entire world apart."

She stepped back in surprise. "You? Jealous of what I was trying to build with Simon? No, that cannot be true. You didn't even notice me before that night."

He gave a wry smile. "Ah, that is what I might have told you too. Before I found…this."

He picked up a leather-bound book from the table beside the door and handed it over to her. She looked at it. "This looks like one of your father's journals."

"It is, in a way. But only of one subject. You and me."

She opened it, and her eyes went wide as she read the words written in the duke's hand. Stories of times Kit had mentioned her, for good or for bad, over years and years. Long before he caught her at her worst with Meg.

"I don't understand."

"When he died, one of the last things my father said to me was to let you be there for me." Kit caught his breath. "And it's because he already knew what I couldn't see. That I love you, Sarah. I have loved you for a long time and put on blinders so the intensity of that emotion wouldn't hurt me. But I feel it, and I know it, and it's true."

She felt her mouth gaping, her eyelids blinking endlessly as she stared at Kit. Took in what he was saying. "Is this…real?" she asked.

"Very real," he said, stepping forward and taking her hand. "Yesterday morning, before Hannah Beckett came and nearly blew our world apart, I was trying to ask you to marry me. It had nothing to do with protecting Phoebe. But I did it wrong because I still wasn't willing to open myself fully. I am now."

He dropped to his knees, and her heart lurched as she looked down into his utterly handsome and completely open face.

"Sarah Carlton, you are everything that my world needs in order to be complete. I would be lost without you. I love you and I want to make you happy every single day until my last breath leaves my lungs. I want to take care of you and let you do the same for me. I want you to raise my sister with me, and our own children, and help me become the duke you seem to think I'm capable of becoming. I want a life with you. A messy, unseemly, entirely wonderful life. Will you please do me the honor of looking past my many, many faults and marrying me?"

Sarah was shaking as she looked down into his eyes. Eyes that held her whole future in their warm, brown depths. And she had no more doubts, no more fears, and no more reason not to smile.

"Yes," she said. "Oh yes, I will marry you, Kit."

He moved to his feet, catching her in his arms as he did so. Their mouths met, passionate at first, gentling as he cradled her against him, and she felt the overwhelming sense of being…home. And realizing that her home had never been a place, but a feeling. With Kit it was safety and joy, pleasure and passion, and a faith that he would stand with her, and for her when she needed that.

Forever.

She parted from him at last, staring up at him with a smile that felt like it could crack her cheeks with joy. His expression was just as jubilant.

"Oh," she sighed, loving how his fingers clenched along her spine. "I should go back to my room."

He chuckled, a low, possessive sound that settled in all her nerve endings. "I do not think so. I don't think I shall ever have you leave my bed again."

He drew her back and they fell together, into his bed, into each other's arms, and she had never felt so happy than she did in that moment.

EPILOGUE

Summer 1814

Kit smiled as he looked out over the ballroom in his home in London and saw all of his friends looking back. They were together again, all of them for the first time since their gathering over a year ago when his father had died.

Tonight, of course, it was for a far happier moment. Sarah stepped forward, Phoebe at her side. She was holding their son, Adam, named after his late grandfather. The baby was still in his christening outfit from earlier in the day. Their friends all cooed as the baby made a tiny fist and let out a squawk so that no one could doubt his debut into the wide world.

As Phoebe slipped into the crowd to greet the other children in attendance, Sarah put her head on Kit's shoulder and let out a little sigh.

"Happy?" he asked as he reached out a finger and the baby gripped it in his tiny fist with a surprising strength.

She nodded. "Happier than I could have ever dreamed not that long ago." She glanced up at him. "I love you, Kit. With all my heart, for all my life."

He brushed his nose against hers gently and then kissed her. "And I love you."

"You'd best go take your boy and show him off to all your friends," she said, shifting the baby into his arms. "And I'm fairly certain that Phoebe is convincing Bibi to run away to the circus, so I should check on that situation."

She squeezed his arm and slipped off in one direction, leaving him to head in the other. He found James, Simon and Graham standing together. Graham had baby Maddie on his shoulders and she was tugging at his hair, though it didn't seem to bother him much.

"A fine son, my friend," James said, chucking the baby beneath the chin with one fingertip. "You look happy."

"I am," Kit said, and looked down into the eyes of his son. The eyes of his father. "I will never not miss my father, but this past year has been happy in so many ways. He helped steer us this way from the beyond."

Simon nodded. "I like the idea that the few decent fathers amongst our friendship circle would be proud of all of us now."

"How could they not be?" Graham asked. "God, I used to think of having children and it terrified me that I would turn into a man I loathed and feared. But…" He glanced up at the little girl who was laughing riotously as she played a magnificent drum solo on her father's skull. "…I could not be more different."

Kit shifted the baby to his shoulder and patted his back as he nudged Graham with his free elbow. "You never would have been like your father."

Graham nodded. "So Adelaide convinced me. Where is that woman anyway?"

His friends roamed away and Kit continued to make his way through the crowd. Matthew and Ewan were standing with their children, as well. Though Jonathon was only two, he was a great talker and could also use the finger language his mother and father had developed as children. Ewan held his daughter, Abigail, sleeping in his arms. When Kit stepped up, the little boy signed to his father, who nodded and motioned toward Kit.

"See the baby?" Jonathon asked, huge blue eyes wide and far too adorable to be denied any request.

"Of course," Kit said. Ewan passed his baby to Matthew, then swung the boy into his arms and tilted him down toward Adam. Jonathon examined the boy a moment and then sighed with contentment. "Best friends," Jonathon declared.

He squirmed in Ewan's arms and Ewan set him down with one of those bright, silent laughs. Jonathon tore off, leaving the men and the babies alone.

"It seems all these children are destined to be friends," Matthew said. "God help us all when they're old enough to get into trouble like we did as boys."

"*God help us when their mothers blame us for their impetuousness*," Ewan wrote on the notebook he always carried.

Matthew grinned. "And rightly so."

Kit chuckled as he strode away toward Baldwin and Helena, Lucas and Diana, and Hugh and Amelia. Diana's stomach extended into the circle of the group as she awaited the imminent arrival of her own child, her first with Lucas. When Kit stepped up, her expression softened. "Oh, he is precious. I'm sorry I couldn't be of help to you during the birth. I think I could have knocked over half the things in your chamber with this thing." She motioned to her stomach with a playful shake of her head.

"Amelia and Helena were wonderful stand-ins, along with the midwife you suggested, and used your guidance well," Kit said. "Though I recognize how rare it is to have a future duke brought into the world by the hands of two duchesses."

Amelia smiled up at Hugh. "We never stand on circumstance in this little troupe, do we, my love?"

"Never have. Cannot imagine we ever will." Hugh put his arm around her waist and tugged her closer. "What fun would that be? Make sure my sister gets to hold the baby, will you? Lizzie is around somewhere here."

"But where are Robert and Katherine? I don't see them in the crowd."

"I think they went out on the terrace," Helena said. "They were talking rather seriously and he said he needed some air."

Kit nodded and waved them off as he moved toward Sarah. She greeted him with a kiss and then took the baby from his arms. "Everyone doing well?"

"Yes. Lizzie wants to hold the baby. Would you mind?" he asked.

She lifted on her tiptoes. "There she is by the punch. Oh, she looks lovely in that yellow dress. Like a spring bloom. I think this may be her Season, Kit."

"I leave that to you matchmakers. I'm going out to the terrace a moment. Robert is out there and I want to speak to him."

"May I join you shortly?" she asked, her blue eyes lighting up with a little mischievous light.

"I will be very disappointed if you don't." He kissed her cheek and then made his way through the French doors and onto the dim terrace.

He saw Katherine and Robert standing in the moonlight. Her arms were wound around his neck and they were kissing as the light fell over them like something sent from heaven. Kit almost turned around and left them to their privacy, but just as he readied himself to do so, they parted and he heard Robert say, "It helps. But my mind is still distracted."

"And I'll do everything in my power to take care of that later," Katherine said. Then she turned her head and noticed Kit standing there. "Oh, Kit. Perhaps you can cheer my husband up. I seem to be at a loss."

Kit laughed despite himself and came to stand on the other side of Robert. "I'm not kissing you," he said.

Katherine patted Robert on the bottom rather cheekily and then headed inside.

Kit tilted his head. "I'm so glad you're home and were here in time for Adam's arrival. We miss you when you're sweeping your bride all over the globe."

Robert smiled. "And I miss all of you, horrible company though you are. And you'll be pleased to know we will likely be home for a while to come. I have some…situations to deal with that will require me to be in London."

Kit wrinkled his brow. "Situations?"

Robert nodded. "A few messes my father left behind." Kit must have looked as worried as he felt. "Don't trouble yourself. It's nothing earthshaking, as Katherine is wont to remind me. Just…annoying. But it means I'll be here, in arm's reach when my friends wish to play billiards or recount stories of our youth."

Kit smiled as he stared up at the moon above. "It is shocking to think that in the last four years, every one of us has not only wed, but married the loves of our lives. That all of us are happy. All of us are settled. I think if someone had told any one of us if this would be the outcome five years ago, we would have scoffed."

"I would have punched that liar in the mouth," Robert said. "But love changes everything."

"It does that," Kit said.

The door from the ballroom clicked behind them and both men turned to watch Sarah step out and look at them with question in her eyes.

Robert nudged him. "Looks like love would like a word with you. I'll go find my bride and make sure she remembers I'm not a boring old married man like the rest of you." He strolled off and inclined his head toward Sarah. "Your Grace."

"Your Grace," she teased back, and then she slid up to Kit and placed her arms around his waist. "Having everyone together again reminds me of how we began."

"The first night I saw you many, many years ago?" he asked, thinking of his father's wonderful list that had thrown in his face the truth he hadn't been ready to see himself.

She laughed. "All right, the time we *truly* began. And this last year has been magical, Kit. I can't wait to see what the next one brings. And the next decade. And the next half century."

He pressed a kiss to her temple and they both looked into the sky together. "Neither can I, my love. Neither can I."

Join Jess Michaels as she launches a brand new series, **_The Scandal Sheet_** in 2019.

One wicked little paper, six stories of the scandals within.

Who will find love?

Who will lose it all?

Read an excerpt from the first book,

The Return of Lady Jane

Jane stared at Colin, her body trembling and her breath hard to find. He was here. He was here in her sister's parlor, standing no more than ten feet away. And God, but he was handsome. He was impeccably dressed in a black jacket that accentuated his broad shoulders and a smart waistcoat interlaced with golden thread. His dark hair was cut close and not a lock of it dared to be out of place. His harsh jaw was smooth and clean, as if he had only finished scraping his blade across any whisker that dared to make an appearance overnight.

He looked every inch the proper, upright gentleman, but then he always did even when there was no need for formality. Only once had she seen him undone and that was the afternoon he made love to her so sweetly.

She tensed her jaw and steeled herself against those thoughts. They would do her no good at present.

"Colin," she said softly.

His expression, which had been focused so intently on her now went hard and bored. She remembered that look all too well. It was the same one that had been on his face when he'd told her she was to go to the country and not return.

"My lady," he said, his tone as icy as his demeanor.

She hardened herself in response, pushing aside her initial thrill at seeing him and reminding herself that not only had he sent her away so callously, but also ignored her for half a year.

"You didn't have to be so cruel to my sister's butler," she said, folding her arms as she glared at him. "You frightened the man half to death."

Colin arched a brow. "I wanted to make certain my intentions were clear."

"Well, you have done that in spades, my lord. As always, no one could possibly doubt your contempt for me. Now, what are you doing here?"

SEASONS

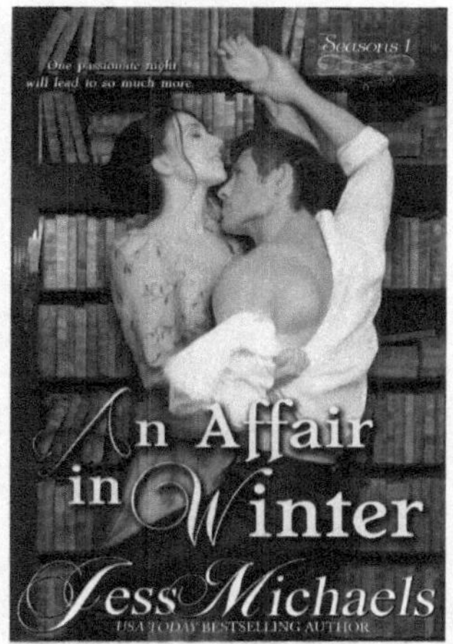

An Affair in Winter
A Spring Deception
One Summer of Surrender
Adored in Autumn

THE WICKED WOODLEYS

Forbidden
Deceived
Tempted
Ruined
Seduced

THE NOTORIOUS FLYNNS
The Other Duke
The Scoundrel's Lover
The Widow Wager
No Gentleman for Georgina
A Marquis for Mary

THE LADIES BOOK OF PLEASURES
A Matter of Sin
A Moment of Passion
A Measure of Deceit

THE PLEASURE WARS SERIES
Taken By the Duke
Pleasuring The Lady
Beauty and the Earl
Beautiful Distraction

About the Author

USA Today Bestselling author Jess Michaels likes geeky stuff, Vanilla Coke Zero, anything coconut, cheese, fluffy cats, smooth cats, any cats, many dogs and people who care about the welfare of their fellow humans. She watches too much daytime court shows, but just enough Star Wars. She is lucky enough to be married to her favorite person in the world and live in a beautiful home on a golf course lake in Northern Arizona.

When she's not obsessively checking her steps on Fitbit or trying out new flavors of Greek yogurt, she writes erotic historical romances with smoking hot alpha males and sassy ladies who do anything but wait to get what they want. She has written for numerous publishers and is now fully indie and loving every moment of it (well, almost every moment).

Jess loves to hear from fans! So please feel free to contact her in any of the following ways (or carrier pigeon):

www.AuthorJessMichaels.com

Email: Jess@AuthorJessMichaels.com
Twitter www.twitter.com/JessMichaelsbks
Facebook: www.facebook.com/JessMichaelsBks

Jess Michaels raffles a gift certificate EVERY month to members of her newsletter, so sign up on her website: http://www.authorjessmichaels.com/

www.ingramcontent.com/pod-product-compliance
Lightning Source LLC
Chambersburg PA
CBHW050614190726
48283CB00007B/2418